SACRAMENTO PUBLIC LIBRARY
828 "I" STREET
SACRAMENTO, CA 95814
8/2022

D0040718

WITHDRAWN FROM COLLECTION
OF SACRAMENTO PUBLIC LIBRARY

I RISE

MARIE ARNOLD

VERSIFY
An Imprint of HarperCollins*Publishers*

Versify® is an imprint of HarperCollins Publishers.

I Rise

Copyright © 2022 by Marie Arnold

All rights reserved. Printed in the United States of America. No part of this book
may be used or reproduced in any manner whatsoever without written permission
except in the case of brief quotations embodied in critical articles and reviews. For
information address HarperCollins Children's Books, a division of HarperCollins
Publishers, 195 Broadway, New York, NY 10007.

www.epicreads.com

ISBN 978-0-35-844904-1

Typography by Celeste Knudsen
22 23 24 25 26 PC/LSCC 10 9 8 7 6 5 4 3 2 1

First Edition

Dedicated to the Black boys and girls who didn't have
a camera to document their trauma and whose stories
we may never know.

I would also like to dedicate this book to my family
and especially to my sister, Cindy, because she's the strongest,
most courageous woman I know. But she hates sappy
stuff like that, so . . .

I dedicate this book to my sister, Cindy, because it's hard for
her, knowing that our mom loves me more.

PS. "I'm so happy." *Joey Tribbiani voice*

Love does not begin and end

the way we seem to think it does.

Love is a battle, love is a war;

love is a growing up.

— James Baldwin

CHAPTER ONE

Afro Rules

I drained all the color out of Harlem. I made the wind so angry it's pounding on the window like po-po at the front door. I even made the tree branches mad—so mad, they bend away from me. Everyone who looks out the window thinks it's just a cold, gray day in September, but I know the truth: Harlem is giving me the side-eye.

But despite my neighborhood's tantrum, I will follow through with my plans. I can't keep putting it off. I had all summer to break the news to my mother and I didn't. I stayed silent. Well, no more.

Do you hear me, Harlem? You can howl and roar all you want; today is the day I claim my freedom.

I nod pointedly at the window and turn my attention back to homeroom. We're only a week into the new school year and most of the students have already broken up into groups.

There's a bunch of guys in the back of the room gathered in a circle. They bounce in rhythm to the music coming from their mini speaker. I call them the Knights, short for "Knights of the Hip-Hop Round Table." They *love* hip-hop and live to argue about every aspect of it. Their discussions are generally peaceful—except for the time they were arguing about who the greatest rapper was and someone said "Drake."

Drake?

Seriously?

Sitting across from the Knights are a group of girls with long nails and even longer weaves. They're perfectly put together, from their sculpted eyebrows to their designer boots. For them, mirrors are a religion and Rihanna is their high priestess. I call them the Narcs after Narcissus, the hunter in Greek mythology who was so vain, he fell in love with his own reflection.

But don't get it twisted—vain doesn't always mean stupid. Last year they held a workshop during lunch called Lace Front for Beginners. They charged twenty bucks a head and cleaned up. And now they have their own YouTube channel, with over three hundred thousand followers.

A few feet away from the Narcs is a small tribe of kids with their heads buried in their textbooks. In addition to their love of all things academic, they have an affinity for old-school stuff —like Richard Pryor T-shirts and Nintendo games. I don't know why, but something about the past seems to make them really happy. So, I call them Vintage.

Standing in the opposite corner are the basketball players and cheerleaders. They don't get a nickname. God already gave them enough.

I look up at the clock on the wall; class will start soon. I go to unzip my backpack, but I feel a sharp pain just below my shoulder.

"Ow!" I shout as I turn to the desk behind me.

"Hello? I asked you a question," my best friend, Naija, says. "What are you doing later?"

"Looking for new friends, ones who don't resort to violence to get my attention," I grumble as I try to inspect the mark she left on me.

"Girl, I called your name three hundred times. And as usual, you were dumbing out." I'm sure she only called my name once or twice; Naija's being extra. It's her way.

I turn toward her and playfully announce, "Queen Naija, oh great one, I'm sorry I wasn't listening. Please honor me with your sacred thoughts."

She rolls her eyes. "Do you wanna come to my house later?"

"I can't. I'm having dinner with my mom. Tonight's the night."

Her eyes nearly pop out of her head. "You're gonna tell your mom today? For real this time?"

"Yeah. I have a plan. I'll tell you about it later."

"Well, knowing your mama, it better be good," she warns me.

One of the girls from Narc—Joy Mitchell—looks up from her pink compact and calls out to me, "Ayo, I saw the words 'How Much?' spray-painted on the back wall of the precinct on One Thirty-Fifth and at the nail shop by my house."

One of the Knights shouts, "My girl Toni said she saw it on a sticker in front of the post office and the supermarket. And yesterday, I saw it on a banner outside the laundromat."

"I've seen it all over the place too. Girl, your mom knows how to get people's attention," Naija adds.

She's right. My mom knows how to get noticed. She's responsible for all the spray-painted signs, stickers, and banners throughout Harlem. They all ask the same thing: "How Much?"

When I walk by anything that's been spray-painted with that question, a pool of ice forms in the pit of my stomach. It's a reminder of what I have to do later today, and it makes me queasy. Thankfully, I don't have to think about it too much, because our new history teacher enters. He's the only teacher we haven't met yet; he was sick and missed the first few days of school. All the kids scramble to their seats.

He's a pale, lanky, middle-aged guy with a receding hairline. He wears dark-rimmed glasses and, for some strange reason, has on red cowboy boots. He tells us his name is Mr. Gunderson and heads over to his desk. Then he makes an announcement and I roll my eyes so hard that I nearly injure myself.

"Instead of you students telling me your names, I'd like to read them off my list. I'm what they call a visual learner," he says in a squeaky voice.

Naija looks over at me. She knows I dread roll call because teachers always mess up my name.

"He might get it right," she whispers.

I shrug. "Yeah, maybe . . ."

But when he stumbles on Naija's name, I know it's a lost cause. He's going to remix my name. But not the kind of dope underground remix that makes you dance harder than the original. Nah, this is the kind of remix that makes you wonder why the person didn't just leave the original alone.

"First name starts with the letter A, followed by Y . . ." he says with uncertainty.

Please, God, let this white man pronounce my name right so no one laughs at me. Or at least get it close enough that I don't have to spend the rest of class under my desk.

I try to help him out. "Mr. Gunderson, you don't have to—"

"No, I can do this."

He can't.

Naija says, "Why don't you just let her tell you?"

He replies, "I got it."

He doesn't.

By now the class is snickering and staring at me. Finally I shout, "Ayomide! My name is Ayomide."

"One more time," he says.

The entire class loudly breaks down my name in unison: "Ay-o-mide."

"Got it."

He doesn't . . .

"Everyone just calls me Ayo: the letter *I* and the letter *O* together. Ayo."

"Yeah, okay. I was close," he says.

I roll my eyes and silently curse my mother for not naming me Lisa. What's wrong with Lisa? It's short. It's uncomplicated. And it fits nicely on a mug.

I'm grateful when he starts to move on to the next name. I can feel the stress slipping from my body. But then . . .

"Your last name is Bosia?" he asks.

I nod slightly as dread seeps back into my body.

"Any relation to Rosalie Bosia? The founder of See Us?"

"Yeah, she's my mom," I mutter.

The thing about being Rosalie's daughter is that people either love or hate her, and they all want me to know about it. I guess that's what happens when your mom is the founder of the biggest civil rights movement to hit Harlem in decades. See Us is similar to Black Lives Matter. It takes aim at police brutality, racial profiling, and an unjust prison system. But See Us specifically targets communities in Harlem.

My mom started it the year I was born, before the Black Lives Matter movement. The movement took off faster than anyone expected. And before she knew it, her five-person operation became a citywide movement with thousands of members. They organize marches, boycotts, and basically an all-points assault on the establishment.

"I saw her on *Good Morning America* a few weeks ago. I love her! She's so well spoken. She's grown into quite a divisive figure, and to that I say, 'Right on!' We need more sassy women like her."

Mr. Gunderson thinks he just gave my mom a compliment. But I'm pretty sure she wouldn't take it that way. I can practically hear her now: *"Does my skin color lead you to believe I would be anything other than well spoken? And did you just call me sassy?"*

Just before he moves on to the next name, he mumbles to himself, "Rosalie Bosia's daughter . . . Gosh, what must that be like?"

What's it like?

Well . . . while other kids made houses with Popsicle sticks, I made posters to free unjustly convicted prisoners. When other kids were playing video games, I was studying Black history with flash cards. And when my classmates were going to their first school dance, I was going door to door with my mom to get people to register to vote.

And yes, many people in Harlem know me, but don't get it twisted; that doesn't mean I have a lot of friends. It's hard to make friends when you invite them over but then your mom won't let them eat until they tell her who was the first Black woman to refuse to sit in the back of the bus. And God help you if you said "Rosa Parks," because that is most definitely not the right answer.

I envied the kids whose parents let them get away with knowing only the basics of Black history: Who is Madam C. J. Walker and what is Juneteenth? My mother was not having it. By the time I was ten, I knew more about Black history than most of my teachers.

That's what it means to be Rosalie's child. And now, I want out.

I'm not crazy. I know I can't opt out of her being my mom. But I want out of See Us and out of the activist life. I've done more than my part. Now, I just want to be normal. My reading list may be advanced, but my social life is so far behind that I'm not sure I even qualify as a teenager anymore.

Most the girls I know are dating, and some are already having sex. Don't get me wrong, I'm not really trying to get down like that, but damn, I'm almost fifteen. I should have been kissed already, right?

Okay, to be fair, I did get kissed one time, but it didn't count because it was really fast and the guy did it on a dare. His name was Keith Hightower. Keith was hesitant because, like many guys in our school, he's kind of afraid of me. Why? One word: Afro.

My Afro makes guys think I'm a badass. Like I'm the younger version of Angela Davis and I don't take no mess. But really, I'm not a badass. I'm more of a "measured" ass. And even though I'd like to say I don't take no mess, the truth is, I take it.

When I go into the CVS Pharmacy on my block, the manager Donna tries to put her hand in my hair. I have to find a way to dodge her probing fingers. Someone should have told me that putting my hair in an Afro would repel guys while attracting curious white women with no boundaries.

According to the unwritten rules of wearing an Afro, I have to put Donna in her place. And also, according to the rules of being Rosalie's daughter, I have to let Donna know why her actions are offensive. But I'm opposed to confrontation. That's why I go to a different CVS, five blocks out of my way, to avoid Donna and her looming fingers of curiosity.

Yeah, I know. I'm a disappointment to badasses everywhere.

When class is over, I tell Naija to hurry so we can go before Mr. Gunderson asks me anything else about my mom. We almost make it.

"Ayo, can I see you for a moment?" he asks. Naija gives me a sympathetic shrug and says she'll wait for me outside. I sigh and put on my best bargain-basement smile as I approach my mom's fanboy.

"Yes, Mr. Gunderson?" I reply as everyone else leaves the room.

"My wife and I have a small gathering—it's nothing fancy. We meet here in Harlem once a month at the café inside Whole Foods on One Twenty-Fifth and Lenox. Your mom wrote a powerful piece for the *New Yorker* about the struggle to combat gentrification in Harlem. It had such an impact on my friends and me. Do you think she'd be open to speaking to our group?"

So far, I know two things about Mr. Gunderson: one, he sucks with names. And two, he's not great with irony. If my mom's article on gentrification had really been a success, there probably wouldn't be a Whole Foods on 125th Street.

"That sounds nice, but . . . she's really busy," I inform him.

"Oh, yes, I understand." He nods.

"Can I go now, Mr. Gunderson?"

"Yes . . . Wait! Is there a way you can get me her autograph? I'm a bit of a collector. I have a church program signed by all of Dr. King's children! I'd love to add your mom's signature to my collection. Is that possible?"

Is this guy joking? Sometimes I have to call my mom's office and make an appointment to get a hug. It's bad enough that I have to share her with all of Harlem; now I'm supposed to share her with my teacher? If I were a badass, I'd say, "Boy, bye."

But I'm not. So instead, I smile politely and mumble something about getting back to him. If I keep going like this, my Afro will rebel against me and turn itself into a perm.

Tragic.

———

Normally the school day takes forever to end. But now that I have something to do after school, something I'm dreading, the day is flying by. And before I know it, it's already lunchtime. On my way to the cafeteria, I spot How Much? stickers on students' notebooks and backpacks.

My mom has outdone herself.

I buy my lunch and head toward Naija, seated at the table near the entrance. We're still waiting for the last two of our crew to show up.

"Ayo, I know you have a lot on your mind, so I forgive you," Naija says.

"Forgive me for what?"

"For failing to recognize my hair and how I'm killing it right now," Naija says proudly. She's not lying; her hair is beautiful. It's freshly styled in Havana crochet braids with pale strands of purple, pink, and gray. It flows down to her waist and frames her round face perfectly.

Naija is beautiful. Her russet-colored eyes are big and sparkle with flecks of gold when the sun hits them. She has full lips that kids used to make fun of but now try to replicate. I don't think Naija's mother actually gave birth to her. I suspect she was created by midnight itself and left on her mother's doorstep.

Her skin color is the reason we met. We were in first grade and a boy was teasing her about her being dark-skinned. I walked up to the kid and dumped my tray of food on him. Everyone laughed at him. I think that was my first and last act of badassness.

After that day, we became best friends. My mom would tell her about different parts of the world where her dark skin tone was worshipped and adored. That helped her self-esteem —maybe too much.

"Hello? Is my hair everything or what?" she asks.

"I love it!"

"Thank you. Now, what's your plan to talk to your mom?"

Before I can reply, the guys make their way toward us. The short kid with deep-set eyes is Dell Rogers. He always wears long, dark jackets and shades. He plays the saxophone and lives for three things: food, girls, and Miles Davis.

The guy walking next to him is Shawn Anderson. He's a tall, muscular basketball player, and all the girls want him. The thing is that he's not into girls. Last year, we were all at my house, playing video games and stuffing our faces, and out of nowhere, Shawn blurted out, "I'm gay."

The words sucked all the air out of the room. The first person to recover was Dell. "You gay? For real?" he asked.

Shawn looked over at his best friend and nodded. "Yeah, I am. I knew for a while, but I didn't want to say anything." He shrugged.

Dell nodded. "I get it, yo. You didn't want to say anything, but now you have to 'cause . . . you have feelings for me."

"Feelings? For you? Nah," Shawn replied.

"Well, damn, you ain't had to say it like that," Dell replied, clearly offended.

Shawn said, "I just meant that—"

"No, I know what you meant. And I'ma tell you something —I'm a catch. You hear me?" Dell informed us.

Shawn walked over to his friend. "So you don't care that I'm gay. You only care that I'm not feel'n you like that?"

"I'm say'n, look at me. I'm fire, baby!" Dell said as he checked himself out in the mirror across the room.

Shawn laughed and then looked over at the rest of us to gauge where we were with his announcement. "What y'all think?" he asked nervously.

"So the thing about gay people having fashion sense, that's all a lie?" Naija teased.

Shawn threw the nearest pillow at her head. I went over and hugged him. The last thing I remember about that night was us gossiping about which guy would be a good match for Shawn, while Dell stood in the background making kissing faces at himself in the mirror.

Shawn hasn't told his dad that he's gay yet. But I don't think his dad will cast him off when he tells him. I mean, it will be hard at first, for his dad to let it all sink in, but in the end, I'm sure things will work out. I'm sure of this because Shawn and Dell have the best dads.

When I was a kid, I remember growing curious about mine. I had a million questions. They bubbled up in my head for a while before I had the courage to ask my mom about him. I remember that day vividly. We had come from Dell's birthday party—one that his dad had arranged for him. I watched the two of them interact, and it made me wonder about my dad.

When I got home later, my mom was in the kitchen, finishing up the dishes. She dried the last one and placed it on the shelf. I entered the kitchen slowly, heart pounding and pulse racing. I had no idea how my mom would react. She never said we couldn't discuss my dad, but she never brought up the subject either.

"Mom, can I ask you something?" I said, voice cracking with uncertainty. "Who's my dad? Is he even alive? Is he somewhere with another family?"

My mom was thrown. I guessed she wasn't expecting us to have this conversation, at least not on that day, or maybe ever. She started to get fidgety, and there was something in her eyes I had never seen before—panic. She walked over to the sink and started to rewash the very dishes she had just washed. It's like she needed something to do with her hands. I followed her to the sink.

She looked out the window, but in her mind's eye, she was far away from here. I could almost hear her heart beat. Her chest moved up and down quickly and her whole body stiffened. I had never seen my mom so rattled before.

"Did I say something wrong?" I asked.

And then something happened that I didn't think was possible: my mom was crying. I had made my mom cry! The uneasiness that filled me would last for days. And even now when I think back to that moment, a chill runs down my body. I never ever wanted to hurt my mom or drive her to the point of tears. I didn't even know that could be done. So I told her I wasn't ready to meet him and I never brought it up again.

Dell pleading brings me out of my thoughts and back to the table. "C'mon, y'all. I need ten bucks to get lunch. Who got me?" Dell asks, dragging me back to the present.

"Nobody but Jesus. So go ask him for money," Naija replies as the guys join our table.

"For real, Naija? It's like that?" Dell says, pretending to be hurt.

"You brought your lunch from home. And you ate it already," Shawn says.

"It's called an appetizer," Dell counters.

"It's called a meatball sandwich," Shawn says.

"Ayo's gonna talk to her mom today about leaving See Us," Naija tells them.

"Is it for real this time?" Dell says.

"Yes, I have a plan," I reply. "Well, I actually have plan A, and in case that doesn't work, plan B."

"What's plan A?" Shawn says.

"I wrote a speech!" They all groan. "It's not just any speech. It's *the* speech," I assure them as I stand up and pull out my notes from my back pocket. I already have it memorized, but having the paper makes me feel better. I picture my mom standing before me, clear my throat, and begin.

"Thomas Jefferson said—"

"Hell nah!" Shawn says.

"Yeah, that's awful," Naija cosigns.

"I just started. How can it be awful already?" I protest.

"You're quoting *Thomas Jefferson*. You want to convince your mom to set you free by quoting a guy who owned slaves?" Shawn points out.

"Damn, I didn't think of that." Now, totally deflated, I sit back down.

"Ayo, don't stress about the quote. Just take that part out," Naija suggests.

"Yeah, and whatever you do, be confident, or your mom will eat you alive," Shawn says.

"They're right. You gotta go hard," Dell adds.

"I gotta go hard," I reply, mostly to myself. "I'll say, 'Mom, it's my life! I do what I want!'"

"You can't say that!" Naija warns me. "You have a Black mama."

Dell shakes his head. "You come at Rosalie Bosia like that and we'll be making funeral plans."

"Be certain, but not rude," Naija says.

"Okay, got it," I reply.

"Just in case you don't got it, what's plan B?" Dell asks.

"The hunt," I reply.

When I was a kid, whenever my mom wanted to get me interested in learning something new, she'd plan a scavenger hunt. I learned about and visited all the Underground Railroad stops in Manhattan; I discovered the journey my relatives took to get to Harlem during the Great Migration and the origins of the Harlem Renaissance.

I hated the hunts in the beginning. But the more I did them, the better I got at them and the more fun they became. Now, every year, I plan a scavenger hunt for her birthday, and she plans one for mine. It's the one time I feel like my mom really belongs to me.

When the hunt is over, I get to ask for anything I want. I've gotten a new iPhone, clothes, swimming lessons, and have had a chance to visit Italy and Thailand. But while the gifts are great, the best part is having something that's just between us.

"My birthday is less than two months away, and my mom is planning my annual scavenger hunt. If I successfully complete the hunt, I can ask for whatever I want. This year, I'll ask for my freedom."

"So if you can't talk your way out of See Us, you'll treasure-hunt your way out?" Naija says.

"Exactly. The only bad part is that I would have to wait six weeks for my birthday to come around. That's why the speech is plan A. It's harder to carry out, but it gives me my freedom faster than plan B."

"So, you're really quitting See Us?" Shawn asks.

The question settles at the bottom of my stomach like lead. I look down at my tray of food, and suddenly, the thought of eating repulses me. My stomach is completely sour. I push the tray away.

Dell looks at me in disbelief. "Um, hello? Young, Black, and hungry over here!"

I slide my tray to him as a new wave of self-doubt crashes down on me. I groan and rest my head on Naija's shoulder. She strokes my arm and says, "Don't worry, Ayo, all she can do is stop loving you."

I know Naija is only joking, but See Us is my mother's legacy, and now I'm walking away from it completely . . .

What if my mom really does stop loving me?

CHAPTER TWO

Handle That

When school is over, I ask my friends if they want to hang out, but they all have things to do. Naija, who knows me too well, says, "Just tell her."

"You're right. I can do this. I'm ready," I reply as I look toward the exit. But while my mouth says I am able, my body disagrees. I can't seem to move. Naija places her hand on my back and guides me toward the exit. "Thanks," I tell her.

I usually take the bus, but this time, I decide to walk, to give myself enough time to gather my courage. As I go down the busy street, I walk past a group of Black women wearing stark white dresses and white head wraps, with Bibles tucked neatly under their arms. They have perfect posture, elongated necks, and judgment in their eyes. I see them all the time; they attend a basement church called the Good Shepherd a few blocks away from here. We call them the Water Ladies because they think they walk on water.

Every time they see my friends or me, they have a comment to make about how we are turning out all wrong. They blame our parents.

"Ayo, you ain't tamed that hair yet?" the leader, Mrs. Curtis, says.

"Nope, still an Afro," I mutter, like I do every time she asks me that, which is every time she sees me.

"Well, that ain't hardly her fault," Mrs. Bell says. "You know her mother; Rosalie is too busy worried about Harlem to tend to her own child's soul. She never makes Ayo go to church."

Mrs. Bell and Mrs. Curtis are sisters. They both have light eyes and fine features. My mom says that's the reason they act like they are closer to God than anyone else.

"I don't know why your mother insists on holding the How Much? march this Sunday. Don't she know that's God's day?" Mrs. Bell says.

The march she's referring to is the biggest protest march ever organized by See Us. There are thousands of people expected. The march came about because earlier this year, yet another routine traffic stop turned deadly and a Black man was shot. The cop claims he thought the driver was reaching for a gun. The driver's name was Davis Brown, and he had just become a dad a week before.

In the weeks that followed, there was a frenzy in Harlem. Everyone was looking to my mom and her organization to speak on their behalf. I thought Mom was going to jump on the issues right away, but she took a different approach. Instead, she organized a massive campaign where thousands of Monopoly dollars were sent to various government buildings in New York City. Soon, Monopoly money was all over Harlem, and each bill had the same two words written over it: How Much?

And for over two weeks, people wondered what it meant. The ultraconservative media outlet Sly News kept trying to guess what it meant. They have nightly guests on that speculate what Black folks could be up to.

But my mom wouldn't comment until everything reached a fever pitch. Then she held a press conference at See Us headquarters. She looked out onto the sea of reporters and, in her usual poised and fearless manner, she addressed the cameras.

"A few weeks ago, I was out with my daughter, having dinner. There was a table nearby with two white men enjoying their meal and recounting how their day was to each other. I overheard one man say to the other, 'I was in such a hurry to get there, I drove like crazy and got pulled over.' The other man groaned and said,

'That sucks, what happened?' And his friend replied, 'I got a two-hundred-dollar ticket!' Both of them sighed and moved on to other happenings in their lives.

"I sat there and wondered, had those been two Black men sitting at the table, would the story have gone the same way? I wish all we had to worry about during traffic stops was the cost of a ticket. I want my child and your child to get pulled over, see the cops, and think, That sucks. I'll get a ticket. But as we all know, when any person of color is pulled over, a ticket is the least of their worries.

"It seems that, yet again, being Black is a crime and we are being made to pay. So on behalf of the slain driver, Davis Brown, and his wife and daughter; on behalf of the two previous cases this year, of drivers who lost their lives, Mr. Larry Ramsey and Mr. Jaylen Jackson; and on behalf of the many people of color in this community who have been detained, harassed, humiliated, and attacked for the crime of being Black, we'd like to ask a question: How much?

"How much to pay for the crime of living while Black? Since being Black is an offense, since the width of our noses, the size of our lips, and the melanin in our skin equates to criminality, it's clear there is a price to pay.

"Our ancestors gave four hundred years of free labor to this country, but . . . that was not enough. They gave up their children, their bodies, and their very breath to this country, but . . . that was not enough.

"So we are here today to ask Commissioner O'Brian and all of the NYPD one simple question. How. Much?

"How much is it going to cost us to finally be treated as equals? How much is it going to take to stop slaughtering us—in the streets, in our cars, and in our very own homes? How much?

"Tell us, so that we can leave here and tell our children, and they can tell their children, once and for all: How much?"

Ever since then, the phrase How Much? has been trending on social media, sprayed on buildings, and popping up all over Harlem. It got so much traction that other foundations joined See Us, and they are forming what is quickly becoming the biggest protest march in Harlem's history. It will take place this Sunday. In addition, three new investigations have been opened involving officer-related shootings. And I have a feeling it's just the start.

I hate that it has to be like this, but I remember the looks on the faces of the families of the victims. They haunt me. It's not fair that they will have to grieve forever just because someone saw their skin color as a threat. And like many people in Harlem, I don't want to think about it. But being a part of See Us means I have no choice.

That's another reason I want to give up See Us. I can't take any more of the sadness that comes with activism life. I don't want to think about the number of ways our skin makes us a target. I want to stay out late, party, and hashtag my way to happiness.

"Ayo, did you hear me? Why does your mom want us to march on the Lord's day?"

"It's on a Sunday because most people don't work on Sunday and will be able to join in," I reply, as I have received that question many times before—usually from the Water Ladies.

"I guess," the sisters say in unison as they make their way across the street.

The How Much? march has taken over our lives. Everyone is working hard to make sure it goes well. I've helped get the youth group ready. That meant getting kids to sign up and also getting them to ask their parents to help out. My friends and I have stuffed a million envelopes, and made as many calls. I've helped make up the signs; I've made cold calls to get donations and printed thousands of stickers and flyers.

I also met Davis's wife. When I first saw her, she looked like a ghost of whoever she used to be. Her husband was shot and killed, and it looked like she just wanted to lie in the dirt beside him. But after getting involved with the march, she's changed. There's a new light in her eyes.

See Us is a good cause. You want out because you're selfish.

No! I will not think that way. It's okay to want to do something fun for once. It's okay to want to have a life. I want to be kissed—really kissed. I want to go on dates. And get invited to parties. Just live like everyone else. Why is that so bad?

"It's not wrong! It's not!" I shout.

"Child, why you out here talking to yourself? You best not be on that stuff," someone says as I walk by.

"Hell no, she would never. Ayo's a good girl. Besides, you know Rosalie don't play that," a second voice says.

I turn toward the voices; it's the group I call the Generals. Five men. Old. Loud. Black. They are in their usual spot—in front of the barbershop. They sit on top of crates, in front of a makeshift card table. They come to the card tables like generals on a battlefield and play a ruthless game of dominoes. Their focus is unparalleled, and their resolve is absolute. They embark on world domination, until their wives call them back home for dinner.

"Ayo, tell your mama I got that Nina Simone on wax she been bugging me about," the leader, Mr. Herbert, says.

"Okay, but you know she could just download it online," I remind him.

They all look at me like I'm crazy. This isn't the first time we've had this debate. Damn, I should have cut through the alley.

"You can't hear the soul on that online music mess," Mr. Herbert says. "You need to hear the soul in a song. You can only do that with an actual album."

"Oh, leave the girl alone. She's young; they into that 'face novel' thing," Mr. Tillman says.

"That's Facebook, Mr. Tillman," I reply. "I can help you set up a profile if you want," I tease, knowing he'd never agree to it.

"Me? Nah!" he says.

"I went on that thing the other day," the oldest member, Mr. Barns, says. "It knew my brother's birthday. How the hell it know that? Nah, I ain't messing with it." Then they all begin to speak at once about the evils of the internet.

"Okay, I will tell her you have the album she wants," I promise them as I try to make my getaway. I'm not far from home now, and I need to go over my speech out loud. I don't care if I look crazy doing it. I skip the Thomas Jefferson part and begin.

"Mom, I know how important See Us is, but I feel like I have done my part, and I want to explore— No, not explore— examine— No. *Argh!* What comes next?" I stop and take out my speech. I look it over again.

"Discover!" I shout once the speech is in hand. "I have done my part, and I want to discover what else is out there . . ."

I'm so into what I'm reading that it takes a while to realize someone is calling my name. I look up.

Devonte Evens.

Oh. My. God.

I've known Devonte since first grade. I shared my pudding cup with him. He smiled at me. It was magic. I thought our love would bloom from then on, but that never happened.

I know you're not supposed to use the word "beautiful" when describing a guy, but there's no other word that fits. Devonte Evens is beautiful. He's tall and lean, with long eyelashes and a lethal smile. His eyes are amber and make you forget to breathe.

All the girls want him—even more so than they want Shawn. I've never seen him without a crowd around him. We're actually dating—in my head. In real life, I didn't even know he remembered my name until now.

He runs up to me armed with that smile. I try to convince my heart not to beat so fast, but it's no longer taking suggestions from me. My hand grows ice cold, my mouth gets dry, and I don't remember my name.

What could he want from me? He's never said hi to me before. Oh my God, does he want me? Does Devonte Evens want me?

"Yo, you good? You hyperventilating," he says as he gets closer.

I nod but can't talk just yet.

Devonte Evens wants me. Life is beautiful. I can see it now—the two of us, going to school basketball games, eating lunch together, and sneaking out of class to make out in the stairwell. Oh hell yeah, I'm down with that!

"For real, are you good?" he asks again.

I nod.

Words. I have lots of words. Where did I put them?

"Cake," I say.

What?

Don't use random words; use words that have to do with what's going on, idiot!

"I mean . . . hey."

Phew, there we go. Words.

"Can I holla for a minute?" he asks.

"Certainly."

"Certainly" is not a cool word. You're not a librarian, and he didn't just ask you to show him the way to the reference books!

"I mean, yeah, what's up?" I ask, trying to sound easy and casual.

"You live by that mural on Lenox Ave., right?" he says.

"Yeah . . ."

How does he know that? Maybe he's been checking for me— Oh. My. God.

I have to call Naija. She will freak out.

"I was around there yesterday. I was looking for you."

Okay, what should we name our kids? Something we can easily find on a mug.

"You good if I walk with you?" he asks.

Seriously, what the hell is happening?

"Sure, okay."

I'm popular now. It's taken fourteen years, but I'm popular now and it has nothing to do with who my mom is. I know they say it doesn't matter what other people think of you, but they are wrong. It matters. And it feels so good!

"I also tried to find you before class but I couldn't," he says.

"I came in early, to sign up to work in the library."

Damn, that sounds wack, right?

"Nah, that's not wack," he says.

Oh, so that last part was out loud? My bad.

Before I lose my nerve, I ask, "Why were you looking for me?"

Well, Ayo, I have been in love with you since the first grade and I was just too afraid to tell you. But now I don't care. I want to be with you. And run my fingers through your Afro, but in a loving, appreciative way, nothing like the CVS lady.

"I know we don't hang out like that, but . . ."

"We don't hang out at all," I reply.

Way to go, Ayo. Why would you point that out?

"That's true, you right." He nods and thinks to himself for a beat. I focus on staying silent and helping my lungs remember to take in air. "Yeah, so, maybe we could change that. And kick it sometimes."

"Yeah, maybe. I mean, it's whatever, you know? It's not like I'm thirsty and begging to hang out. I mean, I have friends. I don't need a social life or whatever . . ."

Shut up, shut up, shut up!

"Yeah, for sure. I know you got stuff going on, li'l mama," he says as he studies me.

His stare makes me dizzy in the best way possible.

"Ayo, I wanted to ask you for a favor," he says.

Oh crap. He wants homework help. Great. That's what all of this was about? No reason to change my social status?

"What class do you need help in?" I ask, deflated.

"What? Nah, I got that on lock. This isn't about that."

And . . . we're back!

"Okay then, what's this favor you need?" I ask, daring to stop and look into his warm amber eyes.

"You know about the Coach Cross situation, right?"

Coach Cross is the track coach at our school. Last year, he had the dumbass idea that dreadlocks were "unsportsmanlike." So he cut Alex Simmons's locs off in front of the whole team. He just said, "My team, my rules," and now See Us is demanding the coach give Alex a public apology.

"Yeah, I heard about it," I reply.

"I'm on the track team, so I saw it all go down. It was foul and everything. But Coach said he was sorry."

"Was it a real apology or a fake one?" I ask.

"What you mean?"

"Is he sorry he did it or sorry he got in trouble for doing it?"

He replies, "That's the same thing."

Okay, so I'll be the one to educate our kids.

"It's actually not the same thing," I reply.

He sighs in frustration. "He said sorry and he meant it, all right?"

"Okay, I guess that's good."

"Exactly! So we should just let it go and keep it moving, right?"

"Certainly."

And the librarian is back.

"This whole beef needs to be squashed. And it would be, but now your mother is demanding more than an apology."

Yeah, that sounds like her.

"She wants the coach suspended?" I guess.

"No. She wants him fired! Coach Cross is the best. We lose our coach, we lose any chance of winning at nationals this year. You feel me?"

I watch as my dreams of being wanted by Devonte melt away before my eyes.

"Ayo! You feel me?"

"Huh?" I reply as the last of my social life fades.

"Coach said he was sorry, and we are all good with that. Alex is the guy it happened to, and he doesn't even care either way. But your mom comes in and then everything gets messed up. Can you handle that?"

"Handle it? How?"

He takes an envelope from his back pocket and hands it over to me. Inside is a single sheet of typed paper. On top is the letterhead from some law firm.

I give it a glance and then look up at him. "This says my mom agrees to accept the apology and doesn't plan any further actions."

"Yeah. Coach gave it to me."

"Why'd he give it to you?" I ask.

"He asked the team if any of us knew you, and I raised my hand. I told him we go way back, since pudding cups."

"You remember that?"

"Hell yeah. Not everyone is happy to share. Chocolate with vanilla swirl, right?"

My face heats up, and my mouth curls into a goofy smile. I nod.

"See, I remembered. Look, you and me go way back. So I told him he could give this to me and that my homegirl would get her mom to sign it. Can you do that for me, baby girl?"

He called me baby girl. *He . . . That's . . . Oh my God!*

He reaches out and strokes my cheek.

Devonte Evens is touching me!

He licks his lips, leans in, and whispers, "Can you fix this for me, baby girl, please?"

I'm lost in the daze of his stare and the feel of his touch. I nod in agreement, although I don't recall what we were talking about.

"Yeah, I can do it," I reply.

"Thanks, Ayo," he says, then he leans in and kisses my cheek.

What the hell just happened?

CHAPTER THREE

Who Are You?

I shove the paper in my jacket pocket. It was crazy to tell Devonte I could help. The fact is that I have no idea how to change my mom's mind about the coach. That's what happens when I look into a gorgeous guy's eyes—I lose my damn mind. Fine, I will try to talk to my mom and see what she says. But right now, I have to focus on my original mission: freedom.

I walk by the mural, the one Devonte referred to, and stop to look at it. It's one of my favorites. It was inspired by Edward Hopper's painting *Nighthawks*. It's of four people sitting at a diner in the dead of night. Dell's dad—Rocky—is an artist and was commissioned to make the mural by See Us.

He reimagined the painting and made it a tribute to some

of the writers from the Harlem Renaissance: Langston Hughes, Countee Cullen, Zora Neale Hurston, and Anne Spencer. I look at them and swear they are nodding encouragingly at me.

"All right, wish me luck."

I turn onto my block and hear music coming from the house. There's always music. My mom keeps soul singers like Nina Simone, Billie Holiday, and Aretha Franklin on heavy rotation. But she loves contemporary singers, too. She plays SZA, Solange, or Jazmine Sullivan a lot. The music coming from our house today is Erykah Badu.

While we play a lot of soul songs, on the weekends, we go deep with hip-hop, new and old. My mom plays Tupac like he just came out. Her hip-hop game is the truth. She's the one who got me listening to Kendrick Lamar, Childish Gambino, and J. Cole. We've seen all three of them in concert. They made donations to See Us and sent the staff concert tickets. My mom and I got all dressed up and acted like fools when we were there.

Okay, Ayo. This is it.

I put my key in the door and hope for the best. There's just no turning back now. I ignore the tightness in my chest and enter.

My house is filled with pieces from up-and-coming Harlem artists. In addition to music, when I enter my house, I can count on two things: the scent of sandalwood and jasmine, and Harriet Tubman's determined gaze.

The painting of Harriet Tubman is done in blues and grays,

with a vivid splash of red. She hangs opposite the doorway with her pistol at the ready. The hard stare on her face says, "Try me."

My mom and I spent days looking for an inspirational piece of art to put in the entryway to greet us when we come home; nothing's more inspirational than our very own Moses.

Although I love the song that's playing, I could use some quiet for what I'm about to do. I use the app on my cell that syncs to the stereo and lower the volume of the music.

"Mom, I'm home."

"Be right down," she shouts from upstairs.

I take a series of deep breaths and tell myself that it will be fine. I hear the door to my mom's bedroom close. She descends the stairs.

My mother is a Maya Angelou poem. She's all pride and all grace; sometimes, I swear she doesn't actually walk, she glides. And God help you if you come into the room after her. No one remembers you were ever there.

She's almost six feet tall, and has perfect posture. Her skin tone has more in common with Naija's than with mine. But where Naija was created by midnight, my mother was created by dawn. And like dawn, her complexion is a rich hue of bronze and copper.

Her wide nose, full lips, and high cheekbones make her look regal. She pins her shoulder-length micro braids into a high, defiant bun. My mother inhabits elegance and has a smile that is distinctly feminine. It makes people think she's fragile. But minutes into a conversation with her, people soon realize that there is nothing fragile about her.

I go over and embrace her tightly. She smells so good. I use her perfume sometimes, but I never smell as good. When I pull away, I look into her face and am greeted by an odd expression.

"Mom, is everything okay?"

She scrunches her lips and looks away. I know that look all too well.

"Mom, what did you do?"

"I didn't do anything," she says, turning away.

I turn around so I can confront her face to face. "Mom . . . ?"

"Okay, I may have watched *Grown-ish* without you."

"What!"

Black-ish is one of our favorite sitcoms. And when one of the characters went to college, they made a new series based on that. It's called *Grown-ish*, and it's funny as hell. But life got in the way, causing us to be a season behind. So Mom and I had a deal: we would wait until both of us were free and binge-watch together.

"Okay, okay. How many episodes did you watch? One? Two, three . . . ?" I ask with growing concern.

She holds her right hand out and flashes it.

"Five! You watched five episodes without me?" She nods and hangs her head in shame. I wag my finger at her. "I am very disappointed in you, young lady," I grumble. "Were they good?"

"Oh, so good! You won't believe who kissed—"

"No spoilers!" I scold her.

"I'm sorry, Getti, I really am," she says. She has called me Getti since I can remember. It stems from my difficulty in saying the word "spaghetti" when I was a kid.

"We had a deal, Mom," I remind her again.

"I didn't mean to. I was only going to watch one episode, but then . . . it got out of control."

"Well, you will need to be punished for this—that's right. I'm taking the last piece of red velvet cake in the fridge. And I'm changing the Hulu password. When you show that you can be trusted, we will reexamine our arrangement," I say sternly.

She nods slowly with mischief in her eyes. I can't help but smile at her.

"I've been working on your hunt—it's gonna be the best one I've ever created!" she says.

"Don't try to make me forget your actions by tempting me with scavenger hunt matters. I can't be bought off."

"I cooked your favorite dinner," she says, her eyes lighting up.

"Okay, maybe I can be bought," I reply. She laughs and makes her way to the kitchen.

I drop my backpack in the hallway and follow her. The scent of greens, mac and cheese, and baked chicken fills the air. My mom doesn't cook often, but when she does, she throws down, for real. My stomach rumbles.

She smiles at me. I know she loves me. I can feel it from

across the table. I'm starting to be more at ease. Maybe this won't be so bad. We'll have a nice meal and then hang out a little. And later, I will tell her everything. And maybe, just maybe, it will be okay. I set the table, remove my jacket, and sit down to eat.

"I know things are heating up with the march so close. Everything all right in school?" she asks.

"Yeah, I think so. Everyone I know is coming to the march. Including the teachers."

"That's good. We need as many people as we can get. We need all of Harlem to ask that same question in one unified voice," she says as she takes a bite of her greens.

"Mom, I don't want to do this anymore," I mumble into my plate.

"What?" she says.

I look up. "Huh?"

"You said something just now, but I missed it. What'd you say, Getti?"

"Oh, I asked how work was."

Coward.

"It went really well. This march is unlike anything See Us has ever put together. We will be out in full force. But that will make some people nervous."

"You mean the cops?" I ask.

"Not just them. We are upsetting a lot of people by asking that our lives be valued just as much as white folks' lives are.

"Do you think only Black people will show up?"

"No, not at all. We have support from some white-owned businesses in Harlem, and support from the Latino community. But still, there's a lot of tension. And we're getting more threats than we ever have before."

"What kind of threats?" I reply.

"The usual," she says, then takes a sip of her water.

"Mom, what are you not saying?"

"It's nothing, Ayo."

"Then say it. What kind of threats?"

"Well, lately there have been some death threats—but that's no reason to worry," she says, putting her hand over mine.

"Actually, that sounds like a pretty good reason to me," I point out. "Maybe we should cancel this thing. Maybe the Monopoly money is enough to get a conversation going."

"Don't do that. Don't falter from your beliefs because some-one is threatening you. We stand our ground in this house. You know that."

"Mom, what if something happens to you? This is dangerous."

"Don't worry. We have more than enough security sched-uled for the march."

"But I am worried. I am." I put down my fork and walk away from the table. She sighs and comes after me as I head into the living room. She sees something on the floor—it's the letter Devonte gave me. I must have dropped it.

She picks up the paper and reads it. Her face falls.

"What is this?" she asks.

Damn. That's not the way I wanted to bring up the subject.

"Devonte Evens gave it to me. He says that the coach wanted him to talk to me about keeping his job."

Mom's face grows dark with anger. "He had no right to give this letter to a kid and ask them to do his work for him. This coach is unbelievable. I'm not even close to being done with him."

"Well, maybe you should be," I dare say before I can stop myself.

"Excuse me?"

Screw it. It's now or never.

"Mom, Alex is the one who got his hair cut in front of everyone. And he's willing to let it go. The coach said he's sorry. The team just wants to move on. I heard he's a great coach, and the team really wants to go to nationals this year."

She looks me over as if she's not sure I'm her child. She tilts her head slightly, and a chill runs through me. "Did you bring this letter home to show me how low the coach will go or to have me sign it?"

I shrug my shoulder but don't say anything. I look away from her. The ease and lightness we shared earlier is gone.

"I asked you a question, little girl. Did you bring this letter expecting me to sign it?"

"I . . . I don't know," I mumble as my feet sweat and my fingers go numb.

"I think you do. Now, I'm going to ask you again—and for the last time. Did you bring this ridiculous letter into this house for me to sign?"

"Fine, yes. I brought it here so that you could sign it. Alex wants—"

"Alex is a victim of a racist, arrogant bully who humiliated him because he dared to come to school with hair that was 'too Black' for the coach's comfort. That boy hasn't even begun to understand the full extent of what happened to him."

"Maybe it's nothing. Maybe you're making a big deal out of it for nothing. Maybe it's just hair!" I blurt out.

She folds her arms across her chest and furrows her brow. "You're saying you think that if Alex had been white, the same thing would have happened to him? How many white kids do you hear getting chunks of their hair cut off at school? How many white kids are being sent home because they dared to come to school with braids? Who are you right now?"

"Mom, I don't want to argue about this," I reply as I go over to the window.

"That makes two of us. You know very well what this is about. The coach did what he did because he wants to stamp out anything that doesn't look the way he thinks it should look. This isn't about hair. It's about having pride in who you are and where you're from. How is it that my child, of all people, doesn't get it?"

"Alex wants to let it go, so we should let it go."

"Well, this isn't about what Alex wants. He's sixteen. He wants to run track, buy five-hundred-dollar sneakers, and hook up with a girl. He's thinking short term. You are supposed to be thinking long term. That's the only way you'll be able to take over for me someday."

I could say it right then and there, but I don't. She comes over and looks out the window with me and doesn't say anything for a few moments. We both silently look out as night starts to fall on Harlem.

"He cried," she says softly.

"Who?" I ask as I turn to face her.

"Alex. His mother told me when she came to the office. He stood there and let the coach cut his hair and he was stoic. But when he got home, he cried and he couldn't even tell his mother why."

"I didn't know that."

"Did you talk to Alex?"

"No, I . . . Devonte said . . ."

"Devonte Evens. He has his father's eyes. Gorgeous. Makes it hard to think when you're around him, doesn't it?"

I shrug and mutter, "Maybe."

She laughs softly. "Getti, it's okay to be distracted by a pretty face and nice eyes. But there's a difference between being momentarily distracted and letting someone knock you off your path.

"Now, I'm sure Devonte batted his pretty lashes at you and tried to get you to do what he wanted. But you should have seen through it. He ran game on you, and you got sucked into it. If you can't recognize game from a skinny kid with the vocabulary of five-year-old, you're in for a world of heartbreak. I don't care how fine the guy is or how much you want that guy to like you. I didn't raise you to be a sucker. Is that clear?"

"Then what is it, Mom? What exactly are you raising me to be? You?"

"Is that a bad thing?"

I laugh sardonically. "Well, then we have a problem. I can't ever live up to you. I will never be as strong, as brave, nor as much of a badass as you are. I'm sorry."

"Getti, where is this coming from?" Tears spring to my eyes. I try to walk away, but she takes my hand. "What's going on with you? Talk to me."

I look at her, and all the words I practiced melt in my brain and ooze out of my skull.

"Ayomide! Speak."

"I want to be normal. I want to be like everyone else."

"You want to walk around blinded to racism and injustice?"

"No! That's not what I mean."

"Then what exactly do you mean? I need some clarity here."

"I don't want anything to do with protests, boycotts, or marches anymore. I love See Us. And I get why it's important, but I don't want to sacrifice my whole life for it anymore. I want to go out and be with my friends and do things that kids my age do."

"So you want to waste your life hashtagging and taking selfies?"

"That's not all kids like me do."

"You're damn right that's not all. They get pulled over for a busted taillight and never make it home. They find themselves getting rounded up and frisked because they 'look shady.' They find themselves with three bullet holes in their chest, taking their last breath on social media. Do you understand what is happening out there?"

"Yes, I get it, but—"

"No, you don't get it. What is happening to kids like Naija, Dell, and Shawn? They walk out into the street, and it's a crap-shoot as to whether or not they make it back home. And you want to stop fighting because you, what—you've missed an episode of the *Kardashians*? You don't have enough time to watch your favorite video on the best MAC lipstick to buy and how to make your butt look bigger in jeans? Is that it? Is that the young lady I'm raising?

"Mom—"

"I am not done! You think all of this I am doing is for myself? This is for you! This is so that when you have children, you don't have to see them in the morgue because of a routine traffic stop."

"I want to be normal. There's nothing wrong with that!"

"Sure, you can be normal. You can start right now. You wanna shop around at department stores and not get followed. You wanna walk around in nice neighborhoods and take in the scenery without being stopped and questioned by the cops. Maybe you'd like to experience what it's like to see flashing lights and not have your heart jump into your throat. You want all that? You got it! Take off the skin you're in. And then you can be as free as you want!"

"That's not fair! You know that's not what I meant."

"Fair? Where'd you get that nonsense from? Someone told you life was supposed to be fair? Why don't you ask the woman who buried her seventeen-year-old son because he wore a hoodie just how fair life can be? Ayomide, you're my child, and I love you. But you ever open your mouth to spout this craziness again, and you and me, we gonna really have it out. Do I make myself perfectly clear?"

I mumble something.

"I don't hear you, little girl."

"Yes! Yes. I understand."

"Good. Tomorrow, I expect you to be at the youth group meeting, bright and early. Now get yourself up the stairs and recalibrate your thinking."

I start up the stairs. She calls out, "And so help me God, if you stomp away like some teen in a damn movie, I'll come up there and drag your behind back down."

I can't process the amount of anger that's passing through

me. I'm livid, and rage flows through every inch of me. It comes out in the form of hot, salty tears and runs down my face. My jaw is clenched and everything in me is tight. It feels like there's a huge ball of fire in the middle of my chest. My mother is watching me. Her face is stern and her hands are firmly planted on her hips. I should just turn away and go up to my room, but I can't.

"Fine, Mom, I'll do exactly as you say. But just tell me this: I've been a soldier in the Rosalie Bosia army all my life. When is my contract up? Or better yet, how much? How much will it take to be free of you?"

CHAPTER FOUR

The Twins

My bedroom is a monument to strong and powerful Black women in American history. There are two beautiful sketches on my desk, one of Sojourner Truth and the other of Ellen Craft. They perfectly capture their defiant stances and determined gazes. And on the wall just above my bed is a bright watercolor painting of various influential Black women, from Shirley Chisholm to the former First Lady.

But the best part of my room is the ceiling above my bed. My friends helped me embed glow-in-the-dark letters that spell out my favorite poem—"Ego Tripping," by Nikki Giovanni. Sometimes, I lie down on the bed and look up at her words and marvel at how magical she makes us Black girls sound. The poem talks about how she built the Sphinx and gave birth to vast deserts by just thinking about them. She also talks about being such a boss that even when she's wrong, she's right. It's so damn cool.

Her words serve as disinfectant, scrubbing out the negative thoughts that cling to me. Some nights, after reading the poem, a stupid smile creeps on my face. I snuggle under the covers and think, *Well, shit. Maybe I am a badass . . .*

But while my bedroom can be a monument to endless possibilities, on days like today, it turns into a graveyard, where all my hopes go to die. And the artwork that once inspired me is now judging me. All the women in my room are looking down on me. I thought Harlem giving me the side-eye was bad, but that was before I got it from Michelle Obama; it's brutal.

I call Naija on FaceTime, hoping she can give me some advice on what to do next. It would be insane to ask my mom again, but I'm desperate. Or should I just wait until next month, for the scavenger hunt? Naija appears on my screen, but where there should have been a face, there's a wall of hair. I caught her right in the middle of her nightly hair routine. She's seated in front of her vanity, and for some reason she's wearing a jacket over her nightshirt.

"Hold on, girl, be right with you," a voice says behind "the wall."

I like watching her go through her nightly hair process. I

find it soothing because her fingers are nimble, her movements graceful.

She uses a large hair tie to gather her braids into a high ponytail and looks into the camera. "What happened? What did she say?" she asks as she reaches over for the jar of edge smoother and gently applies the goop to her edges in an upward motion.

"She said I lost my mind and she'd give me time to find it again."

"Damn, that's messed up," she replies as she picks out one of a dozen silk scarfs hanging on the hook by her mirror, ties the scarf around her head, and then puts on her trusty flowered silk bonnet. She stuffs all her hair under it; it piles up high behind her head, where it forms a dome. She looks like a funky Black Xenomorph, the creature in *Alien*.

Most girls I know would stop there with the nighttime hair routine, but not Naija Harris. She puts on another silk scarf to secure the bonnet. If Naija were on a desert island and could only have three things, she'd ask for her silk scarf, silk bonnet, and her Carol's Daughter Black Vanilla Edge Control Smoother. She'd ask for those things way before she'd think to find food and shelter.

"All that prep work I did was for nothing. I couldn't even get her to sign the paper Devonte gave me."

"Devonte?" she says. I recount that part of the conversation.

She has a bunch of questions. She wants to know if I think he likes me and if there's a chance he's trying to get with me.

"Does it even matter, Nai? See Us will take up all my time. When would we ever hang out? What would I say to him? 'Hey, Devonte, my mom's not home. You wanna come over and write protest signs?'"

Naija laughs. I sigh and drop my head.

"Ayo, relax. You have a plan B, remember?"

"But that's a month away. I can't wait that long. I wanted to start the school year free."

"Is there a chance you can still say your speech?"

"That's why I called. Should I ask again?"

"If you don't want to wait a whole month, then it's your only choice," she tells me.

I don't reply. Instead, I replay the scene with Mom. It feels even worse than it did before.

"Earth to Ayo!" she says as she walks her phone into her bathroom.

"Sorry. Spaced out. I'm back," I promise as I watch her lather her face with African black soap. When she's done, she dries her face off and scoops a small amount of raw shea butter into her hand. She rubs the butter back and forth between her palms, allowing it to melt. She applies it to her face and neck, leaving her dark skin glowing even more so than before.

"If it was the other way around, I know Mom would have held her ground," I add.

"Well, yeah, but that's because any ground she stands on becomes *her* ground. She's an unwavering force of nature, a category-five hurricane that people post warnings about."

I sigh. "Yeah, and I'm a spring shower. The kind people don't even bother running away from." I roll over and plant my face in my pillow.

"I've known you forever, Ayo; you can handle yourself. Remember when you nearly sent Dell to the hospital?"

"Defending my fries from Dell's greedy fingers and taking on my mom are two different things."

"Maybe it starts with fries and it grows," she says in a goofy voice.

I poke my head up from my pillow, deflated and drained. "Great. My mom defends Black people in Harlem, and I defend fries."

She shakes her head and takes on the tone she uses when she's about to school me on something. "No, Ayo, you defend *sweet potato* fries. That's much more impressive."

The more I think about my situation, the worse I feel. I'm in desperate need of a subject change. "Hey, why are you wearing a jacket in the house?" I ask. She shrugs but doesn't say anything. "Landlord didn't give y'all no heat? Damn, that's cold. You wanna come stay here until the heat is back on?"

Before she can reply, her mom calls out to her. She tells Naija to join her and her new boyfriend, Kingston, in the living room to watch a movie.

I first met Kingston about two months ago. Naija and I came back from a block party earlier than we'd planned. We found Ms. Harris and Kingston coming out of her bedroom, wearing robes and looking seriously faded. The smell of weed clung to the air and infected every damn thing in the apartment. Ms. Harris saw us and quickly closed her robe.

"Girls, come meet my new friend, Kingston," she said with a grin. She signaled for him to say hello to us. Kingston is short, heavy, and has skin the color of walnuts. "How you young ladies do'n?" he said. Naija and I exchanged a knowing glance. This scenario wasn't new. Ms. Harris had "friends" come over every few weeks.

Naija's mom uses the same thought process to select boyfriends I use when buying gadgets at the swap meet: I know that whatever I pick up will be defective in one way or the other. I buy it because I'm hoping its flaws are bearable.

Naija turns toward the camera and rolls her eyes.

"Wait, what's up with this Kingston guy?" I ask. "Do we like him?"

She tilts her head to the side, raises her perfectly arched eyebrows, and sighs deeply. I guess that's a no.

"What's wrong with him?"

"Doesn't matter, Ayo. I haven't seen her this happy since she stumbled on a Fenty gloss stick at the dollar store."

There's a knock on my door. My heart starts racing. I whisper into my phone, "It's my mom."

"You think she's changed her mind?"

"I don't know. Hit you back later."

Naija signs off and the screen goes black.

"Come in," I say.

Mom opens the door but remains in the doorway, making no attempt to enter. Her expression is troubled, her eyes crestfallen. There's only one other way I can use to describe the look on her face: heartbroken.

"Ms. Hightower's social security check is late again. I put some stuff aside for her in the kitchen; I need you to bring it to her."

"Okay," I mumble. She starts to close the door. I try to gauge just how pissed she is at me. "Am I still invited to the cookout?" I ask, biting my lower lip nervously.

Her jaw is tight and her body is rigid with disapproval. "Right now, Candace Owens and Stacey Dash would have a better chance of getting in."

Damn.

"Okay . . . that's pretty bad," I mumble to myself.

"It's more than bad. You're verging on Kanye West territory. It's hard to come back from that."

"You think I'm a sellout?" I ask, in disbelief.

"I think you are allowing people in your ear. I think you have gotten off track. And you really need to get back on—quickly."

"Argh!" I shout in frustration.

"I'm right about this, Ayo, and I think you know that. I

started See Us. It's supposed to be your legacy. Walking away would be a mistake."

"No, it's not! You want to know what's insane? Leaving a party because of watermelons!" The words come out of my mouth before I can stop them.

The watermelon argument was one of our biggest. Last year, we went to a party at the MoMA. We happened to be one of a handful of Black folks there, so we kind of stood out. The host encouraged us to eat and mingle. She guided us toward the buffet table. She pointed toward the thick-cut slices of watermelon and said, "I know you two will love these." My mom went off. We had to leave.

"We agreed never to rehash that argument," she reminds me.

"That was before I was kicked out of the cookout."

"You know I was kidding about that."

"Were you? Because I can see from the way you are looking at me right now, you think I'm letting everyone down."

"I don't know about everyone, Ayo, but yes, you are letting me down." My mother's tone can be a healing tonic or a weapon. And right now, her tone might as well be a hatchet.

A lump forms in my throat. My body grows tense and feverish, but I plow ahead and say what's on my mind.

"That's another reason I want out of See Us. I don't want to spend my life having to call out every instance of racism. Sometimes a watermelon is just a watermelon."

Ms. Hightower lives a few bus stops away from me, and given the chill in the air, I should take the M3 bus. But right now, I don't feel like waiting for it. I need to walk; I need to think. So, I head down 125th on foot. Anywhere in the world a group of Black people gathers, a parade of hairstyles follows, and Harlem is no different. I encounter a wide range of wigs—from bargain-bin synthetic to high-priced Brazilian. I walk by a man with thick Rastafarian locs that symbolize spirituality, and a couple with short, spiky, colorful locs, worn for fashion. When you add to that the myriad braided hairstyles, you basically have a runway hair show.

Normally, I people-watch, because here, you rarely see the same look twice. But my mind isn't on that right now. And while I note the hair, I don't see anything else. The parade goes by me in a blur. I don't even remember walking past Red Rooster or Sylvia's Restaurant. And normally, the tempting aroma of smothered chicken and biscuits would draw me in.

Like I said, my mom and I don't argue often. So us having two arguments on the same day is really messing with my head. In the past, when we've hit something we can't agree on, we've found a way to compromise. That's what happened with the situation we would go on to call "the Kenya Barris conundrum."

Kenya Barris is the Black guy who created, among other things, our favorite TV show, *Grown-ish*, the show my mom confessed to watching without me. She pointed out once just how fair-skinned the cast was for both *Grown-ish* and his other show, *Black-ish*. She said it seemed like he went out of his way to avoid casting dark-skinned actors. I didn't really stop to think about it until Naija cosigned.

"I mean, damn, don't he know no dark-skinned people?" she said, rolling her eyes when *Grown-ish* premiered.

I floated a theory around to them: maybe now that Mr. Barris had power in, his next project would be more inclusive. That theory went to hell when we saw the cast for his new Netflix show, called *#BlackAF*. I've seen more color in a blizzard than I have on Kenya's new show.

"I think we should still support the show. It's not the actors' fault that the creator is color-struck," I reasoned.

"You go ahead if you want to, but I'm getting off this 'light is right' train," my mom said.

So we left it at that. When the new show came out, I promised I wouldn't make my Hollywood mom watch it with me; she, in turn, promised not to roll her eyes when it came on.

We met in the middle. Is there any way we can do that now?

"You really young to have such an intense look on your face. What you over there thinking about?" someone says, pulling me out of my thoughts. It's Nate Collard. He's a See Us board member. Many of his relatives were members of the Black Panther Party. He's always challenging my mom on what is best for See Us. And how the movement should progress.

Nate is in his forties. He's handsome, smart and has a laugh that made me giggle when I was little. I always thought he had a thing for my mom. I'd catch him sneaking glances at her. But nothing ever came of it; at least, I don't think it did. I'm kind of glad, because Nate and my mom together would be too intense.

"Hi Nate. I was just thinking about stuff. Nothing important," I lie.

"You're the voice of the young folks at See Us. You can't let trivial things get in the way of that. I warned your mom, you should be homeschooled. That way, you won't get distracted."

I try hard not to roll my eyes, because that would get back to my mom and I'd be in trouble. Nate is die-hard when it comes to the cause, and any time spent on anything else is time wasted.

"I'm running an errand for my mom, so . . ."

"Oh, sure. Don't let me stop you," he replies. I start walking away, hoping it's the end of it. "Youth membership is down this month, I think you can do a better job at recruiting, don't you?"

ARGH!

"Okay, I'll try," I reply without looking back.

A few minutes later, I knock on Ms. Hightower's door. She calls out in the mandatory gruff and uninviting New York tone, "Who is it?"

"It's me, Ayo," I reply.

I hear her footsteps as she comes closer. She opens the door wide and beams at me. I'm all but certain that Adina Hightower escaped from an Annie Lee painting, specifically the one called

You Hungry? And just like many women in Lee's paintings, Ms. Hightower is fleshy, round, and lives for colorful house dresses.

Her hair is dyed a rich, deep copper that complements her wheat-colored complexion. She's in her seventies, but thanks to her wide eyes, baby face, and freckles, the little girl she used to be is never too far from view.

"Oh, so you just gonna keep growing like a weed, huh?" she says, her once-rough tone now warm and inviting. "C'mon in," she says as she embraces me. Ms. Hightower gives the best hugs. It's like being held by a cloud—a cloud that smells like chamomile tea and summer.

Her apartment is a monument to the Apollo Theater. Ms. Hightower worked there for over four decades. On her wall are meticulously framed photographs of her with Jimi Hendrix, Parliament, the Jackson 5, Aretha Franklin, James Brown, and many others. She's arranged them in such a way that it tells her life story.

I can count on two things when I come over to see Ms. Hightower: a cautionary tale and diabetic candy. The cautionary tale she gives me today is her favorite one; it has to do with her most prized possession—a framed, autographed picture of her favorite singing group, Patti LaBelle and the Bluebelles. Inside the framed picture is a train ticket they sent Ms. Hightower. A ticket for a ride she didn't have the courage to take.

Ms. Hightower doesn't just know how to sing—she knows how to *saaaaaang*. This city is full of talented singers who can make you stop and take notice. But to stand out here in Harlem, home of the Apollo Theater, you better bring it. And Ms. Hightower could do that like no other.

"Please tell your mama I plan to pay her back," Ms. Hightower vows as I help her unload the bag of groceries.

"You know she won't take any money," I reply.

"Yeah, I know that mama of yours is stubborn as hell," she says, shaking her head, "but I'm gonna make her take my money. I don't ask for no charity from nobody. You know that."

"Yes, I know, and I'll tell her."

"Good. Tomorrow, I mean to go see them folks at the social security office and see what's what. This is the second time they been late with my check. They lucky I got the Jesus."

"I'm in school when they are open, so I can't come, but if you need someone to go with you, I can ask my mom or someone at See Us. We have a list of volunteers who do stuff like that. Just let us know, okay?"

She smiles warmly and says, "You all are so nice over there. I don't know what we'd do without See Us and your mama. That woman is the heartbeat of this place."

I try to ignore the fresh wave of guilt that washes over me as I open Ms. Hightower's fridge and put in the carton of milk.

"Are you coming to the march?" I ask.

"Humph, just try to stop me!" she says. "And I got the ladies from my Bible study to come too."

"Bible study" is really a weekly card game played with six women who live down the street. They drink wine, gossip, and play a cutthroat game of poker. But whenever one of them wins, they shout, "Yes, God!" so I guess it's kind of like church . . .

"Well, if that's all, Ms. Hightower, I think I'm gonna go . . ."

"Oh no, you gotta eat something."

"I'm not really hungry," I confess.

"No, but you will be later. You too skinny. It's them magazines, giving y'all a complex. Go on and take some pie," she says as she walks over to the counter.

"You know pie is all sugar. It's not good for diabetics."

She waves off my warning, per usual. "Oh, hush. I know I got the sugar. I been had it forever. You don't have to remind me. Now, I ate good yesterday. So I can eat bad today. And besides, I prayed on the pie. God won't let it harm me."

I want to tell her that that's not the way diabetes works, but I know she will do as she pleases.

So I don't say anything. I just take a small piece of pie and go sit at the table. She pours herself a glass of Hennessy and sits next to me. We inevitably begin talking about the pictures on the wall, and that, as always, leads to her Patti LaBelle and the Bluebelles story.

But this time, when she gets to the end, she doesn't talk

about how it was probably for the best or that it was God's plan, like she usually does. Instead, Ms. Hightower gets this pained, faraway look on her face and says, "Sometimes I think the devil had twin babies, one named Fear and the other named Regret. They both ugly and they both scare me. But no matter how big a monster Fear is, Regret is a real mother . . ."

———

The sadness etched on Ms. Hightower's face stays with me even after I get home. She wanted something so badly, and yet she let the chance just pass her by. I don't want that to happen to me. I will not give up on trying to convince my mom to let me go. In fact, I'm gonna talk to her right now.

I walk up the steps to her bedroom. I'm about to knock on her bedroom door when I overhear her on the phone. She's talking to my uncle Ty.

"No, I'm not making too much out of this, Ty . . . Ayo wants to set fire to everything I have built for her. This isn't the girl I raised. I'm so . . . *disappointed*."

It's one thing to think you disappointed your parent, but it's another to hear them say it out loud. A big lump forms in my throat and tears flood my eyes. I feel like someone stabbed me in the heart.

Someone did: my best friend. My mom.

I lean against the wall just outside her bedroom, too shocked to move. My cell vibrates. I look at the screen.

> What up, it's Devonte. Naija gave me your number. Hope that's cool. Did you get your mom to sign the paper?

I look at the text and, suddenly, what was once sorrow and despair is replaced by anger and resentment. What's the point of trying to please her anymore? She wants to be disappointed in me? Then fine, I'll give her a reason to *really* be disappointed.

I march back downstairs to the living room and pick up the letter Devonte gave me. I scribble my mother's name on the dotted line and text Devonte:

> Yeah, we good. She signed.

CHAPTER FIVE

A Warning

The first sound I hear when I wake up is one that is very familiar to me—the sound of Mom putting out fires. It doesn't matter how well a march is planned; there are always last-minute things that go awry. And now that the How Much? march is only four days away, naturally things are coming apart. But in the end, everything will come together perfectly; Rosalie Bosia would have it no other way.

Last night, I tossed and turned and didn't fall asleep until around three a.m. I kept thinking about my mom's call to my uncle. Seriously, what is the point if everything I do falls short of her expectations? Well, I'm no longer going to try.

I get up, go over to my backpack, and take out the letter.

This is usually about the time where I would doubt my decision. I'd second-guess myself, and in the end, I'd "do the right thing." But this ain't no Spike Lee joint. I'm getting off the Pleasing Rosalie Bosia train. I'm going to hop on the Young, Gifted, and Free Myself express.

The very first stop is Forgery City.

I shower, dress, and quickly gather my stuff. I need to get out of the house without running into my mom. I try to get downstairs without making a sound. I'm new to being sneaky, but I'm gonna give it a shot because my mom is the last person I want to see right now. I get down the hardwood staircase and over to the coat rack by the door.

Please, God, let me make it out of this house without being seen.

"Good morning," she says behind me.

Really, God, it's like that?

I roll my eyes and turn around to face my mother. She's dressed for work from head to ankle. But on her feet are fuzzy slippers shaped like the Cookie Monster's paws. Her slippers bring back a vivid memory.

When I was five, the Cookie Monster used to scare the hell out of me. I knew he was supposed to be a fun, playful puppet, but he starred in all my nightmares. In my defense, he had the word "monster" right in his name.

This was around the time that See Us put together a month-long seminar on health and nutrition in the Black community. Every Saturday, a different healthcare professional would speak.

Other kids who came with their moms got to go outside and play. My mom insisted I not only help set up, but that I take part in the workshop.

That summer, I learned more than any kid should about high blood pressure, strokes, and diabetes. I was up on game. I knew that the "lovable" Cookie Monster was nothing more than a sugar peddler.

One night, after a particularly bad nightmare about the blue menace, I woke up screaming and ran to Mom's room. She vowed that she would track down the Cookie Monster, and when she did, I would have to face him head-on.

I was so scared that I almost wet myself. I remember following her out to the hallway, in my Princess Tiana nightgown, clutching onto her. I cried and begged her not to go get the monster. I told her I couldn't face it. She knelt down so that we were at eye level and said, "You will stop crying, right now." Her voice left no room for argument.

I quickly swallowed my sobs and told myself not to be afraid. It didn't work. My mom took my hand in hers and informed me, in no uncertain terms, that tonight I would fight the monster. We headed toward the hall closet, where she said she'd heard sounds earlier.

I pleaded for her not to go inside. But she went in anyway. It felt like forever before she returned. When she came back out, her hair was disheveled, she was breathing hard, and her eyes were wide with shock.

"I found him. Are you ready?" she asked.

I shook my head. "No."

She got on her knees again, so we could keep being at eye level. She interlaced our fingers and said, "Monsters are not new. They will always be here, and they will always come for you. How you handle them now is how you will handle them for the rest of your life."

I wanted to run and hide under my bed forever. She studied the fear and uncertainty etched on my face.

"Child, there are hundreds of people waiting in the wings to help you," she said. "Every one of your ancestors. All you have to do is use your voice and call to them."

So I did as she said. I whispered, "Ancestors."

Nothing happened.

"I don't see them," I said.

"You will, one day. When your voice is strong enough," Mom said. "Until then, you still have a monster to face." She guided me toward the closet.

My heart bounced around my rib cage like a Ping-Pong ball. I felt a chill zip along my spine, causing goose bumps down my arms. My fingers and toes had turned to icicles and I forgot how to let air enter my lungs. She read my fear and said, "Ayo . . . face it. Or face me."

It didn't matter how scary the thing in the closet was — my mom was far more formidable. I took a deep breath and ran inside the closet. The darkness engulfed me and I could feel the hairs on the back of my neck standing up. It was at that point that my shaking hands and I decided it might be best to face my mom instead of the monster. I turned the doorknob to escape, and my mom shouted out to me from the other side.

"Girl, don't you come back out here till that thing is dead and gone."

So, I put everything I had into destroying the foul blue beast. I kicked and punched in every direction, with my eyes closed. I even had a battle cry. A short while later, my mom opened the door and I ran out.

"Did you get the monster?" she demanded.

I nodded excitedly. Mom carefully entered the closet. She came back out holding something behind her back.

"Ayomide Bosia, you better go ahead! You defeated the monster!" she shouted.

"I did?"

"Child, you beat that thing so bad, he ran and left his feet!" she said as she revealed slippers made out of the Cookie Monster's paws. I was beside myself. I came in for a closer look.

"I did it? I got him?"

"You did! I'm gonna keep these to remind me how strong and brave my child is, just like her ancestors," she said.

I beamed proudly. Later, whenever I saw the Cookie Monster on *Sesame Street*, I wasn't shook, because I knew it was just an impostor. I had fought and conquered the real one; my nightmares went away.

I was too young to put it together then: my mom had gone out and bought the slippers in anticipation of yet another nightmare. I was also too young to understand that the monsters would get bigger over time, and that they wouldn't confine themselves to the closet.

"I think we have time for a quick breakfast," Mom says, pulling me out of my thoughts.

"I'm not hungry."

"C'mon, we can be mad at each other *and* eat. There's no need to choose one or the other." She signals for me to follow her into the kitchen, and I do. But I don't commit to anything more than the doorway. She puts two raisin bagels into the toaster, pours two glasses of orange juice, and searches the fridge for the butter.

"I'm really not hungry. And I have to go or I'll be late."

She looks at her watch. "You have some time."

She's right. I can stay here for another fifteen minutes and still be on time for my first period. I feel myself growing frustrated. I admit, "It's not about being late. I just don't want to be here."

"You keep taking that tone with me and you won't be here or anywhere else," she warns me. I feel a tingle spread throughout my body. My muscles tighten and my jaw clenches.

We lock eyes. Her hand goes up on her hip and her head is slightly tilted. She's trying to figure me out. I stubbornly fold my arms across my chest, fearing that she will somehow weaken my resolve. The toaster pops up. The bagels are ready. They will get hard if we leave them there, and yet neither of us makes a move.

She shakes her head. "You have the nerve to tell me that you want out of See Us, and now you're acting like you are the one who should be upset? All right, Ayo . . . ask me," she says.

"Ask me" is a game we play when we disagree on something. She'll tell me who she believes I am acting like, and I'll tell her. In the end, it helps us either come to an agreement or laugh it off. But I'm in no mood to play. I already know what she thinks of me.

"I'm not playing," I inform her.

"Ask me," she says.

"Not playing," I insist.

"Fine," she says, shaking her head again as she tidies up the counter.

I turn around sharply, fully intending to leave the house, but my curiosity gets the better of me. "Okay. Who am I?" I ask begrudgingly.

"Nick Cannon thinking he can battle Eminem."

My mom just called me brain damaged. I'm dumbfounded. My whole body tenses up. There's so much I want to say, but when I open my mouth, all that comes out is "Argh!"

"I'm sorry, Ayo, but that's who you are right now."

"Fine. Ask me."

She takes a deep breath, bracing herself. "Who am I?"

My mom loves throwback nineties hip-hop and R&B. I'm not sure when I started to like it too, but I did. So when we get a chance, we binge-watch shows like *Behind the Music* and *Unsung*. I reference an episode we've watched a million times.

"You're Pebbles refusing to release TLC from their contract."

She folds her arms across her chest and glares back at me. "Really? Well, right now, you are Lil Wayne on *Nightline*."

I have a strong urge to roll my eyes, suck my teeth, and dismiss her. But I don't want to die today. So instead, I let out a breath and head for the door. I turn back to her, and just before I walk out, I pose a challenge. "Ask me."

She says, "Who am I?"

"Azealia Banks."

———

I didn't think it was possible, but as I walk down the block, I see even more How Much? posters through the neighborhood. The posters are mocking me. It's a reminder that no matter how hard I try, I will always be tied to See Us. It doesn't help that I get stopped three times by people who know my mom and have questions about the protest.

No,

you should not bring newborns to the march with you.

No,

we can't change the date because it conflicts with the Real Housewives of Atlanta *reunion special.*

No,

you can't hitch a ride in the senior van if you're not a senior.

When the bus finally pulls up, I'm grateful. All I want to do is get to school without one more reminder of See Us. I step toward the back of the crowded bus and am surprised when I'm able to snag the last seat. I sit and take a deep breath.

The lady sitting next to me is on her cell, watching a televised version of one of New York City's biggest morning radio shows, *The Breakfast Club*, a show about hip-hop culture. One of the hosts—Charlamagne tha God—is announcing his daily segment called "Donkey of the Day."

"Donkey of the Day" highlights people who commit crimes that are too dumb for words. Or just say things that are so asinine and bizarre, it defies logic. To be one hundred, they should just call it "People from Florida," because ninety-five percent of the time, that's where the person they are roasting is from.

Today the Donkey is a man named Guppy. Guppy thought it was a good idea to call the police on his live-in girlfriend because she'd eaten all the blue moon-shaped marshmallows in his Lucky Charms cereal. Then he took off after her using a spoon as a makeshift weapon. And where was he from? You guessed it, Florida. The lady and I look at each other and smile.

Once the host is done with that segment, they move on to talk about the event that is on everyone's lips—the march. They discuss the celebrities coming and how the right-wing news media is vilifying the protest even before it happens. And just before they go to a commercial break, they bring up my mom and how critical she is to the movement.

When I get to class, the bell is just about to ring, so I don't get a chance to update Naija. I also don't get a chance to inquire about her outfit. She's wearing gray hooded sweats that are too big and baggy for her. She has her hood up, and I can barely make her out in the thick cotton fabric.

Mr. Gunderson tells her to take off her hood; she glares at him and does as he asks. Her hair is in a sensible ponytail at the base of her neck. Naija has never been sensible where it comes to clothing or her hair. She's always one for risks, and more often than not, they pay off. But today, her hair and outfit are drab and uninspired.

"Girl, you good?" I ask.

She nods.

There's no time for a follow-up question; Mr. Gunderson is now facing the class. "Before we get to the next chapter, I think it's important to acknowledge that history isn't just what happened in the past—it can sometimes be what's happing right now. And by that, I mean our very own Ayo Bosia will be at the forefront of the biggest protest march in Harlem history. So I thought she could tell us a little more about it. Ayo, get up here."

Someone kill me . . .

I get to the front of the class and quickly tell them about the march, and yes, everyone already knows, but that doesn't stop Mr. Gunderson from asking a million follow-up questions.

When the bell rings, I head for Naija. But before I get to her, Devonte texts me to meet him by my locker.

"Go ahead, Nai, I'll catch up." She nods and goes out the back door. When I get to my locker, Devonte is waiting for me. I have long suspected this, but now I know for sure: this guy gets better looking the more I stare at him.

I take the letter out of my pocket and hand it over to him.

"Yo, I can't believe you got her to sign it! I'm impressed, shorty," he says as he looks me over.

I shrug and say, "I know." My voice is casual, even, and unbothered. It's like, all of a sudden, I'm Beyoncé. And when someone tells Queen Bey she's impressive, she doesn't get all hyped about it—she just nods and accepts it as a fact.

And then he says five words that rip the air out of my lungs: "Ayo, wanna chill with me?"

CHAPTER SIX
Strange Fruit

Wait, what exactly does a stroke feel like? Because I think I might be having one right now. Okay, here's the deal, God: if you take me now, right now, I'd be okay with it, because nothing can top this moment . . . except maybe more moments with Devonte.

And right away a flood of picturesque moments fills my head. They range from small, romantic walks in the park to major events like prom and our wedding.

"Ayo?" he asks.

"Huh?"

"You wanna chill with me sometime or nah?"

I nod.

Oh, look at that, my head still knows how to move up and down. Good for me.

He tells me he'll hit me up later. I watch him make his way down the hall. He uses his swagger and confidence to part the sea of students, like a sexy-ass Black Moses. He got me tripping hard. And now he wants to hang out. That's the start of me having a social life.

Yes!

When lunch finally comes, I rush to the cafeteria, hastily grab a tray of food, and head over to my friends' table. It's all I can do not to skip to them. I catch them up on everything they've missed. When I'm done, they greet me with stunned silence.

"Someone say something," I say.

"You really forged your mom's name?" Shawn asks.

"Well, yeah. But she's so busy with the march, she probably won't notice. And hello, can we focus on the big news: Devonte asked me out!" I remind them.

"What's the point of starting something up with him?" Dell asks. "You only got a few hours until your mama finds out and you end up on a missing poster."

"And you Black, so . . . cops ain't even gonna look for you," Shawn adds.

Naija shakes her head in dismay. "Girl, you did all this for Devonte? I know he's fine, but . . ."

"It's not about him," I promise. She stares back at me as if to say, "Don't even try it." I sigh and admit, "Okay, it's about Devonte, but it's not *just* him." I stab my now cold, limp fries with my fork. "My mom thinks so badly of me already; nothing I do could really make that much of a difference. I overheard her on the phone—she's disappointed in who I turned out to be." I ignore the pain in my chest as I recall her words.

"Everyone disappoints their parents," Shawn replies pointedly. Shawn has been trying to tell his dad he's gay for months now and can't seem to go through with it. I place my hand on his.

"Not everyone disappoints their parents," Naija says. "Sometimes we do stuff for them 'cause it will make them happy. They look out for us, so we look out for them."

"Nah, I'm with my boy Shawn on this," Dell says. "Everyone lets down their parents. One time my dad came home and found me doing something so bad, he wasn't just disappointed; he became disillusioned."

"What happened?" Naija asks.

"It was awful; the kind of moment that changes a man," Dell says as he looks off into the distance. Dell is rarely serious. But right now, he looks dejected and somber.

"What did your dad catch you doing that had him so shook?" I ask gently.

Dell tries to gather himself. "Y'all know how me and my

dad do when it comes to music. He introduced me to the greats: Davis, Parker, Coltrane, Gillespie . . . and I betrayed him—no, I did more than that. I wounded him. I cut him deep . . ." Dell says in a pained, soft voice.

"Yeah, we got that part," Shawn tells him. "Now what did you do to hurt him so bad?"

"He came home and found me . . . listening to Kenny G."

Shawn lets out a groan. I roll my eyes and elbow Dell in the midsection.

"What? It was very traumatic for us, okay? My dad put a lot of work in me, and I throw it away for elevator music," Dell says in disgust.

"We really do need to stop hanging out with you," Shawn says.

Nai shakes her head and looks down at her tray. "Where's the rest of my sandwich?" she asks.

We all turn to Dell. "Oh, you went to the bathroom, and, ah . . . I thought you were done."

"What the hell is wrong with you?" Nai barks. Her tone is so sharp and harsh that a few students turn toward us to see what the drama is about.

"Yo, chill," Dell says, taken aback by her reaction.

She bolts up out of her chair. "Why you so greedy?"

"Why you dressed like a gray crayon?" Dell counters.

"Okay, you two, relax," Shawn says.

"Nai, you can have my lunch," I offer.

"No! I want what was on my tray," she demands. Now everyone is looking over at us.

Dell stands up and tries to reason with her. "You being real extra right now, Naija. It's just a sandwich."

"It wasn't just *a* sandwich. It was *my* sandwich!" She hurls the tray across the table at Dell; it falls over the edge.

"Yo, these kicks are new!" Dell says. He quickly jumps back to avoid the falling debris. It's too late; greasy fries and ketchup land on his sneakers and roll off what used to be his impeccably white kicks.

Naija wags her finger at Dell. "Put your fingers on my food again, I'll break them!" she says, just before storming off.

I find her in the stairwell near the gym. Her knees are hiked up to her chest and her arms are wrapped around them. She buries her head in her knees. Naija is dramatic, but never like this. I sit next to her.

"What's going on, Nai? Talk to me."

She pokes her head out, and her eyes are swollen from crying. "Cramps. That's all," she says.

I know it's not true because she's not inhaling Sour Patch Kids by the handful or launching into her "Why do girls get cramps and boys get nothing?" tirade.

"Talk to me, Nai. Tell me who we gotta beat down," I say.

She rolls her eyes, knowing very well I'm not the violent type.

"What? I'm serious. You give me a name and I'll take care of it," I insist. "I know people with no morals and no fingerprints."

She looks at me doubtfully.

"You say'n I won't?" I reply, pretending to be offended.

She gives me a small smile. That's a win, so I take it. I place my hand on her shoulders and look into her eyes.

"I want to help, but you have to tell me what it is."

"I don't wanna talk about it."

"Okay. Tell me this: Is it a person that upset you or an animal?" I ask. She shakes her head as a silent warning for me not to go there. "Remember that time in second grade—" I begin.

"Ayo, don't!"

I shrug. "I'm just saying, you got really upset and refused to go out into the schoolyard because you were afraid of little bitty animals."

"Those things were huge, vindictive, and sneaky!"

"Those things were squirrels," I remind her.

"They had an agenda."

"You took their nuts," I counter.

"One. Just one. Why couldn't they let it go?"

I can't help but laugh at the conviction in her voice. "And when everyone made fun of you for being afraid to face them, what did me, Dell, and Shawn do?"

"You all made fun of me too."

"Oh yeah, we did—at first. But when we saw that it was

really upsetting you, we all went out there together to face the sq—"

"Terrorists."

I suppress a smile. "Yes, the bucktoothed, furry terrorists came for you, and we faced them together."

"This is different," she says.

"The situation may be, but we're still the same. We got you. And you don't have to talk to me right now, but when you're ready, I'm here."

"Girl, I know," she says, starting to brighten up.

"Also, you think you could guard my food from Dell? I'd pay you. Hell, the whole school would pay you. Kind of a 'Dell protection' program."

"I'll send you my rates," she says. We share a smile. And suddenly, without warning, my best friend places her head on my lap—something she's never done before. I'm taken aback for a moment, and then I stroke her hair and pray to God that whatever is bothering her is something small, like vengeful squirrels.

———

When the final bell rings, I head to See Us headquarters. Naija is still on my mind. She did cheer up for the remainder of the school day, but I know her well enough to know some of it is an act. I'm determined to try again to reach her, because that's what she'd do for me.

"You're late!" a familiar male voice informs me, just before I enter the building.

Milton Moore.

I roll my eyes hard and pray for patience. Milton is vice president of the youth division of See Us. He's at the top of his class and is president of every club he's a part of—except this one. He hates me because I ruined his otherwise unblemished reputation for being a leader.

"The meeting is at three. You're late," he says again, just in case I missed his announcement the first time. I look at the time on my cell. It's five minutes after three and the members aren't here yet. I ignore Milton, getting my keys out and open the door to the meeting room.

"I'm say'n, why do we have to stop at marching? How many marches have we held? They just gonna keep doing the same thing—mistreating us, disrespecting us, and killing us! Let's give it right back to them!" Walter Powell says to me as he comes toward us.

Walter's mom is white; his dad is half white. Walter could very easily pass for a white kid, so he goes harder than the rest of us. He wants the whole world to know he's more down than anyone else in the history of down-ness. His entire life could be set right if someone Black just hugged him and said, "All right, man, we see you! You're Black like us."

Milton isn't done being snarky. "You're supposed to be here before the rest of us. I can't keep covering for your missteps."

I grit my teeth and remind myself that Black-on-Black crime is bad. I step inside, and my jaw drops.

I had forgotten that someone from the adult branch said they'd drop off extra posters for us. And now the room is filled with large protest signs that feature photos of Black people killed by cops: Atatiana Jefferson, Aura Rosser, Stephon Clark, Botham Jean, Philando Castile, Alton Sterling, Michelle Cusseaux: a new crop of strange fruit.

My heart is racing, I'm feverish, and my knees are weak. I know it's because of them. Their eyes are following me as I walk across the room. The members start to arrive and ask me questions, but I barely hear them. I'm too distracted by the eyes on the posters.

Since they can no longer cry out for justice, they need others to raise their voices in protest. They need someone who can give voice to their pain. That someone's voice should be loud enough to travel across the universe and back again, like my mom's. I do not have that voice, and they know it.

I need to get out of here.

I guess the gods heard my prayer, because at that very moment, Devonte texts me. He tells me everyone on the track team is getting together to celebrate the coach no longer losing his job. He wants me to join too. He sends me the address. That's all I needed.

I ask Milton to cover for me for a while. He tries to play it off like it's a huge imposition, but we both know he's full of it. He's glad he gets to take over. It feeds his ego. Whatever, I'm just glad I get to run from the eyes. That's really all that matters.

———

I can hear the music booming down the street. My heart starts pounding, as I get closer. This isn't my first party, but it is my first party after school without any adults around. It's also the first time a guy has asked me to come. And as if that wasn't enough, that guy is Devonte Evens. That's three major events all happening at once. I head up the steps of the five-story building, barely able to contain myself.

Ayo, be cool and tone down your smile. If you enter the party with a big-ass grin, they'll think you're a thirsty loser who rarely gets invited to things like this.

The music grows louder with each step I take toward the apartment. The bass is crazy hard and makes the floor jump under my feet. On the staircase are kids from the track team; some I know, but most I don't. They're talking, drinking, and making out.

Yes! This is where I want to be. This is what I should be doing with my life, not looking at posters of poor souls lost to the battle of racial inequality. Real talk, half these kids don't even know there's a battle. I want to be one of them. I want to know what's out there.

I walk through the door, and it's just like I thought it would be: kids from various schools, wall to wall, bumping and grinding to the beat. They jump up and down, go side to side, and raise their hands high up in the air. It's like they're performing some kind of futuristic African rain dance. The music possesses their bodies and lays claim to their souls.

The smell of sweat, alcohol, and heat mixes with the air of recklessness. It makes for an intoxicating scent. These kids don't give a damn about anything that's going on outside in the real world. They only care about right here and right now.

I spot Devonte; he waves me over. It's at that exact moment that I know there's no way I'm going back to the meeting. I get past the sea of arms and legs and hips. I make it over to him, and he says something but I can't hear. The music is just too loud, and I like it like that. It's loud enough to drive away all thoughts. Devonte pulls me close and starts to dance with me.

I don't have time to use my superpower of overthinking—all I have time to do is take a breath, right before we start dancing. It's a reggae song, and like with most reggae songs, you are contractually required to grind all up on whoever you are dancing with. I take that responsibility very seriously. I'm not sure I'm making all the right moves, but I don't care.

We dance song after song, and with each passing moment, I let go a little more. It feels good. It feels better than anything I have ever experienced. There are no ghosts here. There's nothing to remind me that my skin is a crime for which I could very well lose my life. This space doesn't require me to defend who I am or why I should exist. Here, I'm just one in a crowd of Black bodies that are alive, bodies that can still dance, sing, and give no Fs about the outside world.

I could stay in this crowd forever, but Devonte takes my hand and guides me out the door. The moment our fingers touch, I feel like a bolt of lightning is surging through me. This heady feeling is unreal.

He takes me down to the basement, where a small group of kids are lounging on a few old sofas. I don't know all the faces, but everyone seems really chill. The light is dim, and the roar of the music above has faded enough that I can hear their voices. Someone offers us a drink, and I turn it down and opt for the unopened bottle of water nearby.

"This is Ayo. She that good girl," Devonte explains. I'm not sure if it's a compliment or not. I just smile and sit beside him. We start talking about things that don't matter. I'm taking this all in like a kid on her first trip to Disneyland. Someone offers me a cigarette.

"Hell no, I don't smoke. Cigarette companies disproportionately target Black communities. They spend a lot more money to market to us than they do in white neighborhoods. They also ensure the prices of cigarettes are lower in our neighborhoods so that we keep coming back for more . . ."

Okay, stop right there, Ayo. You don't need to—

"They use Black magazines, hip-hop events, and even civil rights organizations to target us. They try to get to us any way they can because it's an investment. If they can get a Black kid hooked now, by the time that kid is an adult, they become loyal customers. It's so nuts, because when we get sick—which is guaranteed when it comes to smoking—we don't get the same care as our white counterparts. We're basically paying for our own demise."

Damn.

Everyone is staring at me like an alien sprouted from my Afro and is now peeing on my head. I desperately try to save it. "But it's cool if you want to smoke—who am I to judge you . . . Yay, cancer!" I add awkwardly.

I'm relieved when the basement door opens and we're interrupted; two more kids join us. The guy's name is Franklyn. He's in my math class and wears a low fade. The white girl whose hand he's holding has light eyes, blond hair, and a warm smile.

"Y'all, this is Chloe," Franklyn says. Everyone nods politely.

We talk, laugh, and act stupid for nearly an hour. I wish Nai was here; she'd like this vibe. Things are going pretty well, apart from my tobacco company tirade earlier. I'm actually enjoying myself. And even though I haven't had any alcohol or drugs, I feel high. It's a natural high, the kind you get when you feel like you're where you belong.

I should note that by now Chloe has had two beers and is

feeling pretty loose. She aims for a third, and Franklyn suggests that she slow down. She reluctantly agrees and gives him a lingering kiss. Devonte looks at me with this "come close" gaze, and my mind shatters. Meanwhile, my body doesn't need any other hints. I move closer. He leans toward me . . .

I'm about to get kissed. My very first kiss is about to happen. It's cool. I can handle this. I'm not going to freak out in my head. That being said: It's happening! It's happening! It's happening!

And just as his lips are about to touch mine, Chloe plops down right in the middle of us. We pull back and look at each other, perplexed. But one look at the goofy, glossy gaze on Chloe's face and we know she's tipsy.

"Okay, can we be, like, super honest right now?"

"Chloe, chill," Franklyn says, trying to get her to come back over to him.

"What? C'mon, we're all friends here. I just want to ask Ayo a question."

Franklyn tries to dissuade her, but she insists. She turns her focus onto me, taking my hand in hers, and places it over her chest. "You and I just met, but I can tell we're gonna be friends. Right?"

"Okay," I reply with an awkward smile.

There's a chance Chloe could ask something perfectly benign, but history isn't on her side. Never once in all of humanity has a tipsy white girl asked a Black girl a question that wasn't offensive.

My stomach tightens and my hands get sweaty. I try to slow my heart rate down and control my breathing. I know it seems like I'm overreacting, but it worries me that she had to ask permission to ask the question.

I've been in situations like this before, but normally it's because I'm the only Black person in the room. But this time there's a room full of us, and she's the only white girl.

So, I'm thrown. I'm not sure what the rules are in this bizarre, reversed scenario.

"Chloe, it's late. Let's go," Franklyn says.

"Hang on," she pleads.

Devonte has a bemused look on his face. Franklyn is quietly apologizing with his eyes for whatever is about to come out her mouth.

Chloe places her hands together in front of her like she's praying and asks in a sweet, innocent tone, "I've been trying to find someone to cornrow my hair. Can you do it? Or any of you girls?" she says, looking around the room. "I'd pay you for sure."

Girl, no, I can't cornrow your hair! The hell I look like?

I briefly make eye contact with the other girls in the room; they cosign. Their reactions range from slight eye rolling to full-on teeth sucking and turning away.

"I don't know how to do that," I lie. The other girls shrug, letting her know they, too, can't braid hair.

Franklyn takes Chloe's hand and says, "Let's get some air."

"Oh, okay. Be right back," she says as she heads for the door.

Franklyn addresses the room just before he walks out. "She good people. She just loves braids and stuff, so . . ."

We glare at him.

He knows why.

CHAPTER SEVEN

Hulk, 1; David Banner, 0

What Chloe asked was really dumb and side-eye-worthy, but it's not exactly shocking. People say racist mess to us Black girls all the time, without even thinking about it.

Sometimes they say casual racist things that *appear* innocuous but are total insults: "You're so dark, why do you need sun block?" or "You're so pretty . . . for a Black girl." Once, in the library, a cute white boy said to me, "Man, you don't have to work as hard to get into college."

The point is it's just another day, no big deal. But while Franklyn and Chloe go back upstairs to dance, the four couples that remain beside us are not ready to close the door on the subject. I have no idea what anyone's names are. When Devonte made the introductions earlier, I was only half paying attention. So, my imagination takes over in naming them: I call the first guy Fire because he has the rhythm, gestures, and command of a fire-and-brimstone Baptist preacher. He addresses us girls (aka his congregation).

"Anytime you all see us with a white chick, you ready to take our cards. Why can't we be with whoever we want? Why put limits on a brotha? Y'all need to stop being insecure and fall back."

The second guy to speak is Air, so named because instead of looking us in the eye, he fixes his gaze upward as if addressing the ceiling. He twists his lips to the side and pounds his fist into his palm for emphasis. Air's thoughts on the topic of interracial dating are slightly different from Fire.

"Yo, let's keep it one hundred—the reason Black guys go with white girls is 'cause they come with less drama." His thoughts are greeted with deep groans from the girls.

The next guy to speak is Water, thanks to his soft, flowing voice and laid-back demeanor. He's got the whole Black bohemian/Cree Summer thing going on.

"I don't think we should put Franklyn in a box. I mean, every situation is different. All we know is that he came in here with a white girl. But she's more than that label. She's an individual, who might have specific attributes that Franklyn is drawn to. Her race might not even factor into it."

"Exactly!" Air says.

Water adds, "The fact is, none of this is real. Race is just a concept. And we need to stop using it as an excuse for all the things that happen to us."

Turns out Water's an idiot.

The fourth guy—let's call him Earth, because unlike Water, he actually lives on our planet—chimes in, "You need to take that Ben Carson BS somewhere else, man, like for real. For centuries white folks been feeding on and off us."

"I can appreciate that we have opposing points of view—" Water begins.

"Nah, it's not just 'opposing points of view.' You dead wrong. First of all, while Chloe's ancestors were out there building their wealth, our ancestors were denied any opportunity to own land or prosper in any way. And that's after four hundred years of free labor. You feel me?

"Secondly, what we need to ask is why that white girl is with him. She wants to Kardashian him—parade his Black ass around to improve her status. Nah . . . I'll take a sista all day. Every day."

"Just because she's white doesn't mean she thinks like that. Maybe they got that 'deep connection'-type thing," Air counters as he looks up toward the ceiling.

Seriously, why does he keep looking up? What's up there?

Earth says, "Deep? C'mon, like, for real? They probably can't even hold a conversation. Say she pops off and says something crazy. Franklyn asks, 'How Sway?' She won't even know what that means! How deep can their connection be?"

"All Black people don't speak the same way, and for you to suggest we do is ignorant," Water says.

"All I know is, if a white girl is dating a Black guy, something 'bout her ain't right. Some sick stereotype is play'n on a loop in her head," Earth insists.

Water says, "Wait, why we not letting the girls talk?"

What Water doesn't get is that the four girls in the basement have been stockpiling the guys' words, melting them down, pouring them into the mold, and turning them into bullets. In other words, the girls have armed themselves. The first to take aim is Fire's girlfriend.

"Boy, did you just say dating a Black girl is limiting? So what, Black girls aren't good enough for you?"

Shots fired, in rapid succession.

—*"You saying Black girls aren't good enough for you? You have a problem with us?"*

—*"Y'all only have issues with Black girls when y'all start making bank. Then y'all try and 'upgrade' to a white girl. All of you boys in here, steady drinking that 'white folks are better' Kool-Aid."*

—*"Don't trip, boo, we don't need you. You want to be with Becky, go! But don't even think about saying anything when you see us with white dudes. You know how y'all get."*

—*"The only reason y'all want a white girl is because they put up with shit you all know we won't!"*

What strikes me isn't the growing crescendo of protest from the girls. It's the soft, pained melody underneath it. It whispers, "Why are we not enough?" It's a question I'm not sure they even know they are asking. But it's there. And it breaks my heart to hear it.

In that moment, something strikes me about the girls who are here, something I missed before: they have the exact hair and complexion of the women in one of my favorite Nina Simone songs, "Four Women." It starts playing in my head. It's an old song, with a haunting melody that describes the pain and turmoil of four different Black women. The song pairs their skin tones and their struggles.

The girl across the room from me has ink-black skin. In the song, people assume she can take on endless amounts of pain because the darker the skin, the more it can withstand. It's not true. But no one knows, so they heap on hurt after hurt. In the song, they call her Aunt Sarah.

The second girl, the one sitting near the basement window with her boyfriend, Air, could easily be the second verse of the song. She's mixed and has pale, almost yellowish skin. She's too Black for the whites and too white for us. She lurks between two worlds, never belonging anywhere. Her name in the song is Saffronia.

The third girl sits near Devonte and me. Her tan-colored skin and fine hair leave people to believe she's soft and fragile, easy to mess with. She thinks she belongs to whoever is willing to pay, never realizing just how priceless she is. You can find her in the third verse; they call her Sweet Thing.

The last girl stubbornly arguing against interracial dating has brown skin, and according to the song, is bitter to the taste. She's a descendant of slaves, whose pain echoes in her head even now. She's the girl in the last verse, Peaches.

The basement lights dim. The song begins to play. The four girls glide onto the stage and take their place in the soft blue spotlight. They use the soulful song to voice their pain. It feels wrong to hear their deepest thoughts and fears, given the fact that I didn't bother to remember their real names.

Their song causes a familiar ache in the center of my chest. It's the ache that comes when I feel someone's pain and am powerless to stop it. I don't want to listen to the melody.

"Hey, let's go back upstairs," I suggest to Devonte.

"Ayo, what do you think about Franklyn and his girl?" Fire asks. Everyone turns to me.

Seriously, every single person turns to me? Why does what I have to say have more weight than anyone else here?

My mother.

Argh!

I know things like this come up sometimes, but I'm pretty sure the only reason we're staying on this topic is because they expect me to have a strong point of view, given who I'm related to. Why can't I get away from her shadow for just one night?

"We're teenagers congregating in a space with alcohol, weed, and no adult supervision. We should be displaying shockingly bad judgment and self-destructive behavior. Or at the very least, getting pregnant and throwing our lives away. Anyone? Anyone?" I ask, only half joking.

Okay, fine . . .

I shrug. "I don't know. Franklyn can do whatever he wants. If he likes her, then . . . yeah, it's whatever."

And the award for the best nonanswer goes to . . . Ayomide Bosia!

The crowd cheers. I bounce up the steps to accept my dubious award. "I'd like to thank politicians everywhere for teaching me the art of evasion and speaking while saying absolutely nothing. This means so much. I couldn't have done it without you. Thank you! Thank you! Thank—"

"That's all you have to say?" Water asks.

Water, you really need to shut the hell up. You're the most deluded of all four of the elements.

"C'mon, tell us. Is Franklyn sip'n the Kool-Aid white folks made or what?" Earth asks.

It's just my luck that at that exact moment, Franklyn and Chloe reenter the basement. "What y'all talk'n 'bout?" he asks.

"Some people feel a type a way about you bringing old girl here," Devonte says. "And others feel it's cool. We asked Ayo about it because that's, like, her thing."

That's my thing? Debating complex social issues in inappropriate venues is my thing?

I turn to Chloe, hoping a look of discomfort on her face will dissuade Franklyn from pushing me to talk. But she doesn't look uncomfortable; she's eagerly waiting a reply.

Chloe reads the reluctance on my face. "Don't worry. Nothing you say is gonna get to me. My parents raised me to be super open minded. When I see Franklyn, I don't see his color. All I see is the guy I love."

Oh dear God, get me out of here.

"You know what, it's late. I need to get home," I inform them as I get up. Devonte implores me to stay and speak my mind.

He doesn't get it. This is my Bruce Banner moment, right before he changes into the Incredible Hulk. I don't mean the new movie version, where he's glossy green and has a Hollywood shine to him. I feel like the old-school 1980s TV show version; the version that takes the time to show the aftermath of what's left in the Hulk's wake.

In that version, Banner has to deal with the consequences of Hulk's actions. That usually means he's forced to flee yet another town, in hopes of finding a place he feels at home. I just started hanging out with these people; I don't want to go all green on them and have to seek a new hangout.

I never understood some of the daily anger I felt until James Baldwin explained it to me.

He clarified that being Black in the United States and having even the slightest bit of awareness means you're pissed off most of the time. He wasn't wrong. I'm in awe of Baldwin's genius, but it scares me that a man who died over three decades ago can so easily nail how I feel today.

Anyway, I'm leaving before Hulk shows up and ruins everything.

But, of course, that's not the way the story of the Hulk goes. In every episode, he does his best to tell the bad guys to walk away. And they never do. They keep pushing and pushing until . . . red radioactive eyes . . . clothes shredding over massive muscles, and then . . . the Hulk.

Today's "bad guy of the week" is Franklyn.

"Damn, you're nothing like your mom. She's a beast. She would have kept it one hundred, no matter what," Franklyn says.

"Is that really what you what me to do—keep it real?" I ask.

"Yeah, that's exactly what I said."

I shrug and throw my hands up in the air. "Okay, let's be real. Franklyn, I don't know if you're dating Chloe because you want her or because you've been conditioned to *think* she's who you should want. It's damn near impossible to gauge what you feel and what you've been *made* to feel. I have no idea what's going on inside your heart or your head, but the sad part is, neither do you. The fact is, you may never really know what percentage of you is with her because of love and what percentage is with her because it's programmed to view white as better. Again, I don't know. But here's what I do know:

"If you gave a damn about Chloe, you'd talk to her before you took her out of her comfort zone. You didn't think enough of her to school her on her casual racism and microaggressions. Had you dared to have that conversation, maybe she wouldn't be standing here spewing lies about not seeing your color. What the hell does that mean? How could she not see your color? Black is a strength, not a weakness. Why would she not want to recognize it?"

Franklyn starts, "Ayo—"

"I'm not done! Dating Chloe isn't wrong. But there are a lot of things about you she won't know. Things us Black girls were born knowing. No matter how kind, caring, and smart Chloe is, there are things about you she will never understand, like why it's essential you keep your kicks fresh and clean, all day, every day. She'll wonder why you brush, shine, and even fight to protect them—after all, they're only sneakers. But us Black girls know that they are much more than that. We know you cherish your kicks because they are the closest you'll get to owning property in America.

"Chloe doesn't know why your body stiffens when a cop car passes by, even though all you're doing is sitting on the steps of your building. But us Black girls get it because our bodies stiffen too.

"She doesn't get that your grandmother's mac and cheese is medicinal or that shea butter is currency. She'll never understand the swagger in your stride because she can't hear the beat you walk to. But us Black girls hear it, and we should —we created it.

"She'll stand with you in the middle of a high-end department store, gaze into your eyes, and hold your hand lovingly. She'll watch you give a slight nod to the only other Black guy at the other end of the store. She'll think you're greeting someone you know. But in truth, he's a stranger. You give the nod as a way of checking in, because Black people have to check in with other Black people.

"Sometimes it's to gloat, like, 'Yeah, we in this mother!' But oftentimes, a nod is a way of saying, 'There's way too many white folks up in here, and I'm checking to see if you are okay.' Because historically, when white folks outnumber us . . . it's rarely by accident and it rarely ends well.

"Chloe, while well intentioned, doesn't know what we Black girls have known for a long time now: It's not a given that we'll get to see our twenty-first birthdays. What started out as a regular day could find us in the morgue, all because we dared go shop, jog, or play video games in our own homes.

"We know that white girls have pretty, clear blue eyes, full of stars and careless daydreams. But our eyes, while also pretty, are filled with ghosts, ghosts of dreams that are fated to die even before they've lived. But those same eyes got yo back. We're the lookout. We're the tap on the shoulder that tells you to be easy 'cause the block is hot.

"But above all else, the thing Black girls know, that white girls don't, is that to be a nigga in America is to be on borrowed time. It takes courage to face that truth; courage you might not have.

"Black girls are … Basquiat paintings. Vivid. Defiant. Complex.

"We get why you'd rather dive into a Bob Ross canvas. Big yellow sun. Happy clouds. Happy trees.

"We can't force you to look our way. But don't ask us to cosign. Because, mostly, we won't."

CHAPTER EIGHT

It's Your Turn

Our country has a lot of weapons in its arsenal, including missiles, rockets, and nuclear warheads. But no weapon is as powerful or as dangerous as the tears of a pretty white girl. They've started wars and launched a thousand lynchings. Unfortunately for Chloe, she hasn't quite perfected this mystical, salty elixir. And even more unfortunate, she's in the one place where that weapon can be defused—a room full of Black people. But that doesn't stop her from trying. Franklyn comforts her awkwardly.

I have no idea who I'm more annoyed with, Franklyn or myself. What the hell am I doing here? I should have left the moment Chloe asked me to do her hair. I knew better, but instead I stayed.

Argh!

I get my stuff from upstairs and storm out of the building. Night is falling and the wind has picked up. I put my head down as I walk back home. My jacket is too light for the weather, but that's okay. I have self-loathing to keep me warm.

It's not just the thing that happened in the basement that upsets me, it's Devonte. I'm replaying when he first stepped to me. I can't believe I was too dumb to see it before. That smile, those eyes, and the tilt of his head . . . he was playing me. All he wanted was to get that stupid letter signed.

Then why did he ask me to the party even after he got what he wanted?

I hear a faint whisper, but I'm too deep in thought to really focus on it. The questions surrounding Devonte's intention invade my mind. How could I be so stupid? He was never checking for me.

"*Ayo!*" someone shouts as they practically slam into me. I look up.

Devonte.

"I've been calling your name for two blocks, girl, you deaf?" he asks.

"What do you want?"

He steps back as if my words have physically moved

him. "Yo, why you mad at me? I wasn't the one who brought that girl."

"Why did you ask me to hang out?" I demand.

He shrugs. "I don't know."

I roll my eyes, but mostly at myself. Seriously, what the hell was I thinking? I start walking again. He follows again.

"Tell me, why did you ask me here today—and don't say you don't know," I say.

He takes a deep breath and exhales loudly. His beautiful eyes off to the side, he mumbles, "I wanted to hang out with you."

"Why? You don't even like me."

"Who said that?"

"The only reason you hit me up was because of the letter. Tell me I'm wrong."

His silence is so loud that it nearly makes my ears bleed. I'm an idiot. Here I was thinking I was on the verge of a social life, when in fact I was just a means to an end. I am not going to cry.

Okay, I *will* cry, but not right now. I will hold it until I am alone. I pick up the pace. But all my efforts are in vain, because his stride is infinitely longer than mine.

"Damn you and your J. J. Walker legs!" I shout.

He laughs. "*Good Times,* right? Man, my grandma used to love that show. She'd make me watch the reruns with her. What's up with calling the show *Good Times*? I mean, they ain't never had any . . ."

"I know, right? Did you see that dog food episode—"

"Yo, I did! That was crazy."

"And what about the time— Wait! No. We're not doing this. We're not bonding over *Good Times*."

"Why?"

I stop walking and face him. "Because you used me."

He lowers his head and nods. It hurts. I was kind of hoping, despite everything, that he'd have some kind explanation. He doesn't.

"So the only reason you were checking for me was because of the track team?"

He nods.

I try to act all cool, like it's whatever, but the tears streaming down my face betray me. It sucks when your body disobeys you.

"Yo, c'mon, don't do that. I wasn't try'n to . . . It's not like that."

I glare at him.

"Okay, it was like that."

I wipe my tears, take a deep breath, and demand that my legs start working again and get me home. It works. I start moving. He follows.

"All right, I used you. My bad. I'm sorry."

"Noted. Good night," I reply stiffly, only to have him fall in step with me once more. "What is it? Why are you following me?"

"It's your turn to apologize."

"Excuse me?"

He gives me a small smile, as if to say he's amused by the baffled expression on my face. "Ayo, I admit I used you. But let's be real, you used me too."

"How Sway?"

"The only reason you looking my way is because . . . you know," he says, motioning to himself.

"No, I don't."

"Oh, for real? It's like that?" he asks.

"I don't know what you're talking about."

His jaw tightens and his expression turns serious. He folds his arms across his chest and glares back at me. "Ayo, be real. You only feel'n me because I'm fine."

"You make Kanye West look humble."

He sucks his teeth and purses his lips. "It's true. The only reason you like me is because I look good. You don't know anything else about me. And you can spin it any way you want, but you know you're using me too."

"You think I'm using you for your looks?"

"Yes. And to escape."

I scoff loudly. "And what am I escaping from?"

"Your life."

My jaw drops. I have words, but they don't make it to the surface.

"Look, I know girls like you. You always follow the rules and do what you're told. Then you watch one Megan Thee Stallion video and you want your own hot-girl summer. You want to be reckless with it. And that's where guys like me come in. We were both wrong. The only difference is, I said I'm sorry."

I pout like a child and turn away like he's wrong. He's not, but I'm just not ready to admit it yet.

Devonte adds, "And to answer your question, the reason I hit you up, even after I got the letter, was because I was feel'n you. I have ever since the pudding cup thing. I remember after you handed it to me, you said, 'Don't worry. You're not required to reciprocate.' It was first grade; I had no idea what that word meant. I had to go home and look it up."

"I was a nerd even back then."

"Yeah, you were."

I glare at him.

He quickly adds, "That was a good thing. I kind of liked it. But I figured you would only go with nerd-type guys. So . . . I stayed away. And then this track thing came up . . . I thought I could hit you up and get what I wanted with no problem because I was over how I felt about you."

"And are you . . . over it?" I ask, looking at the ground.

"Dancing with you was kind of nice, and back there in the basement, I pushed you to talk because I like knowing what you think. Is that all right?"

I shrug as the blood rushes to my face. I'm not sure what causes the chill down my spine: the sheer bliss from his words or the wind that has just picked up. Either way, I'm cold and shivering.

"You good?" he asks.

"Yeah," I lie.

He laughs. "No, you're not. C'mon, I have an idea," he says, taking my hand in his. Although it's cold, his hands feel warm as they cover mine. There is a real possibility that these might be the last few moments of my life—that is, if my heart doesn't stop racing.

But before we take off, I stop him. "Wait . . ."

He looks at me, not sure what I'm about to say.

"You know what you said about me using you?" I ask.

"Yeah . . ."

I mumble, "Well-I-guess-I-was-kind-of-using-you-or-what-ever."

"An apology should actually have the word 'sorry' in it. I'm just say'n," he replies, clearly enjoying my discomfort.

"Sorry."

He laughs. "Fine, I'll take it, but that was kind of weak. Next time I give you a heartfelt apology, I'm gonna need you to *reciprocate*."

"Oh, you think you cute?" I ask.

"I am."

Yeah, he is . . .

He takes me to a hole-in-the-wall café on the east side, named Mama Jay's. I take a peek through the windows. It's the kind of place where you can touch the walls if you stretch both your arms out. The leather stools were red once; now they are a faded blush color. There're held together by duct tape and prayer. The menu is written on the wall behind the counter. There's only five items.

"I've walked by here a few times, but I've never been in," I admit.

"The food is slap-yo-mama good."

I look at the sign on the door. "It's also closed."

Devonte takes a set of keys out of his pocket and opens the door. He tells me his uncle owns the place and sometimes he comes here to help out. He holds the door open, and we enter. It's small but has a nice laid-back, homey vibe. It reminds me of the diner in my favorite August Wilson play, *Two Trains Running*.

"What's good here?" I ask.

"Everything. But what I brought you here for is my world-famous hot chocolate."

"Oh, real? World famous? That just means you put in milk instead of water."

"Milk and water? Girl, let me put you up on game!" he says proudly as he works his way to behind the counter and into the kitchen. I follow, but he stops me. "Nah, you can't be here while the chef is doing his thing. You handle the music. Pick a Spotify playlist. Remote is behind the counter. Don't pick anything wack."

"Excuse you, my playlist game is strong."

"We'll see," he says, disappearing into the kitchen.

I go over to the radio and choose a fierce playlist that features Summer Walker, SZA, Khalid, and H.E.R. I can't help but peek at Devonte though the window of the kitchen door. He assembles the ingredients for the hot chocolate like a mad scientist. He's so into it that he does a two-step as he gathers everything.

He's chopping something, but I can't make out what it is. He's pouring brown sugar into the cup and taking this very seriously. I don't know if it will taste good, but it sure smells good. The scent of chocolate fills the air and makes my stomach growl. When he comes back to the front of the café, he has two big mugs of steaming hot chocolate. He places them on the counter and motions for me to try it.

"OhmyGod!" I whisper as the strong, sweet, creamy taste fills my mouth.

He beams.

"Devonte, this is really good!"

"Yeah, what you know about that Parisian chocolate?" he asks with a smug look on his face.

"Okay, not bad. Not bad," I admit.

"My grandma showed me how to make it like this. We'd

make a big pot and watch old TV shows on weekdays, and on the weekends, we'd watch *The Last Dragon*. It's about—"

"I love that movie!"

"You know it?" he asks, taken aback.

I jump up off the stool and take a tough karate-like stance. I say in the deep baritone voice of the villain in the movie, "Who's the master?"

He replies like the villain's followers do, "Sho'nuff!"

"I said who's the master?"

And once again, he says, "Sho'nuff!"

I go to sit back down, and he says, "One more thing." He steps closer to me, takes a dramatic beat, and says the quintessential *The Last Dragon* line: "Kiss my Converse."

We laugh until my side hurts; Devonte delivers that line just as silly and over the top as the actor in the movie.

"Who did you used to watch it with?" he asks.

"My mom. She likes silly stuff like that too."

"Wow, I thought Ma Dukes was always serious. I've seen her press conferences. She ain't no joke."

"Yeah, she can be pretty serious."

"So that's where you get it from?"

"I'm not serious. We just reenacted, like, half of *The Last Dragon*. How am I a serious person?"

"You just broke up an interracial couple. Franklyn will never date a white girl again. Why? 'Cause he'll be too scared that they would run into you."

I shake my head. "I didn't break them up."

"Please, right now, Franklyn won't even go near white bread, let alone white girls. You got him shook. To be honest, I was kind of scared of you."

I sigh and play with the rim of my mug, skimming the surface with my index finger. "I don't want people to just look at me and think I'm some raving Afrocentric lunatic."

"Guess that's why you didn't want to talk back in the basement?"

"Yeah . . ."

"If that's who you are, that's cool. I mean, be you."

"But that's not who I am," I protest. "I'm into fun stuff like parties, concerts, and not voting." I laugh. "But seriously, Devonte, when we're old enough, you have to vote. You won't believe how far some people will go to limit Black votes. I mean, everything from closing polling stations in low-income neighborhoods to gerrymandering. And let's not even talk about what the Native Americans go through during elections . . ." My voice fades when I realize I have launched into a speech.

Devonte doesn't stop me. Instead, he listens. "Keep going. This is interesting."

"No, it's not! And that's not what I want to talk about. I want to be wild and crazy. I want to get things pierced or tattooed. Or maybe both!"

He laughs.

"What's so funny?" I demand.

"Those things don't really sound like you."

"I told you, I'm wild and crazy. Pay attention."

He nods. "What wild things have you done—for real?"

I clear my throat and spit out an impressive, albeit sparse list: "We were boycotting this fast food place that supports anti-LGBTQ groups. One day—and I'm not proud of this—I went in and bought a large fry."

He suppresses a smile and says, "That's boss right there . . ."

"Exactly! And one time, I went to a fair for Black business owners—didn't buy anything. Bam! Rebel."

He's no longer trying to hide his laugh. "You are a trip," he says, once he catches his breath.

"Fine, maybe I'm not as wild as I want to be—yet."

"It's all good. But what's it like with a mom that's all over the news? Like, when you were little, what did she tell you about racism? Did she go all Malcolm X on you or what?"

"Nah, actually the lesson on race only took two minutes."

"Really?"

"Yeah. I remember I was about nine. We were at the park and some kid called me the N-word. My mom flipped. The parents said they were sorry, and that they didn't know where their kid heard the word.

"When we got home, I asked if all white people were racist. She went into the cabinet in the kitchen and took out a bottle of cooking oil. She held it up. 'This is racism,' she said. And then she poured it all over my hands. She said in the past, white people where dripping with vile, racist thoughts and actions.

"Today, most white people aren't like that. They've cleaned it up." And then she wiped off all the oil and told me to touch whatever I wanted around the house. So I did. And when we retraced my steps, I realized that while my hands *looked* clean, everything I touched had a smudge, some lingering oil imprint. My mom said, 'That's racism. It touches everything.'"

"That's a dope way to put it," he says.

"I guess, but I was looking for comforting words, not a warning. Never mind that—tell me more about your grandmother. She sounds cool as hell. You said she used to watch TV with you. Did she pass away?"

"Nah, she's in a nursing home in Queens. My uncle and I go see her a few times a month. Yo, they get busy in them old nursing homes! One time I was feeling bad 'cause we hadn't gone to see her in a while, so I went, like, three times in one week. That lady texted me and was like, 'Boy, you can't be stop'n by every day. I got things going on.'"

"What kind of things?"

"That's just what I asked. She texted me back a taco and a hot dog!"

I burst out laughing, and the hot chocolate almost comes out of my nose.

"It freaked me the hell out. So now, when I'm going over there, I give her, like, a three-day heads-up."

"Just because she old don't mean she can't get it in," I joke. We share a laugh, and he shivers at the awful memory of his grandma's text. "So, is making hot chocolate part of your routine to get girls?" I ask as he sits on the stool beside me.

"I only make this for my nana. She can't use the stove anymore, so I make her a pot and bring it over. I've never made it for another girl. And I never bring anyone here after hours. This is the place I go and ponder life's big questions."

"Like what?"

"You know, deep stuff," he replies, making a goofy face. I laugh as his eyes sparkle. He bites his lower lip and makes my stomach dip.

"What are the big questions you ponder when you're here?" I ask, forcing myself to look away and break the spell.

"Pam is fine as hell. Why was Martin always dog'n her out? Was the Dr. King episode on *Boondocks* too far or not far enough? New Aunt Viv or original Aunt Viv?"

"They dogged Pam out because . . . colorism. The Dr. King episode was out of pocket, and original Aunt Viv wins, always. Anything else on your mind?" I ask.

"Actually, yeah, there is . . ."

He gently pushes my mug aside and leans in. His scent is warm and intoxicating, like summer and chocolate. Devonte has always been beauty walking. But after tonight, he's more than just a sight to behold. He's a thief who's stolen stars from galaxies far away and placed them in his eyes, making it impossible to look away. He's a silver-tongued trickster who's convinced Father Time to stand still, just for us. He's a voodoo priest peddling home-brewed oils and herbs that promise to soothe and heal all the anger I felt today.

The thief, the trickster, and the priest lean in even closer. They converge and become one as our lips touch. His kiss is gentle and giving. It consumes all of my thoughts. I'm falling into a glittering black hole of wonder . . .

CHAPTER NINE
Black Girl Magic

The next morning, I stand in front of the mirror and wonder why it's lying to me. It keeps telling me that I am the same girl. But the mirror is wrong. I'm different now. I'm changed. It may take the mirror some time to reflect those changes, but trust, there's been a change. There's an arch in my back, a sway in my hips, and a stride in my step that wasn't there before.

The biggest difference in me is joy. I have an abundance of it. It's so strong and seeks to block out anything that challenges it. It even blocks out the words my mom is speaking into the phone inside her office. All I hear is white noise that I'm certain is related to the march.

The march . . .

I don't want to even think about it because it's a joy killer. I call out a quick "Bye, Mom!" at the closed office door, grab my stuff, and bounce down the stairs.

"Ayo, hang on," she shouts down to me.

Damn . . .

I was lucky; last night when I came in, I managed to make it to my room without waking up my mom. I was hoping my luck would hold and this would be one of the mornings where she had to go in early. But it seems my luck has run out.

"I'm trying to get to school early. I told Nai I'd meet up with her before class," I explain.

"Be right down," she says.

I sigh and go to the kitchen. I might as well find something to eat. I can't wait to see Nai. She was my first call when I got home last night. I ran down everything that happened. But she insisted we meet up before school so I could tell her everything in person.

When I asked her what was up on her end, she changed the subject and then said she had to go to bed. Nai has always chosen juicy updates over getting a good night's sleep. I have no idea what gives, but today I will find out. I will not let her wiggle her way out of talking to me.

My mom comes down the stairs wearing a finely tailored charcoal-gray suit that could easily come out of Olivia Pope's closet. She wears her braids in a high bun, with a sweeping bang. Her makeup is minimal and her only accessory is the small heart pendant Grandma gave her before she passed away. The look is simple but elegant.

"You look great, Mom."

"Thank you. You too, Getti. You're practically beaming."

I smile but don't say anything. I scour the cabinets. "I'm thinking Pop-Tarts, because why not, right?" I tell her as I unwrap the silver shiny foil. "You want one?"

"No, I'm good. How are things with you? Anything I need to know?"

I feel a sharp pang of guilt as I go to take a bite of the Pop-Tart. The truth is I would love to tell my mom about last night. After Nai, she's the person I would usually come to with this stuff. My mom has never been stuffy and reserved, at least not when it comes to things like this. I was seven when we had the sex talk. And by the time I was eight, I could run my own sexual health TED Talk. She said information was power, and she refused to let me go through life powerless.

But things have been kind of funky between us lately. And even if we weren't at odds, I'd have to explain why I was at a party instead of running the youth meeting. Also, there is that little matter of her not liking Devonte. In the end, it doesn't matter how much I want to share my news with her. It's not a good idea.

"Nope, there's nothing you need to know," I reply.

That settles it: if there's a "daughter hell," I'm headed there, first class.

"I've been feeling like you and I are a little off ," she says as she looks over at me.

"Yeah, kind of," I admit carefully.

"That's why I decided to come by the meeting yesterday and take you out to dinner. Thought we could get back on track."

The hairs on the back of my neck stand at attention. My heart rate skyrockets and my life flashes before my eyes. It would really suck to die right after my first kiss. I swallow hard and try to stay calm.

"You came by the meeting?" I reply as my voice cracks.

"Yeah, imagine my surprise when you weren't there. They said you stepped out and would be back. So, I waited for you. You never showed up."

Careful, Ayo . . .

"Oh, I was making copies. It took longer than I thought it would. It kept jamming."

She tilts her head slightly toward the sky as if she's trying to figure something out. "That's strange, because when you didn't come back, I went to the copy room and didn't see you. In fact, I searched the whole building. Couldn't find you. I called you and it went straight to voice mail."

I laugh nervously. "Oh, sorry, my cell must have died. I

think that was around the time I stepped out to get some junk food. You know, I needed a fix."

"Ayo, did you ditch the See Us meeting? The very meeting I warned you not to skip?" she demands. "And before you fix your mouth to lie to me, know that today is not the day to try me. I will snatch you up by your baby hairs and drag you out this kitchen. Do you hear me?"

I'm frozen with fear and shock. It never occurred to me that she would stop by, not this close to the march.

"Did you walk out and leave Milton to do your job?" she asks, already knowing the answer.

"Yes . . ."

Deflated, she shouts, "Ayomide, what's wrong with you?"

"Milton is capable of—"

"I don't care what Milton is and isn't capable of. The meetings are your responsibility. Today is Thursday; the march is on Sunday! This Sunday! Do you know that?"

"Yes."

"Then why would you skip the last meeting before the march? What were you thinking?"

I was thinking I didn't want to spend an hour and a half in a room full of pictures of slain Black folks. I was thinking I'm too damn weak to withstand the judgment in the eyes of the victims. And most of all, I was thinking there are a thousand things I'd rather be doing than turning a conference room into a makeshift tomb.

"I asked you a question. Where were you?"

"I was . . . around," I reply awkwardly.

She comes close and gives me a hard stare, the kind that could turn people into stone. "Are you on drugs? If you are, I'll get you help and save your life. Right after I wring your damn neck. So, are you?"

My jaw drops. I'm shaking with anger. I can't begin to find the words to express my outrage. She takes my lack of communication as a possible confession. Her tone goes from anger to deep terror in a matter of seconds.

"Girl, you better answer my question!"

"You know I would never do that," I tell her.

"I don't know what you would and wouldn't do anymore. That's the problem. I have no idea who is standing in front of me right now. You skip the meeting, you lie to me about it, then you come home late—and yes, I heard you come in. And now, you try to cover up your lies with even more lies. Now I want to hear an answer from you."

I reply between gritted teeth, "I'm. Not. On. Drugs."

"Okay, if not that, then what? Where were you? And just so you know, I'll send you to your maker long before I let you disrespect me with another lie. Now, I'm gonna ask one more time, where were you?"

"I was with . . . Devonte Evens."

She sighs deeply and looks to the heavens. "Good Lord, why couldn't it be drugs?"

"Seriously? How can you say something like that?"

"Drugs you can get off of. Stupid, however, is a lifelong condition, with no cure."

"So I'm stupid for being with him?"

"That boy is just using you to get the letter signed. Don't you get that?"

"He was before, but . . . it's not like that now."

"The hell it isn't."

The anger is growing inside me. The room is red and starting to spin. But there's no way the Hulk could win against my mother—she created him.

"Hold on, did something happen between you two?" she asks.

"Yes—no, I mean . . . We didn't have sex, okay?"

She studies me closely. "But something did happen . . . ?"

My reply should be filled with frustration and anger, given what is going on, but instead, there is whimsy in my tone—actual whimsy.

"I got my first kiss."

"Oh, Getti . . ."

"You can say what you want about him, but he made me laugh. He made me feel . . . special. I won't let you take that feeling away. I won't." I run back upstairs to my room and close the door.

I have no idea why I didn't just walk out of the house. Why did I go back into my room? Well, I'm here now, and I need a few minutes before I go back downstairs and face my mother. I text Nai to let her know I'm running late. My cell dings, and I look down at the screen, thinking it's Nai replying, but it's not.

It's my mom.

She's sent me a text with no words, just an image: the Swiss flag. Waving the flag of Switzerland means one of us is either asking for a judgment-free zone or offering to provide one. When that happens, the other one comes running.

There have been a few noteworthy flag-waving sessions. There was the time my mom ordered a large pizza for dinner and ended up eating it all thanks to an awful case of PMS. I came home and there was an actual mini flag waving on a hook by the front door. I walked in the house knowing that she would need me not to judge what she had done. And I didn't; however, I did limit her carb intake for the rest of that week.

I also waved the flag once when I thought it was a good idea to wax my eyebrows. I ended up looking like Whoopi. There wasn't a single eyebrow hair left. My mom adhered to the rules and didn't judge me. She did, however, pop out of random places in the house, with her index and middle fingers pointed at me, saying, "Till you do right by me . . ." I tried to be mad about it, but she does a great Ms. Celie impression, and I ended up laughing every single time. I text her back and accept her offer, and moments later, she's knocking on my door.

"Come in."

She enters and sits down next to me on the bed. "Okay, tell me about the kiss," she says in a calm and loving tone.

"Really?"

"This boy has to be special if you're going this hard for him. So I'm willing to keep an open mind—but not about the lying. You lie to me again and you'll be grounded for so long, we'll get nursing home brochures with your name on them. Got it?"

"Yeah."

"Now, I want to know everything. Was it bad, just okay, or amazing? Did you see it coming? Were you nervous? What happened right before? I want details."

"No judgment?"

"No . . . but we have to be on the same page about the lying. I mean it. No more lying. We have a deal?"

I smile. "Deal."

"Okay, tell me everything before I have to go back to my office and be a grownup."

I take her through last night, and she hangs on my every word. I make sure to tell her how sorry Devonte was and how we both needed a do-over. She admits that maybe, just *maybe*, he's not a bad guy.

The conversation goes even better than I could have hoped for. I know she's still pissed that I lied, and she's right to be. But we're friends again. I've missed her. A thought enters my mind, but before I can spit it out, I want to make sure of one thing.

"Mom, we are in Switzerland, right? So I can tell you anything without judgment?"

"Yup."

"I forged your signature on the letter for the track team."

My mom jolts up off the bed and her voice goes up three octaves. "You did what? What the hell were you thinking? You've undermined any progress we've made with the school. And what about Alex? How is he going to feel when there are no consequences for the coach? Not to mention the fact that you forged my name! Do you get what a giant mess you've made?"

"I know, I'm sorry. I was just mad because I heard you tell Uncle Ty on the phone that you were disappointed in me. I try so hard, but everything I do . . . It's always going to fall short in your eyes."

"Argh! Ayo, I can't . . ." She rakes her hands through her hair. The bun falls, and her hair is now out and wild. "Ayomide, I was disappointed in your actions, not in you as a person. And if you thought I was so unhappy with you, why didn't you come to me? Hold on, is this all so that you could undermine the organization? Was that your way of trying to get out of See Us?"

Her face cracks and the pieces fall to the floor. I've shattered my mom. I quickly try to explain. "It wasn't like that. I do want out, but the letter wasn't a part of it. I have a different plan to leave See Us. I'm going to earn my way out."

"*Earn your way out?* Child, you done lost yo good mind. How dare you speak about See Us as if it's some kind of punishment!

And how exactly were you going to— Oh, I get it." She nods bitterly as she takes it all in. "The scavenger hunt. So, out of everything you could ask for in this world, your one wish is to walk away from See Us?" Her body stiffens. She turns her back toward me and walks to the window. I don't need to see her face to tell that she's hurt.

"Mom, talk to me."

"I thought this was just a phase you were going through . . ."

"I'm sorry, it's not. And don't blame Devonte. I have wanted this for a long time."

She turns toward me with tears in her eyes. "Why are you doing this? Why are you working so hard to ruin what I made for you?"

I can't find the words; seeing her cry scares me. I would do anything to make it stop. I go to her and take her hands, but she pulls away.

She addresses me with steadfast conviction: "Ayo, we can't stop fighting midway. I know I have not always been the best mom. I've missed a lot of moments in your life for the cause. And yes, I know it's not fair, but baby, that's the price of the ticket. Don't run out on See Us. Don't run out on me."

She pleads with me, growing smaller and smaller with every word. My mom has never been the same size as any other human. She's always been larger than life, and the sight of her shrinking makes my soul ache.

Tears flood my eyes and stream down my face. I shake my

head in disbelief at the woman before me. "How can I run out on you, Mom? You're the love of my life. When I asked you for makeup so I could be beautiful, you handed me the works of Maya Angelou. I asked to dress up as a superhero for Halloween, and you made me an Ellen Craft costume. And when I was confused about religion, you took me to worship at the house of Aretha, Etta, and Whitney. Then we'd find ourselves 'speaking in tongues' as we listen to hip-hop.

"You knew racism, whether casual or institutional, a gust of wind or a tornado, would try to throw me off-balance. So you gave me all those experiences to help me stand my ground. But I'm not strong like you. I'm scared all the time. I'm scared of Sandra Bland's eyes and all the other victims. Their ghosts seek me out. I'm tired of being haunted.

"Mom, you should have told me the truth about Black girl magic; you should have told me that magic is heavy. That carrying it could curve, bend, and eventually break our backs and our spirits. Please, don't make me carry this anymore . . ."

I sob into her arms. She holds me tight against her, rocks me slowly, and whispers, "It's okay, baby. No more weight. No more ghosts. You're free . . ."

CHAPTER TEN

Giants

The world glides by in a rush of bright colors as I pump my fist in the air and shout along with the music. The DJ has the crowd all hyped up. The roller rink is dimly lit; I can barely make out my friends' faces. I just follow the glowing lights coming from the skates of the person in front of me. We all move and stumble in the same direction like a happy, drunken centipede.

The birthday party is for a friend of Dell's from band, Carla. She's into retro glam, so this is the perfect event for her. There's a three-layer cake with a pink sculpted roller skate at the top. All the decorations and party favors say, "This is how Carla rolls." There's a mountain of colorful gifts near the cake being guarded by Carla's rough-looking brother, Thump.

However, the main attraction is the glitzy photo booth. We wanted to go inside, but the line was stupid long. So instead we dance and skate to the point of exhaustion. When the DJ plays the new Lil Baby joint, everyone rushes back to skate. Dell, Naija, Shawn, and I seize our chance and pile into the booth. Every pose we strike is goofier than the next.

When we're done, we hit the food table—hard. Then we spill out onto the street and sit on the park tables across the street from the rink. Dell "liberated" a number of snacks and hid them in various pockets in his jacket; every time we think he's done unloading, he reveals more stuff.

"Damn, yo, how much junk food do you need?" Shawn asks.

"I'm a growing boy," Dell replies. Naija and I exchange a look. Dell stares at her and puts his hands up, signaling he will not get in the way of her taking whatever she wants. I think he's a little afraid of Nai since that day in the cafeteria. She tears into a packet of M&M's, and the rest of us follow. We recall the number of times Dell fell and start to laugh.

"I didn't fall," Dell swears. "I was paying homage to the 'gangsta lean' on roller skates. See, y'all don't know about that," he says as he unwraps a Twinkie.

"C'mon, yo, just admit you fell. We saw you grab hold of Carla's little cousin before it happened. You almost took her down too," Shawn says, shaking his head, amused.

"Did you see what that little monster did when I got back up?" Dell asks. "She kicked me!"

We try hard not to laugh, but then he says, "She hit me in the balls!" We burst out laughing. "Nah, man, this is serious. I might not be able to have children."

The three of us can barely catch our breath, and when Dell vows to sue the little girl, we straight-up die laughing.

When we finally get it together, Shawn turns to me and says, "So, even though you left See Us, you and moms are still cool?"

I nod. "Yeah. I think we're good." I shrug, partly still in disbelief that she actually let me go.

Dell adds, "I'm glad you and your mom are still together, because if you two broke up . . . well, I'll be honest, your mother would win me in the divorce."

"Did she tell the group or did you?" Naija asks.

"She said she'd take care of it. All I know is that Milton is the leader of the youth division now," I reply.

Naija groans. "That's why that fool has been walking around with a superior look on his face. Can't stand him."

Shawn shrugs. "He's kind of . . . cute." We all look at him in shock. "What? I like the preppy know-it-all type," Shawn admits.

"Wait, are you saying you like Milton?" I ask.

Shawn bites his lower lip and gives us a mischievous smile.

"I know that look. Talk!" I say.

The others follow. We demand that he gives us all the tea.

"Okay, well, I was coming back from practice and I saw him coming out the laundromat. We started to talk, and . . . he asked me out."

The table explodes with cheers. Shawn and Dell dap while Naija and I move our hips and arms around, shouting, "Ay!" When the noise dies down, Shawn hits us with a caveat:

"I told Milton I couldn't go out with him until I talked to my pops."

"Are you sure?" Dell says.

"Ever since my mom died, it's been me and Pops. We have always been real with each other. I've been putting off telling him, but now I wanna be honest and let him know what's up."

We all nod with understanding. Shawn and his dad are close. They go to basketball games, movies, and concerts together. Being gay is the only secret he's ever kept from his dad, and we all know how hard it's been for him to do so. But while we understood the hesitation, we get why he kept it secret: Black guys coming out as gay doesn't happen every day around here. And while Shawn's dad isn't super religious, he damn sure ain't "live and let live," so I really hope it goes well.

"Are you scared?" Naija asks.

"Yeah. I am," he admits.

"Telling your parents stuff is . . . Sometimes if you don't find the right words, that's a wrap. You messed everything up," Naija says, mostly to herself.

The guys and I exchange a look. This was the point of the

whole night. I tried the day before to get Naija to tell me what's going on. But she didn't. I could tell she wanted to talk but wasn't sure how to start. So I talked to the guys, and we agreed we needed to get her to relax, and then maybe she'd open up. The party came at the perfect time.

"I get it, Shawn," I say. "I didn't think I'd ever have the nerve to be honest with my mom. I thought for sure she'd regret having me in her life. Like she'd walk around the house secretly hating me."

"She doesn't feel some type of way about it? I mean, you did walk out on all her plans for you," Dell points out.

"Actually, she's gone out of her way not to talk about See Us in front of me. I told her it was okay if she did, but . . . she won't."

"Are you relieved it's all done? No more marches, no more meetings . . ." Shawn adds.

"Yeah . . . of course," I reply. I'm not sure if that's the truth. There is a weight that's been lifted since Mom let me go. I feel lighter, like I can finally breathe. But sometimes, I overhear pieces of conversation taking place between the trees, the wind, and the pavement. They whisper about me. They say, "Child, go where you belong. Go where you belong." It's only when I'm near people that they are quiet. I remind myself that it's only been two days. And freedom takes getting used to.

"What about you, Dell? You ever had to tell your dad something that was hard to confess—and Kenny G doesn't count," I warn him.

Dell thinks for a moment. And when he speaks, I fear he's going to say something crazy, but I'm wrong. "I had to tell my dad to stop calling my mom. He tried for so long to get her to come back. He wanted her to be a real mom to me, but . . . that's not Dina's thing. She wouldn't even let me call her Mom. So what were the chances that I'd come home and she'd be baking and taking care of the house? I knew when she went on her 'find myself' vacation down south, she wasn't ever coming back. But my dad had hope. It was killing him.

"So, I took it away. It was the right thing to do, you know? Hope is a hell of a drug."

It's rare for Dell to be serious. It's even rarer for him to bring up Dina. I never liked that woman. Dell and his dad would do anything and everything to make her happy. But nothing was ever good enough. She was always taking off. She claimed it was because she had a "wandering spirit." I say it's because she's toxic and trifling. Once she was gone, Dell and his dad started doing much better. They were all in for each other, like Shawn and his father.

The guys signal for me to look over at Naija. There are tears coming down her face. She's trying to hide them from us by turning away, but it's too late; we see them.

"Girl, you know you can tell us what's wrong. We won't judge you. Promise," I assure her. I turn to Shawn and signal for him to add something to the conversation.

"Nai, the first people I came out to are all at this table. And everyone kept my secret. We'll do the same for you. Trust," Shawn says.

I assume Dell will add something to the convo, but when I look up, he's nose deep in a Ho Ho. I kick him under the table. He looks at me as if to ask, "What?" Shawn grabs the snack from him and nods toward Naija, who is still in tears. Dell goes over to her side of the table and hands her something from his pocket with the pomp and circumstance a man would hand a woman an engagement ring. At first, I can't make out what he gave her, but then I look closer . . .

"A four-pack of Oreos?" I say in disbelief.

Dell doesn't look at me. His attention is solely on Naija. He looks deep into her eyes and says, "I was saving this later just for me. But you're special, and you deserve nice things. Yeah, that's right—Double Stuf." She laughs in spite of herself. Soon she's both laughing and crying.

I put my arms around her. "C'mon, Nai. Be best!" I tease.

The dumbass Melania Trump slogan has become a joke in our circle. It's basically something you say when there are serious issues at hand and you have no intention of fixing them. It's a slogan that has no value or merit whatsoever.

"You guys know about the new guy my mom is seeing, right?" she says carefully.

We nod, and already a knot forms in my stomach.

She swallows hard before continuing. "When my mom isn't looking, he leers at me like I'm some fruit he wants to bite into. I thought I was tripping at first, but the more time went by, the more he kept looking. I told him I didn't play that mess and that he needed to stop. But he just acted like he didn't know what I was talking about. And when I'm in the shower, he started walking in on me. Talk'n 'bout it's an accident.

"When he's around, I have to stay in my room. I feel like I'm in prison, like, for real. I cover up like I'm a nun, but he stay looking. The other day, my mom went out to the store. I didn't realize she was gone. He came into my room and blocked the entrance. If my mom hadn't forgotten something and come back . . . I don't know what could have happened."

The guys are pissed off right away. They release a litany of curses as I hold Naija close.

"Yo, for real, just tell me where that nigga hangs out," Dell says.

"You not gonna do anything to him," Naija replies.

"I'm not," Dell confirms. "But I know a lot of niggas with time on their hands and no conscience. Let's do this!"

"The hell we sit'n here for? Let's go get him," Shawn snaps.

"No! I don't want anything to happen to him," Nai says.

"Fine, but you have to tell your mom," I insist.

"I can't say anything. She's in love with him. He makes her happy. I don't want to be the one that takes that away from her. Ayo, you took a big risk, telling your mom how you felt. But I'm not like you. I can't take that risk," she says, crying into my chest.

Damn . . .

———

While we don't have a plan for how to fix things for Naija, the guys and I know one thing for sure—there's no way she's going back in that house until that piece of trash is gone. The guys also told her that she could stay with them. They each volunteered to give up their rooms and even let her get a lock if it would make her feel safe. She thanked them, cried a little more, and ate the Double Stuf Oreos. It could be in my head, but I swear Dell is looking at her a type of way . . .

I can't bring that up now. Naija is exhausted. The guys insist on walking us back to my house. Before we say good night, Naija makes us promise not to tell her mom or anyone else. I nod, but I'm not sure what the right thing to do is in this situation. We enter my house and head for the stairs.

"How was the party?" my mom asks.

I didn't think she'd be home, given that the protest is right around the corner. I assumed she'd be in a meeting or an interview.

"You're home?" I reply.

"I'm going back to headquarters. I just wanted to come by and make sure you girls were good—Naija, what's wrong?" she asks as she studies my best friend closely.

Nai shakes her head, swearing nothing is wrong. That won't work with my mom.

"Your eyes are swollen. Were you crying? Lord, don't tell me some ashy li'l boy done broke your heart."

Naija runs up the steps, sobbing.

"What is going on?" my mom asks.

"Um . . . it's bad. Like, really bad. But I told her I wouldn't say anything."

She nods. "Okay. You want to be a young lady who keeps her word. I get that. But if it's that bad, then I will have to know. So you can tell me or I can go up there and find out. Either way, I can't let that child spend the night crying and not know why."

I exhale, not sure what to do. "Have you hung out with Naija's mom lately?"

"No, it's been a while. The last time was at the spades tournament. She was shouting and talking smack. You know how she is about spades."

"Yeah. Well, she's got other things to keep her mind occupied beside cards now."

My mom reads my expression. "I see."

I go toward the upstairs landing and hope Nai will forgive me. "Mom, the new guy . . . He's not all that. Actually, he's a real piece of— Anyway, I don't think she should go home. So she's staying here tonight, and maybe for the rest of the weekend?"

"Of course. I'm gonna go back to the office. Food's on the counter."

"Mom . . ."

"Getti, don't worry. You go take care of your friend. Things will look better in the morning. Okay?" She gives me a hug, and I silently thank God that she didn't disown me for leaving See Us. I can't imagine my life without Mom, my giant force of nature.

I get to my room, and Naija is already in her pajamas. She has slept here so much, she has her own drawer. We put on her favorite TV show—*The Proud Family*—and let it play in the background while I grease her scalp.

We avoid talking about anything heavy. I think that's what she really needs right now. My cell rings—Devonte. I go to decline the call, but Nai says, "Take it. It's fine." I do, but we don't talk long. Devonte tells me about track practice and asks how I'm doing with staying away from meetings. I tell him so far, so good.

He's easy to talk to. I even tell him about the trees gossiping behind my back. I say it kind of like a joke, so I'm not sure he knows I'm being serious. But when I tell him, he jokingly says, "Tell the trees not to mess with my girl. I'll get a chain saw up in this mother." I laugh.

His girl . . .

And then we kissed . . .

"Yeah, I'll be there. Loser pays for the pizza," I say right before I hang up.

"What's that about?" Nai asks.

"Devonte had the nerve to tell me that *Don't Be a Menace to*

South Central While Drinking Your Juice in the Hood is a better movie than *Friday*!"

"What? Is he crazy?" Nai replies.

"I know! So Sunday, we are going to rent both and see who can best defend their movie."

Naija studies me like she's just now seeing me.

"What?" I ask.

"That boy got you open! Y'all ain't doin' it, are you?" she says, her eyes wide with shock.

I laugh. "Nah, girl. You know I would tell if we did anything. I just want to keep it simple right now. Just hang out and chill. You know? This is all new, so, I'm not trying to go too fast."

"Yeah, I get it." And then she gives me a small smile. "Dell has never given away Double Stuf Oreos to anyone, has he?"

"Wait, let me find out that you and Dell . . . Hold up, wait a minute!" I reply, eyes bulging out of my head.

"What?" she asks with a coy smile.

I hurl a pillow at her, and she tackles me. We fall back onto the bed. Her smile fades, then she turns to me and says, "It's going to be okay, right?"

I turn to her and say the words most Black girls don't get to hear too often: "We got you. Everything is going to be okay."

———

A few hours later, the scent of strong coffee wakes me up. I look at my phone; it's just ten after seven. Nai is asleep next me. I put on my slippers and go down the stairs. I sit on the steps and listen to the voices coming from the kitchen. The first voice belongs to my mom and the second belongs to a woman I've known forever—Ms. Harris, Naija's mom. I peek in surreptitiously. The two of them are seated at the table with two steaming cups of coffee, but neither of them has motioned to drink it.

My mom must have told her . . .

"I know she's still asleep, but she's carrying around the crazy notion that you care more about this guy than you do her. So I think it's okay to wake her and straighten things out," my mom says as she brings the coffee to her lips.

Ms. Harris nods but otherwise doesn't move. She drops her eyes to her mug and stares at the liquid.

"Lena?" Mom says.

Ms. Harris looks up and makes eye contact. The corners of her lips turn up into a wistful smile. "You know where we first hung out?" she asks.

My mom shakes her head.

Ms. Harris's smile grows into a full-on grin. "We went to the laundromat! Yeah, I know it sounds crazy as hell, but . . . he'd been checking for me for a while. I stayed away because I didn't have time for another no-good man. And that's exactly what I told him. He asked what I was doing besides work that had me so busy. I said, 'For one thing, I got two weeks' worth of laundry to do. So unless you want to help me do that, you better be going.'

"The next day, he came by with a bag. Inside he had three types of detergent, fabric softener, and dryer sheets. I laughed my head off, thinking he was kidding. But no, he wasn't. We went down there and did load after load. All the while, we talked about stuff like we'd known each other for years. And after he helped me with the last load, he took my hand and we danced right there in the aisle. There wasn't any music, except for him humming softly in my ear . . . Stevie Wonder, 'As.'"

"It's a good song," my mom replies softly.

"Isn't it? I love me some Stevie Wonder . . ." Ms. Harris says as tears spring to her eyes.

My mom reaches across the table and places her hand on top of Ms. Harris's. "Go ahead, go wake that girl up and fix this. Tell her you and Kingston are over."

"She never came and told me. Nai would have told me if things were bad. I mean, if they were really bad."

"Well, Lena, how bad are you willing to let it get?"

"He hasn't touched her."

"No, I don't think he has. But kids know when someone has locked onto them and mean them harm. They always know. And I don't understand the full extent of what is going on in your house—"

Ms. Harris jumps out of her chair. "That's right, Rosalie, you don't. So mind your business."

Mom is unfazed by Ms. Harris's reaction. "Go on, drink your coffee. We'll figure this thing out."

Without saying a word, Ms. Harris sits back down, dejected. And then she suddenly looks at my mom with new light in her eyes, newfound hope.

"Girl, you know what must have happened?" she asks.

"No, Lena, tell me. What happened?"

"You know how some men play too much? Well, that's him. He just gets carried away, play'n around. I'll talk to him and make sure he knows not to play like that. Sometimes people can take it serious, even though he was only playing. You see what I mean?"

She nods, satisfied with her conclusion. She takes a big sip of her coffee. "This is good! It's rich and has nice, bold flavor. Where y'all get this from?"

"Sugar Hill Creamery," Mom says, making no attempt to match Ms. Harris's newfound enthusiasm.

"Well, it's good. I have to go by there and buy a bag. I really like it."

Mom gets up, goes over to the cabinets, and hands Ms. Harris a new bag of whole-bean coffee.

"Aw, you didn't have to do that, but thank you."

My mom nods and sits back down.

"Look, don't worry about it, Rosalie. I'll talk to Kingston. He'll behave. And I'll talk to Nai and let her know everything will be fine from now on. The three of us can still become a family—yes, girl, things are that serious. Once we get past this little thing . . . it will all work out."

Mom smiles and says, "Oh, girl, I know it'll work out. I don't have any doubt about that. Because so long as that man is darkening your doorstep, that little girl upstairs ain't never setting foot in your house."

Ms. Harris's eyes grow wide with shock and her jaw drops. "Excuse you? Naija is my daughter!" she says as she stands up and plants her hands firmly on her hips. She glares at Mom, who is now coolly going about the task of tidying up the table.

"Oh, so you do remember giving birth to her? Well, that's good. I wasn't sure for a minute."

"This ain't just about me, Rosalie. I'm doing this for her too. I want my baby to have a father."

Mom looks at Ms. Harris as she towel-dries her mug and places it on the rack. "Lena, you are not the only single parent around here. I know the picture you have in your mind, the family you wanted and the family you deserve. That kind of want and need can cut so deep into your chest that it leaves a big, gaping hole right in the center of it.

"Now you out here trying to fill that space. I get that. I can't judge that, but you listen, and listen good: you not about to throw Naija down into that chasm on the small chance that sacrificing her will heal your wounds.

"Kingston is a predator. He knew exactly what he was doing when he chose you. You give him an opening and he will leap out and swallow that little girl right before your eyes. Stop worrying about the father you want her to have and start focusing on being the mother she deserves."

Ms. Harris starts laughing and clapping her hands. "You think you can lecture me about motherhood? Please. I know the truth about you, Rosalie. You care more about your cause than you do your own child. So, don't you dare get uppity with me. At least I make time for my kid."

Mom scoffs. "Lena, I put a weight on my child's back no grown man could carry, let alone a child. I've fractured some parts of my baby, and other parts . . . I've completely shattered. But I'll tell you this: if Ayo comes to me and says a grown man is going out of his way to take note of the curve of her breasts or the outline of her hips, I'll fight like hell to protect her from that. And until you are willing to do the same, that girl is staying here with me."

The two women are locked in a standoff. Ms. Harris's hard expression and deadly glare raise the temperature in the room. "You will not tell me what to do with my own child."

"There are very few things in this world I'd gladly go to prison for, and one of them is Naija. Lena, don't test me."

There is no anger in my mother's voice. There's something far more menacing—certainty. This unwavering belief that come hell, high water, or the devil himself, no one is taking Naija away from this house. Ms. Harris knows that too. So she makes her way past Mom and out the door.

It's Sunday; the protest is finally here. The streets of Harlem are alive. The How Much? signs and banners are ubiquitous, even more so than before. Local businesses, churches, and schools all carry the banner, and most are shutting down so they can attend the protest. The excitement is palpable. My house is complete chaos with last-minute fires needing to be extinguished.

Everyone I know is helping out at the march, including all my friends. My mom won't let me lend a hand. She reminded me that I have plans. I told her that Devonte could wait a little while, but she insisted I carry on with what I've scheduled for today. Her voice wasn't cold or cutting, but it still hurt that she sent me away. I get it—after all, that's what I asked for.

We set up for a day of movies, smack talking, and pizza at Devonte's house. His uncle is at work, so it's just the two of us. I think the reason Devonte chose Sunday to do the movie battle was to keep my mind off the protest. I've tried really hard to act like I don't miss being front and center with See Us. But I think he can tell that some part of me misses it.

It's a matter of time. Soon, I won't even miss being part of See Us. It will be out of my mind completely.

I try to focus on the movie, but eventually, I give up. "Okay, okay, maybe we can catch just a little bit of the protest. I want to hear my mom speak."

"All right, I got you." He turns on the news, and I can finally function again.

The turnout for the protest is bigger than any of us could have anticipated; tens of thousands of demonstrators converge on the Manhattan streets. They carry signs letting us know where they hail from. Many of the people are from the outer boroughs, but a great number of them are from out of state.

The victims' families—including Davis Brown—march alongside my mom and other top members of See Us. The front line of the protest is a who's who of Black leadership. It's not only Black people marching—people from all backgrounds are joined together and demand an end to police brutality. The energy of the crowd is electrifying and sends goose bumps down my arms.

The CNN reporter goes over to a group of counterprotesters, a small but seriously vocal group who shout slurs and accusations at the crowd. They accuse the crowd of being antiwhite and anticops. They vow to stop us from ruining "their" country. Their faces are red with ire at what they feel is an attack on law enforcement. The reporter tries to remain professional, but it's clear she's taken aback by the aggressive tone of the counterprotesters.

The reporter asks the cameraman to pan out so the people at home can get a sense of just how large the crowd has gotten. He's right, the crowd's grown and so has the police presence.

We've had many heated protests, but none on this scale. The protest makes its way to in front of the Thirty-Second Precinct on 135th Street, where the officers who shot Davis Brown work. The roar of the crowd grows to a deafening pitch, and my mom is given the microphone. She calmly takes center stage.

She doesn't just settle for naming general groups—she calls out specific people in the police department and in the mayor's office. She warns them the crowd is not there to ask for equality but to demand it. She eloquently gives voice to the rage and frustration of the demonstrators. She points out that the time for asking is over. The crowd goes crazy. She demands that they take instead of waiting to be given the equal protection they were promised. The crowd was already pumped up, but by the time my mom is done, a new kind of fire has been ignited.

I put the TV on mute and turn my back to the screen. I find myself hugging my knees to my chest. I bury my face and form a ball.

"What's wrong?" Devonte asks.

I look into his eyes and marvel at just how warm they are. Then I think about how little it matters. When he gets stopped by the cops, none of it will matter. They won't know that he uses humor to hide his insecurities. It won't matter to them that he holds doors open for girls or makes the best hot chocolate in the world. They will see what most see when they look at him . . . a reason to fear.

I remember reading about the places in the world that are

considered the least racist. I could see myself moving to some of the places on the list. A place where I don't need to stage a protest to simply be allowed to exist. That's it, problem solved. I will keep Devonte, my mom, and everyone else I love safe by moving to another country.

"Did you know Ghana has really impressive runners?"

I'm not sure if that's true, but it might be, so . . .

"You're being crazy random right now," he says.

"They also have something called jollof rice. It's a staple. It's supposed to be really good."

He smiles and looks at me like I'm crazy, but something on TV catches his eye. His smile fades. "Ayo . . ."

I follow his gaze. The protest has become a riot. Protesters and cops are clashing; cars are being set on fire, bottles thrown, tear gas fills the air. I look for her—my lifeline. She's in the center, because where else would she be? I watch, horrified, as a cop yanks a teenage girl by her hair and drags her down to the ground. My mom rushes to her aid, like a ferocious lion. The cop aims his weapon at my mom and shoots . . .

CHAPTER ELEVEN

Into the Deep

A nanosecond after Mom's body hits the ground, my skull caves in and my brain hovers, in fragments, just above my head. Logic says she won't get up; she's just been shot in the head. But logic has not met my mother. While chaos and panic invade both the crowd on TV and Devonte, I stay still and wait. I wait for my mom to get up because she knows I can't do this without her. She will get up.

Except she doesn't.

I'm watching a girl with my face fall onto her knees and sob hysterically. She lets out a guttural wail that comes from somewhere so dark and deep that she didn't even know a place like that existed. The boy she's with tries to help her, but she is beyond his reach. She won't survive; we both know that. The only thing I can gift to the girl with my eyes is the gift of nothing. And so, we both black out . . .

———

The sun tries to lure me awake with its warm, golden rays. No thank you. I will stay unconscious in this cool, dark place. Here, my mom's booming laugh is a colorful dragon I can ride. I hop on and take in the sweetly scented air. It's calming and familiar. But I can't quite place it . . . Oh yes, coconut and jojoba oil. The oils she mixed together before she greased my scalp when I was little. How did she do it? How did she make this whole world smell like washday? Suddenly, my dragon swoops down for a landing . . .

"No, let's stay up here. I wanna stay here!"

"Ayo! Ayo, baby, wake up!"

I open my eyes. I'm back here, in this world where she may not exist anymore. I'm in a hospital room, and a chunky older man is standing over me. He has kind eyes and a salt-and-pepper beard, and worry is etched on his face. He tries to put together something that resembles a smile.

Uncle Ty. He lives in Jersey with his wife; she doesn't get along with my mother, so we don't get to see him as often as we'd like.

"Uncle Ty . . ."

"You okay, Bit-Bit?"

"What happened?"

"You fainted and then when you came to, you were hysterical, so the doctors gave you something. It helped you sleep."

"Mom. Where's Mom? Is she . . . ?" I can't finish my thought. It's just too painful to put those words out into the air.

"She's trying really hard to hold on. Right now, all we can do is pray for her."

"Where is she? Take me to her."

He helps me out of bed, and for the first time since waking up, I hear loud chanting outside: "No justice, no peace."

"What is that?" I ask.

"Just about everybody in Harlem. They are going crazy out there. Now they want justice one way or another." He goes over to the window and opens it just a crack. Everyone is shouting and pumping their fists in the air. They are demanding the cops involved pay for what they did.

When I think about the man who shot her and his partner, who just let it happen, the ire is overwhelming. There isn't space for both prayers for my mom and hate for the cops. It's not that I can't summon both, but one would take over the other, quickly. And if rage won out, I would be too busy burning the police station to the ground to really be there for my mom.

So for now, I choose to put all my energy on her. I don't know how long I can hold back this kind of fury. That's the thing: all the Black girls I know have rage in one way or another;

no one tells us where to put it. And sometimes we are left to improvise . . .

"Bit-Bit, the cop and his partner have been fired. But you know good and well, them white folks could easily let them go with no more punishment than that. The cop's name is—"

"No. He doesn't get to have a name."

———

When I passed out, I was taken to the same hospital as Mom —Mount Sinai. We get up to her floor, and a nurse tells us why I won't be allowed to see her. I see her lips moving, but very little of what she says means anything to me. I head for Mom's room, and a doctor blocks my path.

"You're the daughter, I understand? I'm Dr.—"

"No names. Please. I need to go in and see her."

My uncle tries to convince them that it's okay to let me in. They tell us we can't enter because they are prepping Mom for surgery. The doctor does offer us an update. "Luckily, the bullet didn't do nearly as much damage as it could have done."

Yeah, that's exactly how I feel—lucky.

He tells us there's swelling in her brain and they need to relieve the pressure. My uncle demands I get three minutes with her. The two of them debate. But soon, their voices are mere background noise. I march toward her room.

"You can't go in," the doctor insists.

I turn back and look at him, and whatever he sees makes him back off. I enter her room.

She's not in there. She's been replaced by a small, fragile, grayish woman, a woman who could be swayed and bent by a gentle breeze. I don't know who this woman is, not by looking at her. But what my eyes can't recognize, my heart knows. This is my mom. I don't let the tears or the lump in my throat stop me. I pull it together. I'm not here to cry for her. I'm here to remind her of something.

"Okay, Mom. You remember when I got lost on Halloween and I couldn't find my way back? I thought I was so grown, wanting to trick-or-treat alone. You followed me. And when I started crying, you came out and took my hand. You said, 'Stop crying. You are never alone in this world. Now, fix your face and start focusing on finding your way back.' Well, it works both ways, okay? So stop crying and find your way back. If you love me, don't take my air away . . ."

———

It's hours before the surgeon comes back out to talk to us. He says it went well. That should mean my mom will come out of surgery like nothing ever happened. That's what my heart wants. But that's not what the guy with the degree tells us. He says all we can do now is wait to see if she wakes up.

Wait to see if my soul is alive or dead? Sure, doc, shouldn't be too hard to do . . .

I live on the ocean floor. The only reason I come up to the surface is to visit my mom. I see what's going on in the real world but have only a casual connection with it. I can hardly make eye contact with Nai, although we live in the same house. It's not just her; I barely speak to my uncle, or anyone, for that matter. I avoid news because they like to play the footage of my mom getting shot. They always say, "Please be advised, this footage is graphic . . ." but they're so damn quick to play it.

Members of See Us are calling for the arrest of the cop. I know I've heard his name, but my mind refuses to let it in. The media has made this their hot story of the moment. They swarm all around the neighborhood and ask questions. Uncle Ty, much like his sister, isn't one for foolishness. I'm thankful he can keep them at bay.

Devonte gets up early to ride with me to the hospital before he goes to school; we don't talk. He knows that all words would fail. Both my friends and neighbors try to find a way to connect. But they can't, because I'm not in the same world as them.

When I'm at the house, everything feels strange. Someone removed all the specificity from my life. The mint was stolen from my toothpaste, the oranges drained from my juice, and the seasoning siphoned from my eggs. Everything in this world feels dollar-store generic and doesn't belong to me.

In the week that follows, the women in the neighborhood

swear that I'm rail thin and wasting away. They bring over food throughout the day, enough to feed all of New York City. The older guys on the block want to help, but some of them are too old for the fire and brimstone of rising protests happening outside. So they come over and fix things—things that aren't broken. Meanwhile, my uncle plays bodyguard and keeps the media and random nosy people at bay.

Up above my head, things are happening. Nate Collard is making the rounds in the media, voicing outrage and disgust. But when I walk into a room and see him on CNN or any of the major networks, my mind relegates him to the background. There's no more room inside me. I can't let anything else in, not even updates on my mom's case.

My uncle knows how disconnected I am but still, he tries to keep me engaged by telling me the latest news on the cops. The more the city resists charging them, the more pissed off Black folks get. Some make a cozy knit scarf out of their rage so they can wear it to keep them warm as the temperatures drop. Some people liquefy their rage, mix it with their tea, and sip it slowly. And others, like my uncle, breed their rage into attack dogs, ready to launch at anyone, anytime.

When I was a kid, my mom's friend took us to church. The pastor said that if we were worried or fearful about anything, we could call Jesus on the main line. I mistook that for an actual phone call. So when someone was mean to me, I'd ask my mom for God's number, so I could tell on them. She told me that God probably wouldn't answer for little things like people teasing me at lunch.

I wonder if my mom getting shot counts as a big thing to God. Or is it a regular old Tuesday for him?

I close my eyes and fall asleep not long after just waking up. The next day, I do the same thing. I vaguely recall brushing my teeth, or it might have been a movie I watched where the Black girl was getting ready. I can't remember. The calendar app on my cell tells me that two weeks have gone by. I guess I can't really object—the calendar tends to win those arguments —but for me, time is still.

Earlier this morning, Uncle Ty entered my room to tell me that more info about the officers has leaked out. Both of them have multiple complaints for excessive force over the years. One person filed a complaint saying the officer who shot my mom had called him the N-word just before putting him in the squad car. In addition, reports are that both officers were over-heard referring to us as "savages." The uproar over the cops' past behavior got to be so much that by the end of the day, the city announced it would be convening a grand jury.

My uncle and my friends thought that piece of good news would get me to come back to life, but it did not. And now, they are really worried about me. They all try to help in their own way. Uncle Ty lets me eat whatever I want for dinner, but most times, I end up just picking at it. Nai tries to keep my mind off everything by sending me random clips of trashy reality TV shows. Dell makes goofy videos he calls "In White-Folks News." The best one was a loony white woman who vowed to stage a protest against the Bronx Zoo for refusing to let her in the lion cage to take a selfie.

Shawn sends silly TikTok videos that actually made me smile. And then there's Devonte.

He got the entire track team to send me a message saying they are praying for my mom. And he calls me every night. I tell him I won't be great company, but he says he just wants to hear my voice.

He found a joke book that was like a hundred years old at a flea market and insists that out of the three hundred or so jokes, one of them has to be worthwhile. So right before we hang up for the night, he tells me one. They all suck. But what I love is the hope in his voice, right before he tells me the joke. He's always so full of hope . . .

Normally, I would try to fix the situation, get up just because I'm told to do so. But the thing about life on the ocean floor is that you don't have to do a damn thing you don't want to do. That includes getting out of bed. So when they try to get me to face the world, I grunt and go deeper into my covers.

School is unhappy that I have not been to class in weeks. They've called the house and insisted I go to a counseling session. My uncle said it seemed like a good idea. Man, you know it's bad when Black folks have to go see someone. I tell him that

I don't want to go and he says I should at least give it a try. In the end, I only agreed to go because Uncle Ty spoke in his "Ain't no body here play'n with you" tone.

So, now we are headed for the therapist's office in Midtown. My uncle took me, fearing I wouldn't go otherwise. We enter the waiting room; everything from the dusty-blue color palette to the water fountain mounted on the wall suggests that I should be calm or, at the very least, should pretend.

I made a deal with my uncle: if there were three things that feel wrong about being there, we could go back home. So after walking over to the water fountain, I spot something and walk back toward the reception desk.

"Does a dead bee in the water fountain count as one?"

"Bit-Bit, that's just nature," he says.

"I guess, but you ask me, it was self-inflicted. That bee chose a watery grave rather than being stuck in here."

He drops his head in disbelief but then says, "All right, Bit-Bit. That's one."

"Thank you."

He rolls his eyes and smiles playfully. He hasn't smiled in forever, so it's nice to see that on his face. I don't need my smile back. I'm good with losing it. What I want back, surprisingly enough, are my tears. I ran out of them a long time ago.

The lady behind the reception desk has a name tag informing us that she is Darlene. Darlene is in her late fifties, wears fuchsia lipstick, and has a framed picture of her cat near her desktop. When she's done gathering up the multitude of papers, she battles a stubborn stapler, hoping to keep the stack together.

We take a seat across from an elderly man and his wife. They are having an argument but doing so in a whisper. She looks like she's rethinking every decision she's ever made in life, and he looks like he'd sign away his soul for an exit—any exit. I guess the calming blue has failed to actually calm anyone.

My uncle plows through the paperwork, and I turn my focus on the coffee table in the center. I smile to myself, because I think I might have found reason number two.

There are three magazines on the table, all of them face-down, only the ads on the back showing. I turn to my uncle.

"If I turn these magazines over and there aren't any Black people on there, that makes it number two, right?"

"Okay, but not just the cover. You have to look through the entire magazine."

"Deal."

I turn over the first magazine—*Harper's Bazaar*.

We skim the pages.

Strike one.

"The next one could be O. You know how Oprah do," he says, filled with hope. He turns over the second magazine—*Redbook*. It's worth a look, and so we dive in.

Strike two.

The final magazine is mine to turn over. My heart actually

skips. I need this to get me a step closer to getting the hell out of here. I turn the magazine over—*Town & Country.*

Ha! We don't even need to open it—Gwyneth Paltrow is on the cover.

The light from the inner office spills out onto the waiting room and a woman enters the waiting area. She's a white woman in her early sixties. She has clear gray eyes and wears a tasteful gray blouse and pencil skirt. My uncle stands up and prods me to do the same.

He leans in and whispers, "She's already here, so no, there is no time for strike three. The school says she's helped other students. Try it, Bit-Bit."

Damn it. There has to be a way to get out of this . . .

She extends her hand to me and smiles warmly. "Hello, my name is Dr. Wolkoff. It's nice to meet you."

We shake hands. I try something. "Hello, I'm Ayomide."

"Hello, Ayomide," she replies.

Damn.

Perfect pronunciation.

My uncle grins because he knows he's won. We begin to head back toward her office, but then it hits me . . .

I call out to her, "Doc, I've had this song stuck in my head all day. Do you know what it is?"

"Hum it," she says.

I look over at my uncle, who senses trouble, and begin to hum a tune.

She listens carefully. My uncle frowns.

She says she doesn't know what the song is and asks me to hum it again.

I do, three times.

"I don't know that song," she admits.

"It's the Black national anthem." My uncle groans in dismay.

She says, "There's a Black national anthem?"

We never even make it to her office.

CHAPTER TWELVE

Gather

I know going into Mom's bedroom will only make it hurt more. But that is exactly where I find myself. It's a little after midnight, and the urge to be around her things has become irresistible. I stand in front of her closet and run my fingers through her clothes. They have her scent, and each item comes with a memory. They aren't big, dramatic moments; they're small ones that I would've dismissed before all of this.

When I was a kid, she read and reread many books to me in here. It took us weeks to get through *The Bluest Eye*. But that was to be expected of a Toni Morrison novel. We'd pull her words apart and rearrange them so that us mortals could understand them. Then we'd put them back the way she wrote them and marvel at her brilliance.

This is also the room where my mom let her guard down and was like the rest of us, especially when it came to reading horror stories. If books are food for thought, then Stephen King books are the dessert we gorge ourselves on. We read *Cujo* here in this room, and every time we got to scary parts, we'd both dive under the covers. It's because of *Pet Sematary* that we never got any pets in the house; thanks to *The Shining*, we'd cross the street anytime we see twin kids. And there was no way in hell anyone in this house would ever, ever go to the circus. *It* kept us up for days.

I get up on her bed and reach for what I know is there—a book on her nightstand. She was reading *Your Blues Ain't Like Mine*. I pick it up and read the handwritten notes she made for herself. I start reading, and soon my eyes get heavy and sleep takes me.

I wake up half an hour later. I see her Cookie Monster slippers looking back at me from the open closet.

My uncle wasn't happy that I didn't give therapy a chance. He scolded me on the train ride home and said I needed to talk to someone. He made arrangements for me to see a Black, female therapist next week. But if the point is to talk to someone, I think I have an idea. I go over to the slippers and put them on. I walk out into the hallway closet where my mom made me confront the monster in my dream years ago. She said the ancestors would protect me. Maybe they're in there right now, in which case, I can find someone to talk to.

Once inside the hall closet, I go to turn on the light, but on second thought, I leave it dark. Maybe they like it that way. I close the door behind me. I have no idea how much sense this makes, but it can't hurt to try. Maybe they really are in here, and while they never showed up for me, they'll show up for her.

"Ah . . . hello? I don't really know what to call you guys . . . 'Ancestors' sounds . . . really formal. How about aunties and uncles? There, that's better, right? I don't know if you know me. I'm sure you know my mom. She puts a lot of faith in you guys, and, um . . . she could really use your help.

"You have never appeared to me because I'm not strong and courageous like my mom. She taught me to see, I mean *really* see, the world, and it scared me. They say knowledge is power, but it's much more than that—it's weight. And it just got too heavy for me. I guess that makes me fragile, and it looks like you guys don't have time for people like me.

"It's cool. But my mom isn't weak. She's the strongest person I know. And she really needs your help. So all of you aunties and uncles from yesterday need to gather at the river; sing your songs and send up your prayers; save her. She's not just *my* light; she belongs to the whole neighborhood. Don't dim the lights of Harlem . . ."

After speaking to the aunts and uncles, I go back to bed. I feel lighter. That's not to say I am better, because I will never be better until she's awake. But I go to sleep feeling like maybe I will soon have help.

When I get up, it's almost noon. My uncle looks seriously concerned when I come down the steps. I assure him that I did talk to someone—in fact, I talked to a lot of people. He looks confused. I hug him and tell him that I won't be sleeping all day anymore. I'm hoping that getting up and even maybe going to school will show the aunties and uncles that I have faith in them. It's a long shot, but it's all I have.

I go to see her. She's in the same condition I left her in; seeing that is more painful than anything else I've encountered. But I take her hand and tell her not to despair. I tell her that help is coming. And as I kiss her goodbye, I hope to the heavens that what I said was true.

Once I'm home and enter my room, I find the same heaviness waiting to greet me. I know I can't turn back the clock and undo what's happened, but for just one moment I long for things to be like before. I can close my eyes and pretend like my mom's at work, and she's gonna be home late. And my heartache is slightly less acute now. So I keep going with my grand delusion that everything is fine. Now, what would a normal, trauma-free teen do on a night where her mom is working late?

Well, if that teen has a funny, kind, and hot-looking boyfriend . . .

Devonte knocks frantically on the door. I let him in wearing a big smile. He's not sure what to make of it. He looks me over head to toe. He's looking to see if I'm in one piece. I'm not. But that's exactly why I called him over here. Since I vowed not to stay in bed all day and fill up on sadness, I have to fill up on something else—anything else.

"You texted me 911. What's wrong? You good?" he asks.

"Yeah, I'm fine. Come in," I reply.

He's about to say something, but I don't give him the chance. I open the door wider and insist he gets inside.

"Is it news about your mom? Is she . . . I mean . . ."

"No news yet. And no, this ain't about her. I just wanted to see you. Can't a girl ask to see her boyfriend?" I reply as I head toward the stairs.

"Where is everybody?"

"Uncle Ty is at a meeting and Nai has tutoring. It's just us," I say as I get to the top of the landing.

"All right, you wanna go get something to eat at—"

"I'm not hungry. Follow me." I catch the look on his face just before I disappear into my bedroom. Normally, I would be filled with anxiety and self-doubt in a situation like this. But there's nothing normal about my life anymore.

Devonte has long legs and could be in here in seconds, but

instead, he's coming up slowly, as if he's thinking over every step he takes. That's fine; it gives me a chance to look myself over in the mirror. My collarbones are more pronounced now; I haven't been eating much. There are dark circles under my eyes and an aura of hopelessness surrounds me.

It's not all bad, though. Yes, my cutoff jean shorts are worn, but they are still cute. And yeah, my T-shirt is faded, but it's A Tribe Called Quest, so I'm good. The last thing I check out is my hair. Thanks to my girl Nai, it's freshly braided like Alicia Keys circa *Songs in A Minor*. All in all, not bad for a girl who just wants to stay in bed and never get up.

He knocks on my bedroom door, although it's already open. I find that adorable. Why would he knock? Could he be nervous? I mean, he's probably done this a bunch of times, so why would he even think to be nervous?

"Come in."

"For real?" he says.

I roll my eyes. "Yes, come in already!"

Devonte carefully crosses the threshold of my bedroom. Once he makes it inside, he lets out a sigh of relief.

"What is it?" I ask.

"Man, I thought, knowing your mom, she might have rigged your room up so that any guy who crosses the doorway gets sent to the cornfield."

I'm about to have sex with a guy who can make a decent *Twilight Zone* reference. Respect.

"The only reason that kid acted like that was 'cause he didn't have a Black mama," I point out.

We both laugh as he takes in my room. He nods with approval. He asks about some of the posters. I walk over to him and place my arms around his neck. I lean my head back and gaze into his eyes.

"I didn't bring you up here for Q&A. I brought you here for T&A," I tease.

"Oh, shoot, wordplay," he says, then we kiss. It's a casual kiss at first. But then it grows more and more seeking. This is usually the point where we would pull back. Okay, this is usually the point where *I* would pull back. He would follow suit.

He's waiting for me to halt the make-out session, but I don't. And as the kisses intensify and our hands wander, the darkness that threatens to swallow me whole is held at bay . . .

Yes, it's working . . .

He tries to slow things down by literally taking a step back. I don't let him get too far. I don't really know much about seduction. I figure now is as good a time as any to learn. I kiss his neck and slide his coat off and onto the floor. My heart is pounding loudly in my ear; the contact we're making is pushing all the ugliness away.

More, I need more to make it all go away . . .

He pulls back from the kiss and takes another step back. This time it's a big, decisive step, one that ensures a solid distance between us. He exhales loudly and swallows hard. His eyes are dancing with desire and longing. I know for certain he wants this too. I can hear his heart from here. Not sure why he stopped.

"What's wrong?" I ask.

"Ayo, I don't think—"

"Don't think," I order him, then engage his lips again. I back him toward my bed and boldly push him down onto the mattress, an action I can only take because he's caught off guard. I straddle him and remove my shirt.

All that's left is my black cotton bra and shorts. I wish my bra was silk or lace, like in the movies or the romance books I'll never admit to reading. But hey, I will work with what I have. I lean down toward Devonte. Our lips are only inches apart. He's about to talk, but I stop him—with my tongue.

"Yo, hold up! Hold up!" he says as he sits up and effortlessly removes me from on top of him. He puts me down next to him and quickly grabs his coat to cover me up.

I stand up and come close to him. He reaches out to me—I think maybe he's changed his mind, but instead he zips up the coat he placed on me. Now I'm all covered up. Damn, that's not the direction I intended this to go.

"Devonte, what's the problem?" I ask.

"You went dark for three weeks and now you just wanna go hard like this? Plus, it's your first time. And I know this isn't the way you wanted it to happen."

"Who cares what I want?"

"I do."

"Argh! Can you just do what I ask?"

"So you're really asking me to have sex with you right now?"

"Yes! Are we going to do it, or do I have to find someone else?"

He rakes his hands through his hair and interlocks his fingers behind his neck. His jaw is clenched and a vein in his temple is throbbing.

"Ayo, I'm not 'bout to take advantage like this. And if you feel you gotta go to someone else, then I guess that's what you gotta do."

"Get out!" I shriek.

"Ayo, let's talk, okay?!"

I grab the nearest thing—a crystal jewelry box—and fling it at his head. He ducks. It shatters on impact. I throw everything at him as he tries to reach me. When he gets close enough, he pulls me into his embrace. I do the ugly cry.

"All I feel is sorrow. It's in the enamel on my teeth, in my hair, under my nails . . . It's all I am now."

I don't remember how I got to the floor; maybe he put me there or maybe my knees gave out. All I know is that we're there now. He's holding me from behind, my back against his chest. He can't stop my tears from overwhelming me. But he refuses to let me drown alone.

It's nightfall now. The house is pretty quiet apart from the sound of the TV coming from downstairs. I can make out Nate's voice, along with one of my mom's favorite commentators, Rachel Maddow. I guess tonight, Nate's doing MSNBC.

Back in the room, Devonte's made no move to let go of me, and I'm more than okay with that. I saw him text someone earlier. I think it was Nai, because even though I heard her come into the house, she didn't come in my room like she normally would.

My throat feels raw, and when I try to talk, my words come out as a harsh whisper. "I'm sorry."

"For what?" he says, as if this was just a normal event in our lives.

"For being a mess. If you want to break up—"

"Stop it. I'm not about to leave you because of this. If I leave you for anything, Ayo, it will be because you put mayo on your eggs."

I try to laugh but don't quite succeed. Instead, I reach back and elbow him in his ribs.

"That's how they do it in France," I reply proudly.

"Also, you go hard for untalented band members."

"I'm telling you, Pras has untapped potential."

He groans. "And worst of all, you have a thing for generic cereal."

"You never even tried Fruit Rings!"

The more I protest, the more he laughs at me. "The point is, Ms. Ayo Bosia, none of those things will make me bounce. So hush and let me be here for you."

I turn to face him and find tears springing to my eyes, tears I thought had long dried out. "She can't die. She just can't."

"Die? No, not your mama. She's a boss. You know that."

"Yeah, I know. Hey, thanks for . . . you know."

"All good. But when and if we ever get here again, you should know, I need to be wooed. I mean it. I want flower petals, scented candles, all that!"

I laugh at his silly ass, and Nai calls for me to come down.

"Coming!" I reply as we scramble to our feet. I get dressed and we head downstairs. Ms. Hightower is standing at the door with a package in her hand.

"I swear it gets colder every year! I might go down to Florida and stay with my sister," she says. She threatens to leave New York City every year, but she never goes.

"Come in, Ms. Hightower," I reply, giving her space to enter.

"Nah, I can't stay. I came to drop this off to you," she says, showing me the box. "Your mom hid this with me because she didn't want you to stumble onto it before your birthday. She called the day of the march to say she was coming to get it to give it to you early before your special day, but . . . she never made it to my house. Been waiting for her to wake up, so . . . anyway, thought I'd bring it by."

I take the package and mumble a quick thank you. Nai and Devonte say good night to Ms. Hightower and close the door behind her. They look on as I open the package. Inside is a box, roughly twelve by nine, with beautiful blue and gold African-print wrapping.

There's a note on the box, and my breath catches in my throat. I excuse myself so I can read the note alone. I feel like this is just between my mom and me.

I go to her office and lock the door behind me. I sit on her favorite armchair by the window and open the handwritten letter.

Dear Ayomide,

This hand-carved box has been specially crafted for you and has three locks; each lock requires its own key. In order to find the keys, you must follow the clues written below. This undertaking is more involved than previous years have been — perhaps allow your friends to help you in your search. Once you open this box, you will uncover the source of my strength . . .

Good luck!

PS: Nothing is by chance . . .

I read the letter three times. I can't believe this. I'm finally going to learn her secret to being strong and courageous. Could it be a book she read, a song she sings to herself, or some ancient proverb? All I have to do is complete the hunt and I'll finally learn the true source of her strength.

I unwrap the box and gasp. It's a wooden box carved to depict the cover of my favorite Black folktale, "The People Could Fly." The figures hold hands as they magically fly away from a life of slavery. The locks on the box are heavy and made of dark metal. The keyholes at the center are made to fit antique keys. An elegantly handwritten note is attached to the first lock:

> The King's death gave me life.
> My father is first, in two places.
> Give me everything and I will give you wings.

CHAPTER THIRTEEN

Mrs. Wright

I put my focus on the treasure hunt. I quickly shower and get ready for life above the surface. I'm not just floating around in a black void anymore. I have a mission.

It's that mission that is keeping me away from going to see my mom in the hospital. I'm terrified that what little hope I found with her letter will be undone when I see her nearly life-less face. So for now, as difficult as it is, I stay away from my mom so I can focus on the task at hand.

On my way down the stairs, I hear two voices coming from the kitchen. In addition to Uncle Ty, there is another male voice: Nate. He's arguing with Uncle Ty, though they're trying to keep their voices down. I lean in close so I can overhear.

"You have to let her do this. You don't have a choice!" Nate says.

"I ain't got to do nothing but stay Black and die. You know that," Uncle Ty says.

"This is what Rosalie would have wanted. You need to let this happen."

"She's not ready to do anything like that. We just got her to agree to go back to school."

What are they talking about? What is it Nate wants me to do? Why doesn't Uncle Ty think I'm up to it, whatever it is?

I can't stop myself from taking a quick peek inside the kitchen. But I do it carefully, because once they know I am there, they'll stop arguing. Nate is pacing up and down the kitchen, and Uncle Ty has his hands balled up in fists.

"I know how you feel about Ayo," Nate says. "I feel the same way. I want to protect her too. But we don't have a choice. It's not just me asking. Do you have any idea how many calls we're getting at See Us? Everyone wants to know what she's thinking, which direction she wants to go, because we all know that's what Rosalie was grooming her for. This is her destiny. Why are you standing in the way of it?"

"She's hardly fifteen. She doesn't have a destiny; she has homework. She has friends. She has a mother in a coma. She doesn't need you to add the entire race on her shoulders."

"That's not the way Rosalie saw it! She had a vision. You know that!"

Uncle Ty stands up so quickly that his chair falls over. "And where the hell did that get her?"

"So, that's it? You're letting those cops off?" Nate asks in disbelief.

"No! The trial hasn't even started yet."

Nate laughs sardonically. "Brother, that trial started and is almost over. It has nothing to do with the courtroom. The only court that matters is the court of public opinion. That's where we need to score a win."

"You want me to put my niece up there and have her cry for the media's approval? Is that what you want?"

"No!" Nate says, slamming his fist down on the table. "I want her to look grateful. White folks love when we look grateful, even though they are only giving us the bare minimum. That's the only way this works."

"She's smart, she's clever, and she's well read. But none of those things change the fact that she's just a kid. Her childhood shouldn't be—"

"Childhood? Man, please! Who the hell told you our kids would get one of those?"

"She has barely gotten out of bed. She's lost her whole world. I ain't gonna add to her trauma."

"There's no way you can keep her from trauma; she's a Black girl in America!"

"You need to go, you need to go right now before I forget my good mind and throw you out!"

The two exchange a dangerous glare. The tension in the room clings to the air like grease after a fish fry. Both men stand their ground.

"You heard the things the cops and their lawyers have been saying about Rosalie," Nate says. "It's only going to get worse. The only weapon we have is Ayo. Use her or get ready to explain to her why the cops who shot her mom are getting off."

Nate turns on his heel and walks out of the room. He passes me in the hallway. Our eyes lock.

"Hi, Ayo."

"Hi, Nate."

—

My uncle doesn't want to discuss what the argument was about, but I threaten not to go to school. He could easily drag me there; he doesn't play when it comes to stuff like that. But I think he sees in my eyes just how much I need to know what's going on. I've spent so much time below; coming up to the surface means I need to be caught up on everything—no matter how bad.

He tells me that the cops and their families have been doing the morning show circuit. They're painting my mom as some kind of outlaw who was hell-bent on terrorizing the city. The way they put it, they were saving New York City from an anarchist.

I need to see it for myself. So I check out some of the clips on YouTube. The cops and their families came dressed in their

Sunday best. The sadness and regret in their eyes remind me of designer handbags sold on Canal Street. It seems genuine until you look closer. You can see the flaws in the seams.

My uncle abruptly takes my cell away. I look up at him, and he signals for me to look down at my hand. It's bleeding. I cut into my palm with my nails and didn't even notice the pain. Now that I'm back on the surface, things like rage and bitterness are just as easily accessed as hope and purpose.

"How dare they blame her for what they did to her? She's fighting for her life and she still has to defend herself?" I shout as my uncle places my hand under running water.

"You know they'll say anything to excuse what they did. But we know what happened. And we won't let them change the story. The good news is they are going in front of a jury. Let's hold on to that for now."

"We get to shout and beg for scraps of justice. I'm so sick of scraps! Those cops put a bullet in my mother's head. And we're supposed to overlook that because they coach their kid's little league team? For real?"

"See Us is not going to let them blame your mom. I promise you. But per our deal, your job is to go to school and focus on the hunt. See Us will take care of this. Now promise me you're going to school."

"I want to do it, Uncle. I want to speak out about my mom. If Nate thinks it will help, I'll go," I say.

"We might do that, but for right now, I just want you to try to get back to something . . . normal."

Normal? What the hell is that?

I reach out and hug my uncle. We both know normal is gone and done. But I appreciate that he worked hard to fix his mouth to say the word.

———

I want to just focus on the first set of clues to finding the keys. But I can't stop thinking about all the awful things being said about my mom. They're playing in my head on a loop. And by the time I get to school, my palm is bleeding again.

It's my first day back at school and I'm relieved to see Nai. She's been sleeping at her cousin's house most nights, so that I can have some space. I feel really bad that I haven't been much of a friend to her lately. It's hard to reach out from the ocean floor. But things will be different now. Nai hugs me so tight, I might need medical attention when it's all over. I push back tears. "Yeah, yeah, I missed you too," I manage to say, with what little air I can get into my lungs.

"Girl, I know you have a lot on your mind, but I have tea —its piping hot and so good!" Nai says, excited.

I'm not really in the mood for gossip, but I can tell it means a lot to her. So, I find a smile and spread it across my face. "Okay, I'm ready. Go!"

"My girl Titi overheard Devonte talking to his boys and he called you his girl!"

"No! For real?"

"Yes!" She runs it all down for me. One of Devonte's friends was trying to set him up with a girl he knew and Devonte declined, saying he had the girl he wanted. She said he was beaming when he said my name.

I knew we were official because Devonte didn't pull back at all since things went down. In fact, we've only gotten closer. This morning he took me to visit my mom. We talked about the crazy stuff on the news and he made me promise to come find him in school if I was feeling overwhelmed.

"I got you," he said. It was a simple statement, but it meant the world to me. On our way to class, I quickly text Devonte:

Me: So, I hear we're official now.

Devonte: You didn't know?

Me: I did. Still nice to hear it out loud. We should celebrate our "official" status

Devonte: Like w/ a kiss?

Me: I was thinking more of a pinky swear situation but a kiss will do.

A few moments later, I fake having to use the restroom so we can meet up in the stairwell by his locker. He makes good on the kiss. I mean really, really good. When he pulls away, I groan softly. He laughs. "Same, yo." I guess he didn't want to stop either.

He looks me over, but not in the "are you okay" way everyone else has been. This look is more passion than pity. I like it.

"Man, I always forget *just* how beautiful you are until I see you. And then its . . . wow."

I bury my face in his chest and wrap my arms around him. And for a moment, all my heartache goes away . . .

Later, Nai and I head for lunch with the guys. When I encounter Shawn and Dell, they too suck the air out of my lungs. When we sit down, it looks just like old times, but it's not. I can *feel* them feeling sorry for me. And even though there's all this food on the table, no one feels like eating, not even Dell.

I wanted to keep things light, but I end up ranting to them about all the stuff in the news. They admit they've seen it, and they wonder if it will actually work and if the cops will get off. We all say, "Hell nah." But we say it knowing just how wrong we could be.

After lunch, the guys walk Nai and me to Mr. Gunderson's class. We enter, and all eyes turn toward me. Everyone is studying my face, not sure what they expect to see.

"Ayo, it's nice to see you back in class," Mr. Gunderson says. "We all wish your mother a speedy recovery. And we're sorry this happened to your family."

I nod quickly, hoping that will be the end of it as we take our seats.

Please, God, let him just teach the class and not focus on me. Pleasepleaseplease.

"It looks like the more rallies See Us has, the more unstable the situation becomes. Do you think See Us is taking a more violent route? If so, do you agree with the new direction?" he asks me.

I must have sent my prayer to white Jesus, because it did not get answered. Nai reads the torn expression on my face. Her hand flies up in the air and she says, "Mr. Gunderson, can we go over the homework? I didn't get it at all."

He tries to put it off for later in the class, but Nai is insistent. Mr. Gunderson reluctantly has us take out our books and go over the homework from the night before. I squeeze Nai's hand and mouth, "Thank you."

—

I barely make it through all my classes, and when the bell rings, I'm weak with relief. But before we all gather in our spot—the small classroom across from the gym—I make a quick run to CVS. Nai, Shawn, and Dell have dropped everything to help me find the three keys, and the least I can do is provide the necessary fuel: junk food.

I would normally skip the CVS because of "Probing Finger" Donna, but I'm short on time, so I go in. One quick look inside tells me she's not in today. Good. I grab the snacks and place them in the red basket. I'm standing on line when I feel someone's hands digging into my Afro.

The next thing I know, I'm shaking the mess out of her, yelling, "Don't you ever put your hands on me!"

The crowd is too stunned to make a move at first. By the time the crowd understands what's going on, my hand is already at her throat. My rage has never been this clear and this present before. I don't even see Donna's face anymore. All I can see is the bright red haze that accompanies my rage. I'm going to choke the living hell out of this white woman if someone doesn't stop me!

The crowd and the staff manage to pull me off Donna. One of the managers goes to call the cops, and someone in the crowd says, "The hell you will! Do you know who this girl is right here? That's Rosalie Bosia's daughter. I *wish* you would call the cops. You won't make another sale in this neighborhood ever again."

I follow the voice. It belongs to an older lady, Mrs. Wright. The man standing an aisle over cosigns: "Hell nah! After what they did to that woman, you call the cops and we will be boycotting this CVS. Trust."

"I'm glad she got beat down! That lady stay touching my hair too!" a Black girl with bantu knots adds, rolling her eyes and sucking her teeth. It doesn't take long for a shouting match to erupt between the staff and the Black customers. The small amount of Black staff watches it play out, standing back and nodding to themselves as the customers talk.

"And why you holding her like that?" a Black man in a suit says to the manager, who has me by my elbow.

"Let that child go!" Mrs. Wright demands. "She was just defending herself against your employee, who came up and touched her without her permission. We can leave it like this, or we can get See Us down here. And you can explain to them why you think it's okay to touch your customers without their permission."

"Look, we don't tolerate anyone touching anyone else without permission. That's not a policy of—"

"Yeah, well, best let her go, and then you can tell my son, the civil rights attorney over there, all about your policy," Mrs. Wright says, pointing at the man in the suit.

The man nods and folds his arms across his chest. The manager releases me. Mrs. Wright whisks me out the doors before I get a handle on what the hell just happened.

"My friends are waiting for me to—"

"Let your friends know what's going on. And tell them you'll be late," she orders. I text my friends but don't go into any details. I just tell them that I'm with Mrs. Wright and will join them as soon as I'm done. Mrs. Wright starts walking down the street and signals for me to follow her.

"Don't you want to wait for your son?" I ask.

"I don't know that man," she replies.

"He's not your . . ." One look into her smiling face lets me know it was all a bluff. "Why did that guy go along with your lie?" I ask.

"Girl, did you think we weren't going to stand up for you after all the things your mama done did for us?"

"No, I guess not," I admit.

"That big-headed uncle of yours told us to give you some space, and we have. But ain't no one around here willing to let anything happen to you and yours, you hear me?"

I nod, still unable to really wrap my head around what I did. My hands are still shaking as she takes out her keys.

Mrs. Wright is full figured, over six feet tall, with onyx skin, deep-set eyes, and full lips. She used to own a small restaurant near here that served Nigerian food. That's pretty much all I know about her. She opens the door to her apartment and lets me in.

And right away, I know something else about Mrs. Wright: she's a Trekkie!

She has a wall-to-wall display of *Star Trek* memorabilia. Her collection includes 3D puzzles of the USS *Enterprise*, figurines of major characters, and a throw pillow of Spock.

"Wipe your feet," she says.

I look down at the mat beneath my feet; it's a braided oval with the words "Please Don't Trek Your Dirt Inside." I wipe my feet and enter what is basically a museum to all things *Star Trek*. But the decor has to take a back seat as I recall what just happened.

"How could I attack her like that? I've never had a fight in my entire life! But when she touched my hair . . . I don't know, I just . . . lost it."

Mrs. Wright looks over at me and says, "BISeH'eghlaH'be' chugh latlh Dara'laH'be."

And now, I think it's pretty clear that I must be suffering from some kind of head injury, because I have no idea what she just said.

She reads my confused expression and says, "It's Klingon. It means, 'If you cannot control yourself, you cannot command others.'"

"Oh. Okay . . ."

I get a text from Nai and reply, letting her know what happened. She asks if I'm okay. I have no idea if I am or not. But I let her know I will be there as soon as I can.

"Come on into this kitchen and get something hot inside you. It'll be good for the shock."

I follow Mrs. Wright into the kitchen because her tone doesn't really allow room for arguing. She asks how my mom is, and I don't reply. I guess that tells her everything she needs to know.

She puts a pot on the stove and lights the burner. She has me sit at the table, where Captain Kirk is looking up at me from a coaster.

"Now look, that white woman had it coming. She's been doing that for a while now. But she's not the one in the wrong —you are."

I hang my head. "Yeah, I know. I can't believe I launched at her like that."

"That's not what I'm talking about."

I look up at her with a blank stare.

"Look, when white folks leave the house, they make sure that things are the way they should be. They check to see if they got their house keys, if they turned off all the lights, and once outside, they check the gauge on the gas tank. Do they have enough to take them to work and get them back home, or do they need to stop at the gas station?

"We do the same things, except we have an extra step. We gotta stand in front of the mirror and ask ourselves one very important question: What is my white-people tolerance level today?"

"I guess I didn't today. If I had, I'd have stayed home," I admit.

She goes over to the stove and pours a white powder into the boiling water. It soon makes a sticky white paste. Mrs. Wright fixes me a plate of fufu and fish sauce. I wasn't going to eat, but she insists, and the smell of all the spices makes my mouth water.

"You think I'll get in trouble?" I ask before taking my first bite.

"With everything going on, no one can blame you for going crazy. But it's not a place we can afford to live in. You hear me? Get your mind right."

"Can I ask you about . . . this whole *Star Trek* thing? How long have you been into it?"

She puts her spoon down and surveys her collection on the display wall. "I wasn't, before. But my niece, Melody, was really into it. I raised her when my sister got sick. She loved everything to do with *Star Trek*. When she got pregnant, she actually had me make onesies with Spock's face on them. I used to tease her about it."

"Did you find out what she liked about it?"

"No, I only know why I like *Star Trek*—because in all seventy-nine original episodes, never once did a life-form refer to us as sassy."

"Where's your niece, at work?"

Mrs. Wright's face falls and she looks away. "Mel is gone. She died in childbirth. She was always saying that no one listened to her at her property management job, and she fought like hell to be heard. Turns out, they don't hear Black women in the medical profession either. She tried to tell them that something was wrong. She was in pain and they didn't believe her. By the time I raised enough hell . . ."

"I'm so sorry."

"I never wanted to be called the 'angry Black woman.' But that night, good Lord, I raised hell. And for five years, I thought I just didn't raise hell enough. But last year, I read how Serena Williams damn near died giving birth to her child because the doctors didn't believe her when she said something was wrong. That's when I knew . . . If the best athlete in the world can't get her voice heard, what chance did my Melody have?"

CHAPTER FOURTEEN
She Did What?

Devonte surprises me by coming to pick me up from Mrs. Wright's place. He figured I got stuck helping Mrs. Wright with a chore and came to see if he could help too. I told him what went down as we walk to his family's restaurant. Since they're closed on Mondays, his uncle has agreed to let us use it. He texted my friends and told them to meet us there. I didn't even know he knew them like that until he explained they'd started a friendship while I was in my abyss.

We're a block away from the restaurant when I tell Devonte once again that he didn't have to come get me.

"I came to get you for selfish reasons. These streets are dangerous. I might need a bodyguard," he jokes.

"Yeah, not funny," I reply.

"Man, I would've paid cash money to see you throw down!" he says excitedly.

"I lost control. How is that good?"

"I don't know if it's good or not, but I'm glad you had some kinda reaction. You've been faded to black for weeks . . ."

He doesn't finish his sentence. I decide not to push the issue. We cross the street and are just outside the restaurant when he says, "I didn't know what to say to make you feel better."

"Wait, do you mean there's no Hallmark card for this? Are you sure?"

He laughs. "Nah, yo, I looked."

"It's okay. If things were reversed, I wouldn't know what to say either. But maybe we don't use words. Maybe you just kiss me."

He tilts his head up toward the sky, like he's thinking really hard. "Well, I guess I better because . . . I'm a little afraid of you." He comes close, takes my face in between his hands, and kisses me. It makes me feel light, like I could float away. You don't get kisses when you live on the ocean floor. This is definitely a good reason to come to the surface.

When it's over, I open my eyes and realize we are being watched. My friends have their faces mashed up against the window, spying on us.

"We better go in," Devonte says, shaking his head.

He takes my hand, and we enter the restaurant. They start

asking questions all at once. The story got around really quickly, and each time someone told it, I guess an element was added. To hear it told now, I put the CVS lady in the ER after breaking her nose, arms, and legs.

"Yo, let's get on these clues," Devonte says, rescuing me.

Nai takes out her tablet. Shawn, Dell, and Devonte do the same.

I can't let this start without saying one thing first: "I just wanted to thank you guys for helping me."

"This is not about you. I don't really like you," Shawn says playfully.

"Yeah, it's about your mom," Dell says. "Remember when I entered the national jazz festival and didn't win, and I was about to give up on music? But your mom called me over to your house and introduced me to Wynton Marsalis. We played together. Do you understand? *I played with Wynton Marsalis.* All because of your mom. And when the session was over, she made us soul food. *Soul food.* That woman gets me."

"I can't believe I forgot about that," I reply.

"And your mom is letting me stay at your place," Nai says. "She didn't have to do that. She also didn't have to go down to the school and demand that they get another photographer for picture day."

"Oh yeah, I remember that! In the first set of pics I couldn't even find you, the light was so bad," Dell says.

"Ms. Bosia was not having it. She insisted the school get someone who knew how to light dark-skin people. And when we got the second set of pics, it was so much better. I know it was only a fourth-grade class picture, but that meant a lot to me."

"Was it her idea for you to wear a tiara?" Dell asks.

"No. It just felt right," she replies. We all look at each other and try hard not to laugh at her.

"The last time I saw your mom, she was threatening to take my life if I mistreated you. And telling me where the condom drawer was in your house," Devonte says.

My heart stops and my eyes are wide with shock. "She did what?"

"Yup, I ran into her at the corner store," my boyfriend replies.

"Why didn't you tell me?"

"Nah, she wasn't try'n to do me greasy. I mean, she did vow to end my life if I hurt you. But she also warned me about leaning too hard on track, and then . . ."

"Let me guess, she gave you a book?" I ask.

"Yeah. It's about using what you know to get seven streams of income, if running doesn't work out. She said, 'You can be Black. Or you can be broke. God help you if you're both. Here, read this.' And she shoved it in my hand."

"Did you read it?" Dell asks.

"Yeah, and so did my dad. And now we have a meeting set

with my guidance counselor, so we can discuss my future," he says with a deep groan. I playfully give him a sympathy hug while he shakes his head in dismay.

"I came out to my dad two weeks ago," Shawn says.

"You did? Why didn't you tell us?" Dell asks.

"I wanted to wait until Ayo was here."

"How did your dad take it?" I ask.

"Much better than I thought, because last year, your mom made him go with her to a workshop sponsored by the Trevor Project. She said it was research for See Us. And since he's a member, she dragged him along. They heard stories from kids who got support from their family and kids who didn't. My dad said the ones whose parents pushed them away were really messed up. And he didn't want that to happen to me. I mean, he's not throwing a party that I'm gay, but he's not judging me. And this morning, he asked if there was anyone I liked. That's huge for my dad!

"Your mom didn't come right out and tell him I'm gay, but she tried to prep him. That made a big difference. So yeah, I'm here for whatever she needs."

"You told your dad—does that mean you and Milton are going out?" Nai asks.

"As soon as we find the keys," he says, practically blushing. We tease Shawn like the immature people we are, and then get down to business.

"Let's start with what we know," I say. "All the keys will be found somewhere in Harlem. My mom would only hide things in this community."

"Also, it will have something to do with Black folks, since, well . . . you know your mama," Nai adds.

"Yup! And one last thing: the keys will most likely be somewhere we can legally get to so we don't get in trouble," Shawn says.

"Is there any chance they're at the soul food spot?" Dell asks. Nai takes a textbook out of her backpack and hurls it at him. He ducks. "Hey, I'm just being thorough."

I place my notebook on the table. "Let's take the first clue in the set: *The King's death gave me life.*"

That clue doesn't take us too long to figure out. The only "King" that's been to Harlem and that matters to Black history is Dr. King. The day he was assassinated was April 4, 1968. That gives us a place to start. So we all begin looking up events that happened in 1968 in Harlem.

We look up famous people in Harlem born in that year, but nothing fits. It's a half hour later that Shawn suggests maybe we aren't looking for a person but a thing; maybe a business or some kind of charity. There are fifty or so companies that sprang up around that time. We run down the list and see if any of them fit the other two clues:

My father was the first, in two places.

Give me everything and I will give you wings

We split up into two groups. Nai, Devonte, and I take the second clue and try to break it down. When would someone be the first to do something? We look up various competitions that took place at that time. They had contests every weekend at the Apollo, but the Apollo opened in 1913. There were other contests, but nothing major, and none were in the right year. Meanwhile, Dell and Shawn try to work out what would give someone "wings."

It's two hours before we take a hot chocolate break. The break helps me get fresh eyes. It allows me to see what I should have homed in on to begin with:

"We're looking at companies that were created in 1968, the year Dr. King was killed. But it had to take the company some time to form, right? Let's expand our search to companies that opened in 1969 in Harlem," I suggest. The team gets right on it. Nai is the first to find the list of business, and right away, I see one that could work.

Everyone leans in and looks at my screen. This could be the one. The guys look up the history of the company. Nai and I read about its founder, Arthur Mitchell. When we're done, we all look at each other with big, goofy smiles. We got it!

Dance Theatre of Harlem!

The King's death gave me life: *The death of Dr. King inspired dancer Arthur Mitchell to form the Dance Theatre of Harlem.*

My father is first, in two places: *Mitchell was the first Black*

principal ballet dancer to perform in New York City Ballet, and his
company was one of the first American ballet companies to perform
in Russia after the fall of the Soviet Union.

Give me everything and I will give you wings: *The dance*
company requires its dancers to dedicate their lives to the craft for
years before they can perform on the main stage, where they make
elegant, gravity-defying leaps.

We quickly get going to the red brick building on 152nd. The top layer of the building is in black and white and has a statute of a posing dancer. It's gorgeous. We enter the lobby and look out at the large framed photographs of past and present company members. Someone on staff tells us that there is no show tonight, only rehearsals.

We tell them we have a project for school and just want to take a look around. They say no. We start to plead with them, but then another staff member enters the lobby. She takes one look at me and says, "You're Rosalie's daughter, right?" Her name is Jennifer, and her whole family is a part of See Us. She tells us we can look around for as long as we want.

"But you can't go upstairs—that's where we hold classes," she warns us.

I see what I'm looking for directly across from us—an exquisite portrait of Arthur Mitchell midleap. We head straight for it. And when Jennifer's back is turned, I take a peek behind the large painting.

"I see it!" I whisper to the team.

"A key?" Dell asks.

"No, an envelope. The key has to be inside," I reply as I stretch as far as I can to retrieve the envelope that is taped to the back.

We thank Jennifer and quickly run out of the building. My hands are shaking as we stand outside and look down at the white envelope. "Hurry, open it! It's cold," Dell says. I swallow hard and rip it open. The first thing I see are torn pages ripped from a journal. In addition to a black antique key and small white business card. I want to dive into everything all at once. But I know my mom. I know she arranged things in the exact order she wants me to view them. So, I start in with the first thing she placed for me to find—the journal.

March 15, 1988

My mama gave me this book and said I could write anything I want. She even said I could cuss in it! But something about the way she said it told me I better not. She said I'm supposed to start with "Dear Diary." But I don't know anyone named "Diary," so why I wanna write to her for? Instead, I'm writing to my favorite superstar—Janet Jackson!

Dear Janet,

My brother Ty thinks he's all grown up because he's turning fifteen and he won't hang out with me as much anymore. I told him I'm grown too. But he says ten ain't as grown as fifteen. Ty isn't a bad brother. He helps me with my homework, we play cards sometimes, and he won't let anyone on the block step to me.

My daddy is a mountain. He's tall, wide, and can't nothing move him! We play "bit-ball." It's like football, but I'm the ball! The only time Daddy is serious is when he first comes home from work. He's been working in construction since before I was born. He says he does twice the work, yet gets half the pay. He starts swearing and Mama makes us leave the room. Then when we come back a little later, he's not mad anymore. I'm not sure what made him feel better, but I think it's my mama. She always knows how to cheer everyone up.

We have a few friends on the block we hang with, but Ty says we'd have a lot more if Mama weren't so uppity. He can't say that to her face because she'd take a switch to his behind real fast. I guess it's true —Mama can be uppity. But she's not mean or anything. She just acts different than the rest of the people around here.

She hides money in a big metal coffee can and puts it under the sink. I know lots of moms who do that. But they usually save extra money for stuff like a nice dress or maybe perfume. But for Mama, that's her book money. Sometimes she takes a little of the grocery money just to buy a book. She has a library card but says it's not the same thing. She says some books become part of your soul, and what sense does it make to give back a piece of your soul?

My mama is as serious about books as my friends' moms are about church. She says, "Everyone in the projects is quick to hop a train, looking for a way out. There ain't but two stops on that train: coffin or prison. Not my babies." So she makes us read every day. And if the book is hard for us, she makes us read it to her out loud and go over it until we understand.

We hated it at first, but now it's not so bad. Ty loves the books about race cars, and I love the fantasy ones. My favorite one is *The Lord of The Rings*. It took a lot longer to read it, but it was so good! We had a homework assignment last week from my English teacher, Mrs. Nelson. We were supposed to write about our environment. I asked and she said I could make it a fantasy, so I did:

North of New York City there sits a small kingdom called Heirloom. The people there live in crumbling towers held together with straw and bubblegum. The people nicknamed the towers "Knot-Ah" because "not a thing" works the way it should. The elevators don't move, the heater is busted, and the water is brown.

The people work hard but don't make a lot of money. They can't afford to travel to nearby lands because it costs too much to fly a dragon. Instead, they have to wait for metal boxes to come pick them up and drop them off on the other side of the kingdom. The metal box is always late and runs too hot or too cold.

Although life in the kingdom is hard, the residents of Heirloom are happy because of one thing: everyone in Heirloom has their own personal sun. That's why the people are called the Sun Bearers.

And with this magic they can summon joy from deep sadness, conjure herbs and oils to cure illness, and replenish their strength. But most importantly, the sun guides the Sun Bearers so they never get lost in the darkness.

One day, the Sun Bearers witnessed candy falling from the sky! But not just any candy — Dragon's Teeth. Dragon's Teeth is candy with colored jelly in the center. Some centers are green like money, some are Kool-Aid red, and others gleam like gold. The candy was so pretty and smelled so good that the Sun Bearers ate it.

It was better than anything they had ever had. It wasn't just that it tasted good; it made them feel good. Some said it was like a hundred paydays back to back. Some said they felt like they had the power to control things around them. But what most people said about Dragon's Teeth was that it set them free.

Sun Bearers couldn't afford dragons, so they didn't know much about them. They had no idea that when dragons shed their teeth, it turns into a hard candy with a poisonous center. And by the time they found out, it was too late. The more they ate, the dimmer their sun became. Until eventually, it faded. Sun Bearers who no longer had a sun would come to be called Shadow People.

Shadow People hang around in dark corners, thin and limp, like boiled spaghetti. They have black lips that don't know how to smile and holes where their eyes used to be. There are small, dark dots throughout their bodies to remind them that they belong to the shadows. They spend the day scratching what's not really itching and replying to questions no one asked. Some are angry and quick to fight. Some are slow and don't remember how to use their necks to hold their heads.

They wander throughout the towers, looking for the only thing they care about — Dragon's Teeth. But now the candy isn't free anymore. It costs. So the Shadow People do anything to get their hands on some money so they can get more.

Shadow People surround the kingdom. They lurk in doorways, hallways, and sidewalks.

They come out from behind the alleys, seep through the floorboards, and latch onto the pipes. They crawl along the walls of the towers and peer inside for candy. And if they can't find it, they will trick a Sun Bearer into joining the shadows and are rewarded for bringing one more person into the darkness.

Sun Bearers have to leave the house in pairs, get home before dark, and watch over their children carefully. When the Sun Bearers see relatives they used to know, people who are now shadows, they cry. They want to hold them in their arms, but instead they cross the street because they know shadows feel nothing.

The Kingdom of Heirloom is now the city of shadows. But some people still remember the days of magic and light . . .

My homework came back and my grade was ninety-two. I was supposed to be happy, but I wasn't. Mama asked me why, and I didn't have an answer. She wanted to cheer me up, so she took me to her friend's apartment — Mrs. Ross. We went up to the roof, and Mama pointed to a large window a few blocks over. It's a ballet studio where Black dancers are gracefully flying through the air!

"Those dancers are from Dance Theatre of Harlem. They just started rehearsing in this studio. There's some beauty in this world, li'l bit. You got to learn to look for it," she said. She was right; some things in the kingdom are bad, but some things are pretty good — like Black ballerinas and front-row seats with Mama.

Later, as I was getting ready for bed, it finally came to me: the reason I was unhappy with my story was because it's actually a mystery. And it leaves me with two questions I don't have the answer to:

Who dropped the candy from the sky?

And why?

CHAPTER FIFTEEN

Top Five

I didn't jump to find the next clue on the card because I liked spending time with the kid version of my mom. I wanted more time with her, even if it was only through the pages of an old journal. Later that night, after rereading it for the hundredth time, I was finally ready to move on to the third item inside the envelope: a card with the second set of clues. And just as I am about to read the new clues, my uncle enters my room and informs me that I can't continue with the hunt until after my math test. I argue, but it's no use. He takes the box away and says he will only return it after the math test.

I reminded him that there were things far more important than school at the moment, but he wouldn't listen. He pointed out how disappointed my mom would be if I let my grades lapse. I know he's right, but it doesn't make it any easier to hear. I did think about pushing the argument, but my uncle looked emotionally drained and exhausted. So, I gave in and went to bed.

When sleep finally comes, it plays tricks on me. I dream about shadows coming for me. And no matter how far or how fast I run, they always catch up to me. In the dream, they grab hold and pin me to the ground, that's when I wake up screaming. Thankfully, Uncle Ty and Nai are sound sleepers. I'm sweaty and take a full minute before I can control my breathing again. It's been a while since I thought about Alex getting his locs chopped off by the coach. He was in my dream; he was one of the shadows. I owe him an apology and it's way overdue.

I look at the time on my cell; it's just after midnight. Alex and I are friends on Facebook. I send him a message asking if he's around to meet up. He agrees. An hour later, we meet in front of the mural, just across the street from me.

———

He comes wearing jeans and a thick leather jacket. His hair is in a low Afro. All the other times I've seen Alex, he's been mostly happy. He's a really chill guy, or at least he was. Now he looks . . . somber.

"What's up? Why'd you need to see me?" he asks.

"The letter that coach sent to my mom . . ."

"Yeah, what about it?"

"She didn't sign it. I did."

He smiles. I didn't expect that. "I knew it! I knew she wasn't gonna do me dirty like that. When we talked in her office, she got what I was trying to say even before I said it, and then . . . Yo, why would you do that?"

I lean on the mural and hang my head. "Just . . . being a self-ish jerk, only thinking about what was good for me. Turns out that's a gift of mine."

"Nah, don't just say it like that. Why did you sign it? Are you taking the coach's side?"

My head snaps up quickly. "What? No. Why would I do that?"

"I don't know. Why would you forge your mom's signature?"

"Because I wanted someone to like me, and that's what I had to do to make that happen. So I did it. It was wrong. I'm sorry."

We both stand there, leaning on the colorful wall in silence. I don't think he's going to forgive me. It's okay. I'm not even ready to forgive myself. That was so wack. What was I thinking? I flash back to that day when I signed the letter. It seems like years ago, not weeks.

"Devonte?" Alex says. I look up at him, confused. "The guy you did it for—was it Devonte?"

I nod.

"He's been into you for a while, like, since back in elementary school."

I shrug, not sure what to say.

"So, she really thought what the coach did was wrong," he says, mostly to himself.

"She's not the only one. It was wrong, Alex. That's why I messed up when I signed the paper. It made the coach think what he did was a little thing, but it wasn't. Please believe me. Coach was wrong. And so was I."

He nods slowly, like he's unraveling a mystery only he can see. "I thought about shaving it all off. You know, just no hair at all."

"Is that what you want?" I ask.

"No, I want my locs, but it won't be the same now, you know?"

"No, it won't. They'll grow back stronger because you're stronger. That's what they tell me about bad stuff happening to you. It makes you stronger."

"Do you believe that?"

"Not sure yet."

He exhales deeply and runs his hands through his hair.

"So . . . do you think you can forgive me?" I dare ask.

"No, I can't."

"Oh . . ." I say, hoping the lump in my throat goes away.

"I'll forgive you . . . just not tonight, okay?"

"Sounds fair."

He starts to walk away. I call out to him, "Don't be mad at Devonte. He was trying to help the team."

"I figured," he says. "How's your mom doing?"

"Same," I reply as the lump gets bigger and tears spring to my eyes.

He comes back and leans on the wall alongside me once again. "Coach is afraid of her."

I smile. "That list is long."

He laughs. "And I'm fo' sure on it!"

I laugh. "Listen, if you want to start growing them again, I know a few people who could really hook you up."

"Locs are expensive."

"It's okay. I'd pay for them to start it," I promise him.

"I don't mean money. I mean locs cost—a lot."

———

I'm wearing my mom's perfume today. It's a light citrus scent with a hint of vanilla. It always smelled much better on her. I also wore her scarf. It's her favorite because it's the softest one. I remember her hugging me while wearing it. It sounds nuts, but having her things near me make me feel like she's there. I think I'll put something of hers on every day, anything to take away the daily flashes I get of her lying in a bed, unresponsive.

Before I went to see her this morning, I picked out a book of poems from her shelf—*Just Give Me a Cool Drink of Water 'fore I Diiie*. It's Maya Angelou's first book of collected poems. My mom loves it. Devonte took me to the hospital and I read some of the poems to her. I tried to focus on the words on the page and not the loud silence that comes with coma victims. I was able to read a good chunk of the book, but I had to go before school started. I promised her that I would be back in the morning, with a new book. I'd like to think she heard me.

I'm late for first period but manage to make it in time for second period, English. On the first day of school, we were given a syllabus for each class. I had highlighted a lesson plan called "Race & Society"—that's the day the class would have to review Ava DuVernay's documentary *13th*, in addition to Ta-Nehisi Coates's *Between the World and Me*.

I highlighted that section because I knew there would be some kind of drama and I was going to skip that day. My English class has only a handful of people of color. As far as Black folks go, it's me, Milton, and another member of See Us, Denise Winston. This unit wasn't supposed to be coming up for another few weeks. However, thanks to current events, the lesson was moved up.

I discovered this when I walked into the class and saw what was on the whiteboard. And now that I have already entered, I can't skip it. Can I ask to use the bathroom and then not come back? Does that make me a poor student, or worse, a bad Black girl? Will my card get taken away if I bail?

"Ayo, take your seat," Mr. Cutler says.

I remember Mrs. Wright's warning about checking my "white folks tolerance" gauge. I checked it this morning, and it was low, but not dangerously so. But now that we are here, about to discuss race with a mostly white class, I'm left to recalibrate. And it's just as I thought: I don't have enough in me to sit through what's about to come.

"Ayo, is something wrong?" Mr. Cutler asks. I like Mr. Cutler. He's French and has a melodic accent that makes everything sound fancy, even if it's not. He's in his late thirties and has bright red hair, a thin goatee, and kind green eyes. The reason I love his class is the very same reason I know I will hate the lesson today: after the lesson, he encourages open dialogue and lets kids say whatever they want, so long as they aren't cursing or outright insulting each other.

"Ayo?" he says firmly.

I take a seat and hope that maybe if I stay quiet, I can make it out of this. I look over at Milton. He knows what's coming. And judging by the wary expression on her face, so does Denise. The three of us silently agree to brace ourselves.

We're about halfway done with the lesson, and so far, it's not that bad. The reason it's not bad is that all the kids, consciously or otherwise, have opted for politeness instead of honesty. I know it sounds messed up to say, but given where my gauge is, I'm good with it.

We hear blanket statements like "Racism is wrong" and "It's unfair to be treated differently because your skin color isn't right" for the first half of the class.

The three of us nod along and wait for it to be over.

And then Sage Mildred raises her hand. If you curled her hair and put her in a puffy gown, Sage would be a perfect antebellum poster. She has clear, bright blue eyes, long, cascading blond hair, and a smile that is always working overtime. She's also smart as hell; I will always give her that. We've debated in class before, and sometimes she wins and sometimes I do. I can't say that we're friends, but I don't think we're enemies. We hang in different circles, but we're usually cordial and say hello to each other.

I'm not sure what she's going to say, but the fact that she clears her throat and begins to speak in a whisper is a bad sign.

"Mr. Cutler, I want to ask a question, but if I do, some people are going to get mad. So I'm not sure I should say anything."

The three of us exchange a knowing glance. But we remain silent.

"Well, Sage, we are all for honest conversation in this class," Mr. Cutler says. "These are obviously sensitive issues, so watch how you phrase things, of course, but this is a classroom, and questions are welcomed."

"All right. First, I'm not racist."

Well, that just put my mind at ease.

She continues as my heart begins to race. "I think everyone should be treated fairly, and I don't think color should have anything to do with it."

Wait for it . . .

"Here's my question. Slavery was a long time ago. It was one hundred percent wrong, and I'm glad it's over."

Aw, me too, Sage!

"But I didn't take part in it. Why do I have to walk around feeling bad because something happened that I had nothing to do with?" she asks.

That opens the door. There are four or five white students nodding slightly. And two others raise their hands because they too want to ask questions about race. The three of us Black students do not speak. We know this isn't the end of it. We have to listen to all five classic tracks from the "Ballad of the White Folks" playlist.

Track #1—"I never oppressed anyone!"

Track #2—"Slavery was a long time ago, let it go!"

Track #3—"Black people are proud to be Black, so why can't I be proud to be white?"

Track #4—"They commit a lot of crimes, that's why so many of them are in prison."

Track #5—"Racism is rare in America now."

With a bonus track, featuring the cool stylings of Sly News:

Bonus track—"Why are innocent white people always being targeted?"

The first person to give up her silence is Denise. She gives in to temptation and rolls her eyes. That invites Mr. Cutler to say,

"Denise, you have something to say? We'd love to hear it. This is a safe space."

When he says that, it's all I can do not to roll my eyes too. Milton, on the other side of the room, has decided to mentally go somewhere else.

"I'm sick of hearing people say racism isn't a thing in this country. How the hell would you know?" Denise asks.

"I treat everyone the same," Sage counters confidently. "Ask Milton. Don't I treat you just like everyone else?"

Milton ignores her. I think his gauge might be lower than mine.

"See, right there! It's not Milton's job to put a 'not racist' stamp on your forehead. And if you are sitting up at night trying to figure out if you are or aren't racist, let me save you some time, Sage—yes, you're racist."

Sage bursts into tears. Her friend comes over to her desk and comforts Sage. Denise looks very close to slapping the hell out of Sage for using her nuclear weapon, and so soon.

"See, this is why I don't like talking about this stuff," Ashton, the guy sitting behind me, adds. "We can't agree on anything. All I know is that I haven't done anything to anyone. And I'm tired of Black people trying to make me feel bad for my skin color."

"You shouldn't even talk, Ashton," Denise says. "When we did our project together back in junior high, you had me come over for dinner so we could work after. And it was only after we had eaten that you admitted your parents call people the N-word when they get mad."

"Yeah, that's why I wanted you to come over, so they could see that you were cool, so they wouldn't say that word anymore. I was trying to fix the problem," Ashton barks back at her.

"I don't want to be your token Black friend, and you should have told me that your mother was a racist bi—"

"Okay! That's enough—from everyone!" Mr. Cutler shouts over the noise.

The classroom is silent, but the sound and fury of unspoken thoughts rings loud. Mr. Cutler is facing an internal struggle: The academic in him loves this honest discussion. However, he knows it won't take much more for the whole thing to so south.

Decisions. Decisions.

"Now, if we agree to no name calling and no shouting, I will let this go on for another few minutes before the bell rings. Can we all agree?" the teacher asks.

The class quietly agrees. The first person to speak is Ashton. "I wasn't trying to upset you. My parents aren't always great with the whole race thing, but I thought if they met some of my friends, then they'd start getting better at it. My parents aren't bad people. They only say the N-word when they're mad."

"And you all say the N-word too, in, like, every song!" Sage says.

Dear God, make the Southern belle shut the hell up.

The girl who is comforting Sage looks over at Denise. "I don't think you have a right to call Sage racist. You don't know her."

Sara, a small, meek white girl with a short haircut, chimes in. "Everything that happens isn't about race. Like if you don't get a certain job or if someone is rude to you. Not everything is about that."

"You have no idea what you're talking about!" Denise says angrily.

I gauge my meter. It's not better, but it's not on empty either. Why is that?

Mr. Cutler says, "Well, I think we need some new voices in this conversation. Milton?"

"Does this affect my grade?" Milton asks.

"Ah . . . no. It won't. But I'd like your input," Mr. Cutler adds.

"If it really doesn't affect my grade, I'm choosing to abstain from this . . . conversation."

Normally, Milton gets on my damn nerves, but right now, I love that boy! I suppress a smile and look over at Denise. I give her what I have come to call the "Harriet Tubman nod." It basically says, "Dear white folks, we out!"

She starts packing her stuff. I never unpacked, so no issue there. Milton is already up and ready to head out. Mr. Cutler says, "We still have five more minutes, guys. And we'd like to hear from everyone."

"You want to hear from everyone Black on this issue, and we get that," I reply with a smile. "But here's the thing, Mr. Cutler—Sage and the rest of the class is right: There is no racism in America. Everyone is the same. There's equal housing, equal pay, and yes, justice for all." I head toward the exit.

But sarcasm seems like a bad way to end things, and again, I really like Mr. Cutler. So, with my hand on the doorknob and Denise and Milton not far behind me, I address my teacher. "The only problem is that Sage and the rest of the class are talking about *their* America. You know, the one where they can protest peacefully without fear of retribution? The country where the wealth their ancestors amassed gets to stay in the family. You know what America I'm talking about—Sage's America, Ashton's America, and yours too, Mr. Cutler."

Denise chimes in, "Now, we'd love to sit and tell you about *our* America—you know, the one where Black mothers watch their kids leave for school, knowing they might not ever come back? Our America, where we get attacked by culture vultures who put more value on our hairstyles than they do our lives?"

"The same America that 'freed' us in ten ways and found a thousand ways to systemically strip that same freedom from us," Milton says matter-of-factly.

"The America where my mom gets shot in the head and is somehow made to be the bad guy. That's our America," I add.

"And once you see it—if you dare to see it—you'll get uncomfortable. Then you run back to Sage's America. And act like nothing happened.

"Well, our guides are exhausted, weary, and fed up. So as of now, all tours of Black America have been canceled."

CHAPTER SIXTEEN

Forever Midnight

The tree branch outside my window wags its bony finger at me. It wants me to stop what I'm about to do. The tree is not alone in objecting. There's a small colony of ants on the tree, and I swear they are forming a "no" pattern as they crawl along the trunk. The squirrels at the base of the tree aren't any subtler. They hold their acorns in their mouths and dart their heads from side to side as if to say, "Don't you do it!" But now that I am back on the surface, I have to know what's going on. And that means going back on social media. So, despite nature's strong objections, I log on to Twitter.

Most of the tweets aimed at my family are supportive and kind. They mention praying for my mom and hoping our family is able to make it past this. But there is a small but very loud group that wants us to know how much they hate us. They call my mom all kinds of horrible names and paint her to be some domestic terrorist with evil intent.

Seriously?

Are they talking about the same woman who put a funny voice to the bottle of cough syrup so I'd take my medicine? The woman who tears up watching *Toy Story 4*, no matter how many times she sees it? The very same woman who has yet to cash a paycheck and not hand some of it to someone in need?

My mom, evil?

So, stop looking, Ayo. Stay away from social media!

But I can't stop. I keep looking deeper and deeper into the chasm. I tell myself to log off, but I can't. I click on a link from one of the users who tagged me; it leads to a homemade GIF of an old-school video game, where the duck has a target on its face. The person has replaced the duck's face with a picture of my mom.

I run to the bathroom, hug the rim of the toilet bowl, and throw up everything I ate today. And just when I think I am on empty, I throw up yet again. I hug my knees and rock back and forth in a futile attempt to calm down. I vow to myself that I won't cry. I remind myself that hate isn't new; only the packaging changes. But that doesn't make it hurt less. Nothing makes it hurt less.

It's another hour before I leave the bathroom. I had to wait for my tears to dry and the swelling around my eyes to go down. All I want to do right now is crawl into my bed, put the covers over me, and not wake up until morning. But I know that if I give in to this urge, I will sink back to the ocean floor, and this time, I will stay there. I don't have it in me to pull myself back to the surface again.

How could anyone think that's funny? How could anyone make light of something so devastating? I thought about calling Devonte but I didn't because he has a chemistry test to study for and I don't want to be the reason why he fails. And besides, I'd kind of like to be alone.

I go downstairs in an effort to distract myself. Nai is doing homework at the kitchen table and Uncle Ty is fixing dinner. I mutter something about needing fresh air and quickly make my escape before they can have a chance to ask me any questions, or offer to join me.

Harlem hits me hard in the face with its icy breath. It's trying to knock the stupidity out of me. I knew better than to go online, but I did it anyway. My city isn't happy with me. I don't really have a direction in mind when I leave the house; I just need to put some distance between me and my cell phone, hence why I left it at home.

"Ayo! Ayo!" someone shouts as I walk down the block. I turn around and come face to face with Nate. He runs to catch up with me. We embrace, since this time he hasn't just come from fighting three rounds with my uncle.

"Hi, Nate."

"Where you headed?"

"Not sure," I reply, wishing I had chosen a different direction. Nate is going to talk about See Us and me stepping out front. My uncle has an issue with that, and since I've been tripping lately, I'm not sure it's a great idea either.

"I saw your mom this morning. There's been no change, as you know, but she's a fighter. She'll make it out of this. In the meantime, we need to talk," he says, leading us down the block and around the corner to Lenox Coffee Roasters.

He gets us a small table and orders two black teas, then begins to make his case right away. "We need to put a face to this. The other side is already out there telling the city their version of the story. Membership in See Us has risen by nearly twenty percent. The rallies are getting bigger, and we have the city's attention. But that's not enough. You need to get out there, just like your mom would. Every major outlet wants to speak with you. We can arrange it."

I wrap my hands around the hot mug; it feels good. I wish I were swimming in it. That way it could warm me up all over.

"We need to use this moment to our advantage. Black folks need to be encouraged and white folks want to feel good. If you speak up, our people will be assured. And white folks will rally behind you and put pressure on the system to do right by your mother. Then they can go to bed thinking, *Yay, I fixed racism.*"

I suddenly picture a mini version of myself swimming inside the mug, swimming away from all the noise and the drama. Mini-Me swims like her life depends on it. She's desperate to get to the other side of the mug.

Go, Mini-Me, go!

"Ayo, you need to send out a clear message, just like your mother would do."

Nate becomes a distant white noise as I focus all of my attention on the surface of the tea. I blow softly on the tea, hoping the breeze will help her get to the other side.

C'mon, Mini-Me, you got this!

"Ayo, are you listening?" Nate says, pounding his fist on the table. The ripple causes a huge wave on the surface of my mug.

She's drowning . . .

Mini-Me, fight! Fight to come back up . . .

Oh no! She's gone under . . .

She doesn't make it to the shore. Maybe none of us ever do.

I grit my teeth, take a deep breath, and push my mug away.

"How can you be so easily distracted? I'm trying to talk to you. Did you hear anything I said?" Nate asks.

"Yeah. You need me to go to the media with a message," I reply dryly.

"Not just any message. I need you to make this city cheer for you. You need to give them hope."

"Then give me some!" I shout out of nowhere. My heart is hammering against my chest. My mouth is dry and the familiar red haze begins to surround me.

I lean in closer and lower my voice. "You want me to find words that'll reassure Black folks, while soothing white folks' conscience? Okay. Tell me what magical words I'm supposed to string together to make that happen."

He leans in close. "We have people at See Us who can craft a statement for you. We'll choose the right words; you just have to say them."

"My mother never used anyone else's words. She used only her own. She led with messages that came from her heart. I have to do the same thing."

"Yeah, that would be ideal, but given that you don't have a message, you need to use the one we create for you. That grand jury will be coming back soon. And you know as well as I do that there's no guarantee they will do what's right. We have to get America on our side."

The laughter that escapes my throat is so sudden that it startles me. I don't realize just how loudly I'm laughing until other people in the café turn to look at me. There are tears in my eyes, my side aches, and I can't catch my breath, all because I'm cracking up so hard.

I flash back to the GIF of my mom. It should make me cry, but instead, it makes me laugh even more.

"Ayo, enough!"

I try to stop, I swear I do, but I can't. The longer this goes on, the more obvious it becomes that this isn't a joyful event. Everyone is looking at us, and Nate tugs on my coat in an effort to get me to stop chuckling, but it doesn't work.

Everything hurts: my mom's absence, the possibility of losing her forever, and seeing the worst thing in my life as a joke for internet trolls. But my body has its wires crossed. What should be sobbing is still cackling. The manager comes over to warn me about keeping it down.

"This isn't a joke! How dare you act like this? You are not the child your mother wanted to raise!" Nate says.

"Nathanael Collard!" someone says behind us. I turn around and see Mrs. Pascale. The laughter dies in my throat.

We didn't notice when she entered, but we certainly notice her now, as does the entire café. Mrs. Pascale is over eighty and don't take no mess, no way. Her puffy Afro is stark white, like a winter wonderland. She's short, with freckles, and has been known to strike people with her cane. And although she's elderly, her aim is surprisingly accurate.

"I know you not sit'n here attacking this poor child," she says.

"Mrs. Pascale, I was just—"

"I was headed for my weekly meeting with the ladies, when I looked in the window and see you going crazy on this child. She don't need nothing more put on her. Her mama ain't here; it's on us to look out for her, not yell at her and say mean-spirited things, like what you just said. Now, go on and tell her you're sorry."

He looks at me, and I try my best to save him. "He doesn't have to apologize," I say.

"Hush, child." She doesn't even look at me. She keeps her gaze steady on Nate.

He lets out a deep breath and says he's sorry.

"Much better. We here to build up, not tear down, am I right?"

"Yes, Mrs. Pascale."

"Now, Ayo, you come with me. You look empty," she says, making her way toward the door.

"Thank you, but I'm not hungry."

"I wasn't asking you. And I wasn't talking about food."

———

She takes me to Mrs. Celie's house. There we are greeted by Ms. Hightower, Mrs. Jacobs, Ms. Doris, and of course, Mrs. Celie. This is their weekly poker game. They have a buffet all laid out, and the card table is ready.

The minute they see me, they examine me from head to toe. The results are in: I'm too thin, I need to deep-condition my hair, and although I am not ashy, I am "ashy-adjacent" and therefore need more shea butter in my life.

It sounds as if they are picking on me, but it's actually the opposite. When they take me in, the care and concern in their eyes is unmistakable.

"I found Miss Thing at the café over there, crying," Mrs. Pascale says.

"I wasn't crying. I was laughing," I remind her.

She gives me a side-eye and whispers, "Oh, is that what that was?"

I smile slightly but don't say anything. One of the ladies fixes me a plate, and another one calls my uncle and tells him I'm with them. And when he asks what they plan to do for the night, they tell him, "Get drunk and get tattoos." Once Uncle Ty gets off the phone, the game starts.

I thought I would be a witness to a nice old-lady card game; I was wrong. This is a cage-match situation. The women talk trash and try to psych each other out. All the while debating everything from the best card player to whose grandchild is the smartest. They go hard on everything, from politics to dressing recipes. But under the trash talking, it's easy to see just how much the ladies love each other.

There are a few things I do not anticipate them getting into, like stock tips and the best place to get edibles. But my favorite part of the night, the part that makes me laugh the hardest, is when Ms. Doris tells us about the *fiiiiiiine* new neighbor who moved across the street, and how he does not have curtains in his bathroom.

"He's a handyman," Mrs. Doris says, full of mischief. "He's coming over tomorrow to fix my garbage disposal."

Ms. Hightower replies, "Your disposal is new. It's already broken?"

Mrs. Doris smirks. "No. But it will be when I get home."

I don't know how they've done it, but they've made me happy. It feels so good to sit among them. I feel truly safe.

Between the four of them, they have eighteen children and twenty-two grandchildren. They tell me that this entitles them to give me advice. So I listen closely as the night comes to an end.

"You young people run into some problems and you want to just give up," Ms. Doris says. "Good Lord, if the ones before you had done that . . ."

"There ain't a place darker in this world than the soul of some white folks—not all of them, but enough of them to make it feel like it's gonna be midnight forever," Ms. Hightower adds.

Mrs. Celie cosigns. "Humph."

The last word of the evening is from Mrs. Pascale, the eldest of the group. "Ayo, you listen, and you listen real good: There's nothing that shines a light in your world like knowing someone loves you. And that mama of yours, she loves you. You hold on to that; that's your flashlight. Hold on real tight, because I'm old and I said so."

CHAPTER SEVENTEEN

Weight

My math test is over. I've never been so happy to be done with an exam in my life. I text my uncle to let him know, at which point he kindly reminds me that taking the test is only the first part of a two-part deal. I'm not allowed to go back to hunting until the test results come back. I get that he's trying to help by making me focus on school, but it's frustrating because all I want to do is work on the hunt. I lean against my locker and sigh as the students make their way to class. I should get going too, but class is the last place I want to be.

"I need to talk to you!" Dell says as he grabs hold of my arm and practically drags me into a stairwell.

"Okay, okay, Dell! I've grown fond of my right arm, and I'd like to keep it."

He looks around to make sure that no one is coming.

"I was at the laundromat last night with my dad, and we were just about to leave when I heard some ladies from Nai's building talking about the huge argument Nai's mom had with her boyfriend. The two of them broke up!"

"They did? That's great! We have to tell Nai." I motion to move, but I'm frozen in place by Dell's stern expression.

"What is it?" I ask.

"They broke up weeks ago," he replies.

"Why hasn't she come to get Nai?" I ask.

Dell doesn't answer; he doesn't really need to. We both know what it means if Nai's mom hasn't come to get her. My heart sinks as I think about how hurt my best friend will be.

"You think Nai already knows?" he asks.

"No, this morning she said she didn't want to go back home to get her hair supplies and risk running into Kingston. So she's shopping for new hair stuff after school."

"Good, she doesn't know yet. That means we still have time."

"Time to what?" I ask.

"Duh. Go over to Ms. Harris's house and find out what she's thinking."

"What makes you think she'll talk to us?"

"She has to! She can't just walk out on Nai. That's not gonna work for me."

I step back and look him up and down. Who is this guy in front of me? I have never seen Dell act this authoritative. I respect his sudden, newfound gangster attitude.

"All right, Dell, so what's the plan?"

He starts pacing as the bell rings. "We go over there and we do whatever it takes to get Ms. Harris to act right."

"All right, after school we can—"

"No, Ayo, now. We can't let her find out Kingston's gone and her mom didn't say anything. We have to fix this for Nai. If we don't, she'll be devastated."

I study his face. There's something more than casual concern in his eyes. It's more serious than that. The only time I have ever seen him this worked up was when his autographed *Birth of the Cool* poster got water damage. This might be even more important than that.

"You really like her, huh?"

He shrugs it off, but we both know he's falling hard.

"So, can we ditch the last class and go now? Shawn has practice. It's just us two."

"For my girl, hell yeah. Let's go."

⸺

We turn up at Ms. Harris's apartment, but no one is home. Thankfully, her neighbor directs us to the church a few blocks away. Ms. Harris doesn't go to church often; she normally only attends during major holidays. She always said, "God is like family—you don't have to see them all the time, but it's good to check in a few times a year."

We peer inside the small storefront of the makeshift church. It's half full, mostly women. The pastor is saying something about not letting ego stop you from getting your blessings. We scan for Ms. Harris. I find her because, as always, she's the best-dressed woman in the room. I point her out to Dell and we agree to wait until the service is over before we approach.

When the service begins to clear out, we make our way toward Ms. Harris. Before we even start to talk, she ambushes us with questions about Nai.

"Is she okay? Did something happen? Oh God, where is she?"

It takes a few minutes for us to convince her that Nai is fine and that we just came to speak to her. Once she finally believes us, she makes us go back into the nearly empty church, as the wind has picked up and fall in New York City is no longer charming.

The pastor sees me and comes over. He tells me that the church sent up prayers and that they have been by to visit Mom. He jokes that the line was so long outside her room that there was a waiting list. He leaves after Ms. Harris promises that she'll lock up. Now it's just the three of us. On the way here, Dell and I agreed to go slow and ease into what we want to say.

"Yo, why you do'n my girl dirty?" Dell barks.

Wow.

Shocked, I turn to Dell to see what the hell he's thinking.

But judging from the look on his face, he's just as shocked as I am. Ms. Harris gives us the mother of all side-eyes. She folds her arms over her chest and waits for the sense to ooze back into our skulls.

"I'm sorry, Ms. Harris, that's not what I was gonna say," Dell says.

"Well, tell me what you *meant* to say."

I'm not sure he's ready, so I chime in: "Ms. Harris, Nai really needs you. We thought maybe you'd come by and take her home now that . . ."

She shakes her head. "This neighborhood got a big mouth."

"So you two really are over?" Dell asks.

"Boy, what you do'n in grown-folk business? Have you lost yo mind? Do I need to go see your father? If you think you finna sit up here and disrespect me—"

"It's not like that, Ms. Harris, I promise. It's just that Nai misses you," I tell her.

She relaxes her combative expression and looks down at the Bible in her hand. "I miss my baby too. But I can't just come and get her."

"Why?" Dell and I ask in unison.

She's taken aback by how firm we are. "I know you all care about her. And you coming here is really nice. Although I know you are missing a class, because school don't get out for another half hour," she says, giving us yet more side-eye. We avoid her gaze.

"I've wanted to come get her, but what kind of mother would make the decision I made? I didn't know how to show up to your house, Ayo, not after choosing a creepy fool over my baby. Nai deserves someone like your mom, someone who'd stand up for her."

"But that's not what she wants," I say. "She wants you. You're the one that held down three jobs so she could take dance classes and go on school trips. You taught her how to wrap her hair and keep her outfit game tight. That's not a little thing. You gave her confidence to step out the door, knowing she was fire. My mom didn't do that, you did."

She snorts. "Your mom. I went to go see her yesterday. Humph. That woman looks strong even when she's in the hospital. How does she do that? She was always like that, you know? Uppity," she says bitterly to herself.

I think Ms. Harris has long since left the room and is now living inside her own thoughts. There is a clear moment when she remembers that we are here and that my mom is fighting for her life. "I'm so sorry. I didn't mean to say . . . Your mom is a lovely—"

"It's okay." Actually, it's not, but this is for Nai, so I let it pass.

"She knew right away that Kingston was no good. But I didn't see it. Or didn't want to see it. She was right about keeping Nai with her. Maybe I shouldn't change that."

I can hear rage tapping on my door, demanding to be let in. *Ayo, stay calm.*

"Your mother never would have made the mistake I made. I don't know what I was thinking. But leaving her with you could be the best thing for her, right?"

Rage bangs louder and louder, demanding I let it inside me.

Ayo, do not go off!

"And besides, at your house she gets exposed to all that culture and book stuff. We don't do that at my house. So maybe she belongs with you," Ms. Harris says.

Think of Nai and how she would feel if you went off on her mom! And if your uncle finds out, you will be grounded for the rest of your life—after he beats your behind for telling off an adult.

Yes, but how can she think that anyone would be better off without their mom? Who says a thing like that? I'd give anything to have my mom back, any way I can get her. And here this woman is, just running away from the child that loves her more than anything. What is wrong with this lady?

Tension coils itself around my neck and shoulders. I begin to see a familiar red haze, and Ms. Harris's words are fading into background noise. The rage is inside now, although I don't remember letting it in. I look over at Dell, and to my surprise, he gets it. He places a hand on top of mine, signaling for me to chill the hell out.

"Ms. Harris, I don't believe what you say'n," Dell says. Just before she goes off on him, he stands up with his palms out. "I don't mean any disrespect. I'm not saying that you're lying. I'm saying I think you're reading this thing all wrong."

"Oh really, how am I wrong? You so grown, go ahead and tell me."

He looks at me. I shrug. I'm still working on keeping my temper in check. I can't bail him out. Dell takes a deep breath, swallows hard, and tries to salvage the situation.

"No one knows this about me, but . . ." He clears his throat. "I knit."

What?

Dell reads my shocked expression. "Yeah, that's right—I knit, and my poncho game is strong," he replies proudly. "Anyway, knitting itself isn't really that hard. The hard part is when you have to go back and fix a mistake in the pattern. It's hard and frustrating. But when the work you did so far is that impressive, it's worth going back to fix.

"Ms. Harris, when you created Nai, you made the most beautiful and complex pattern I've ever seen. You dropped a stitch. You made a mistake. You don't have to throw away the whole project. Just go back and fix it. Isn't that what the pastor was saying—about not letting your ego get the best of you and block you from your blessings? Your blessing is at Ayo's house. Go get her."

———

The next day, in the cafeteria, I rush to update Shawn before Nai shows up. "Dell?" he says in disbelief. "You mean *our* Dell?"

"Yup," I reply as I dip my fries into a puddle of ketchup. I left out the part about Dell knitting because we made a deal that I would keep his secret and, in return, there would be a hand-knit hat in my future. But even without the detail about knitting, the story of Dell taking charge is still pretty surprising.

"I can't believe Dell did all that," Shawn says.

"Yeah, he has it bad. And I think she does too."

"Should we push them to go out or nah?"

"Let's give her a chance to get settled back in with her mom and then see."

When I get home later, Nai runs down the stairs to tell me all about how her mom called and begged her to come back home.

"She said she was sorry and that she loves me. Ayo, she . . . she didn't forget about me," Nai says, choking back tears.

"Um, how could she? You're amazing! Girl, don't you know that? I'm so happy for you." I hug her and feel the stress leaving her body. It's as if she's been holding her breath for weeks, and now she finally gets to let it out.

—

The next morning, I went to math class where I got some really good news: I scored eighty-five on my math test! That's nothing to gloat about, but it's enough to get my uncle to give in. I call him and tell him my grade. He's happy and says I can have the box when I get home later.

"No, please. I can't wait any longer. Can you bring it to me?

That way my friends and I can get right to brainstorming?" I beg. He agrees and stops by after school. I thank him and take off to the back of the gym, where we all agreed to meet—it's the only place we can go, since Devonte's family's restaurant will be too noisy for what we need.

I'm the first one to arrive; Shawn comes along a few minutes later. And while we wait for the others to come, I realize I haven't really checked in with him. "How are things with your dad?" I ask him.

"It's still awkward, but it's getting better. He had this life planned out for me, and now he has to adjust. Big adjustment," Shawn says anxiously.

"He can do it. You know how parents are—we have to be patient with them," I joke.

I flash back to the huge argument I had with my mom. The words come back and haunt me in ways I couldn't see coming.

"Fine, Mom, I'll do exactly as you say. But just tell me this: I've been a soldier in the Rosalie Bosia army all my life. When is my contract up? Or better yet, how much? How much will it take to be free of you?"

I wanted to be free of her and now I am, maybe forever. I choke back tears and prevent them from spilling over. But the lump in my throat isn't as easily managed.

He smiles. "You ready for the second set of clues?"

"Yes! I need to find out what makes my mom so tough. And maybe I can use that for myself."

"If you become any more like her, we won't be able to tell you two apart."

Nai and Dell enter together—holding hands. Our jaws drop. Well, I guess its official; Nai and Dell are a thing! I take out the small white envelope and read the contents out loud to everyone.

Key #2
I was born to no one.
I taught him French; he showed us Evidence of Things Not Found.
My Incident is set in stone.

My mind is racing and my heart is pounding. I know one part of the phrase, "Evidence of Things Not Found," refers to one of James Baldwin's essays. So, we decide to start there. We look to see who taught Baldwin French, but nothing comes up.

Damn!

We try to pull the clues apart. We look up the words "I was born to no one." But nothing useful comes up. It's not a poem or an essay. We do searches using variations on the phrase and get nothing.

"Maybe we're overthinking it. 'Born to no one'—that could simply mean he was an orphan," Dell suggests.

"Yes! That could work. So an orphan who worked with Baldwin," Nai replies.

"Guys, look at the word 'incident.' It's capitalized. It's not just a word, it's a title," I shout. "Duh! It's a poem by Countee Cullen."

"And you just happen to know that?" Shawn asks.

"Ah, yeah. Doesn't everyone?"

They all roll their eyes at me, signaling that I am alone on this one.

We dig a little more and find out that Cullen used to teach at Frederick Douglass Junior High, where he taught Baldwin as a kid. It all fits.

"So the answer is Countee Cullen?" Dell asks.

"Yes, and I know exactly where to find the next key!" I reply.

———

We rush through the doors of Countee Cullen Library, located on 136th Street. We enter loudly, and the librarian greets us with a scowl. We slow down and look around for what we came for. It's in the center of the library—a bust of Countee Cullen. His poem "Incident" is etched in stone at the base.

I get down on my knees and lean in really close. I spot a small gray strip of paper taped to the base. It's about the size of the strip inside a fortune cookie. I carefully peel it off.

"What's it say?" Dell asks.

It's a series of numbers in the Dewey decimal system. I know exactly where this book is—we head straight for the African American Lit. section and take out a large book titled

Countee Cullen: Collected Poems. In the center of the book is a white envelope.

I pull it out and hold my breath as I open it.

Just as before, there are three things in the envelope: key number two, a smaller envelope that will no doubt give us the last set of clues, and some more pages ripped from my mother's journal. I kiss the second key and put it in my back pocket, along with the clue for the third key. Right now, I want to read the journal. If this entry is as telling as the first one, I will get to know my mom in a whole new way.

June 24, 1995
Dear Janet,
A few weeks ago, I was thinking about getting a perm. I've been asking my mama to let me get one forever, and she always says no.

She says, "All perms do is take the fight out of your hair. You a Black girl; you gonna need all the fight you got."

I said, "There's nothing wrong with having soft and gentle hair!"

And then she goes, "The world don't take kindly to anything soft or gentle. Best not aim for that." I mean, like, for real? Do we have to go all "Fight the Power" even for hair?

Well, I got tired of waiting for Mama to agree

with me and started thinking about doing it anyway. I didn't really have a plan or anything, until . . .

My homegirls and me were hanging at Ladonna's house, talking about guys. Tia was talking about how romantic her boyfriend was and how he's not try'n to rush her into anything. All us girls looked at each other, because we knew better. Her man was working real hard to get her to give it up. That's why he had "I'll Make Love to You" on repeat.

We talked about guys some more, but then Biggie's "One More Chance" came on Hot 97 and there was only time to rap along — loudly.

Later, we started talking about how we planned to wear our hair for the prom. Tia wanted a Nia Long cut, just like the one she has in *Friday*. Michelle wanted to rock Moesha micro braids, and Joy isn't sure what style she wants but says it has to be something that lets her show off her baby hair. I don't know who she fool'n; she ain't got no baby hair.

When it came time for me to share my plans, I confessed that I wanted a perm. I asked my girls what getting one was like, and they said it tingles. But they also said that if I could stand the tingling, I would get silky, bone-straight hair, the kind of hair that can swoosh around from side to side like them white girls on the hair commercials. I let my homegirls talk me into it.

We played a bootleg videotape of Bad Boys in the background while Tia scooped out a big white glob of perm and spread it over my head. It was really cold at first, like ice on my scalp. Moments later, I ran screaming into the bathroom to wash it out!

The next morning, when I woke up, I found clumps of hair on my pillow. The perm wasn't in my hair for long, but it'd had enough time to do major damage. My hair was rebelling against me for trying to tame it. It wanted me to know that it no longer trusted my judgment, and as punishment, it was giving me bald spots. All this, and prom was two weeks away.

The crazy thing is, my mama didn't get mad or even give me that "I told you so" look. Instead, she took me to a friend of hers who does natural hair, and we talked through the best way to make my hair healthy again. I had to cut all my hair off and start again. She told me what oils to treat it with and the best wigs to get in the meantime.

After my visit to the hair lady, my mom asked to talk to me. I thought, Okay, here we go with the lecture. She sat next to me on the bed and told me about the time she had a date and wanted to straighten her hair. She got some crazy hair mixture from a friend and ended up completely bald. She told me that my hair wasn't just hair. She said it has history and roots. And since we've been displaced and uprooted for generations, anything that holds our history is sacred.

I asked her if she was saying that having a perm is bad and what that means for the Black women who have perms — are they wrong? She said, "It's not the perm. It's the reason why you want it. Be careful, li'l bit. Every day, in a hundred ways, you're being told you're not good enough. You're not pretty enough, light enough, or smart enough. I don't want you to echo that in your head or in your heart."

We spent the next few days looking at wigs, trying to figure out which one I should go with. I thought my mama would aim for a natural wig with braids, but she came over to me with long, silky black hair from Brazil. It was more expensive, but she thought it might be what I wanted. I put it on, and there I was: long, shiny, soft hair that could swoosh. I looked pretty, carefree, and new. The new part bothered me. I wasn't new. I was the latest. The wig — naturally — had no roots. I opted for the lace-front wig with short twists. It felt more like . . . me.

The guy who asked me to the prom a few days later was Matthew Simpson. He's in all of my Advanced Placement classes. People talk about him because he's always checking his watch so he can get to where he's going half an hour early. He always carries a bigger backpack than anyone else. That's crazy because we have lockers we can put our books in. So, why is he carrying them around? He says it's because he wants to always be prepared. His obsession with time and being prepared makes people laugh at him.

I think he asked me to the prom because no one else would ask me. The guys I like think that I'm stuck up or that I speak like a white girl. And the girls Matthew likes think he's too odd to even consider going out with. He asked me and I said yes. It's not exactly a romantic story, but at least we get to go to prom.

We thought that before the big day we should hang out, just to get to know each other more. So we planned a date to the movies and then to get some food after. When I got there, Matthew was waiting for me, backpack in hand. He told me he'd arrived thirty minutes early.

"Why you always come half an hour early and why you always have a backpack on?" I asked.

"I'm not always half an hour early; sometimes I'm twenty minutes early and other times I'm an hour. It depends."

"On what?" I asked.

"On how many times I get stopped by the cops."

I'd never even considered that.

He explained, "When we're at school, people think I'm a nerd, and I like that. I study really hard, so I like getting that word put on me. Yeah, I'm a nerd. But when I hit the streets, I'm a threat. My GPA, test scores, even my college acceptance to NYU mean nothing."

He wasn't sad about it, Janet. That's what made it even worse. He was so . . . resigned. It broke my heart. I knew I shouldn't ask what was in his backpack, but I had to know.

He said, "First-aid kit, for when the cops come at me hard. My inhaler comes in handy if they make me put my face in the ground — sometimes it triggers an attack. Also, I have kneepads I put on if I know I'm about to get stopped. The concrete is hard on my knees; I injured one as a kid, so . . . the pads help. I also have a card with phone numbers I need to call in case they take me in, and lastly, I carry this."

He then showed me a large book titled *Countee Cullen: Collected Poems.* He told me he's been carrying it around because of one poem, "Incident." He showed it to me. It's about an eight-year-old boy who gets called a nigger for the first time in his life. The poem haunts Matthew because something like that happened to him on his way to the science fair when he was eleven.

"I can find that poem in smaller collections, but I like this big book. When the cops order me to face the wall, I feel weightless, like a brown paper bag they can kick around. But this book gives me weight. So I won't just crumple and fly away . . ."

CHAPTER EIGHTEEN

Let's Party!

I find myself thinking about the second journal entry while in class the next day. The fact that my mom was ever less than confident is strange to me. The fiasco with her hair sounds like more of an Ayo thing than a Rosalie thing. It's hard to see my mom as a teen who was just as confused as I am.

When I read her journal, I feel close to her. And while the most important thing is to get all the keys, the journal entries have become priceless. I find myself researching the years the entries were written and looking into what was happening around that time.

For example, I read about New York City's "stop and frisk" law, which was basically the "Black equals criminal" law.

They're still doing that mess, but nowhere near as much as back in the day. I can't imagine what it must have been like for her and her friends. I wonder what happened to Matthew.

The bell rings and jars me out of my thoughts. I step out into the hallway and join the parade of students heading for their lockers. Some of them look at me funny as they look up from their phones. Nai runs up to me like it's life or death and says we have to go out tonight.

"Why?" I ask.

"We need to do something fun. We haven't gone roller-skating in a while. Let's go!" she says, practically dragging me from my locker.

"The Water Ladies organized a prayer meeting for my mom, and Uncle Ty and I have to be there. Anyway, I'm not really in a skating mood," I reply. Once again, a student walking by me looks down at their phone and then up at me with pity. "What's going on? Everyone I make eye contact with is looking back at me like I'm some sad puppy."

Devonte comes up and embraces me from behind. And right away he offers to treat us to dinner at his family's restaurant, right now. I remind him that he has practice, and he says he will blow it off.

"Okay, that's it. What's going on?" I ask. "And don't say 'nothing.' You never blow off practice. And why are people looking at me funny?"

Devonte and Nai exchange looks. Well, this can't be good.

"For real, just tell me."

"There's this video . . ." Devonte starts carefully.

Nai quickly warns me against watching it. But it's no use. I need to see it. She gets the clip on YouTube and plays it for me. Some hate group added sound effects to the video of the shooting, cartoon noises. And when my mom lands on the ground, there's a laugh track playing.

My chest tightens. I can't seem to get any air in my lungs. I'm nauseated and the room is spinning wildly. Nai is talking, but I can't really focus on what she's saying. What's happening?

"Ayo. Hey, it's okay, baby girl. You're okay." Devonte's voice is faint in my ear.

"I can't . . . breathe . . . I . . ."

"You're having a panic attack. But you're gonna be okay. Just do what I say."

I nod as I try not to give in to the sheer blinding terror rushing through me.

"Take deep, slow breaths. Okay? Deep and slow."

He starts breathing with me. Other students start to crowd around me. Nai shoos them away.

"I need y'all to fall back!" she tells them. Her tone works. The students move along—mostly. There are a few determined to watch this play out.

Devonte continues to take deep breaths along with me. It slowly starts to get better. But the room is still loopy. He sends

Nai to the girls' bathroom to wet some paper towels. When she comes back, he places the cool, wet paper against my face. It feels good.

I'm finally able to catch my breath again. "That's it. Just keep taking deep breaths." Once I assure Nai I'm okay, she goes down the hall to get me a bottle of water from the vending machine. It's just us two now.

"Oh my God, what was that?" I ask.

"Panic attack."

"I've never had one before. It's awful."

"Yeah . . . it's scary as hell."

I lean against the wall, feeling lightheaded and empty inside. "How could anyone be so cruel? I don't get it. They don't even know her."

"People are for-real messed up," he replies sadly.

"So this is all over the internet now?"

"See Us is working on them pulling it down. They are threatening legal action. Most of the sites have agreed to take it down, though it will still be online. It just won't be as easy to get to."

"How do you know that?" I ask.

"I called your uncle when I saw the video."

"Oh. I didn't even know you had his number," I say.

"He gave it to me. Said to keep an eye on you."

"He thinks I can't handle it." I laugh sardonically. "And I guess he's right."

Devonte shakes his head. "Nah, it's not that. He just wants to make sure you're okay. I gave him my number for the same reason."

I look him over, grateful that both him and Nai are with me. "How do you know what to do for panic attacks?"

"I used to get them. I was always anxious as hell that I would never be fast enough to get away."

"From what?"

He doesn't reply. But he doesn't need to. I realize how dumb my question was. I just asked a Black boy in New York City why he's anxious. Duh.

———

I'm home alone when Nate calls to tell me the news: the grand jury decision is coming. I turn to CNN. The bright red banner across the screen reads, *Grand jury decision in Bosia case imminent.*

My stomach dips. I feel heavy. My insides are churning and I'm close to throwing up. There are large goose bumps forming up and down my arms. I can barely make out what the news anchor is saying because my heart is pounding so loudly in my ears. I tell myself to have a seat, but I can't really move.

"The grand jury has decided not to indict."

I stand there, mouth open, bewildered. The reporter's words are a rusty knife under my belly slicing me open. My guts are out to the world. There's nothing left on the inside.

No, I'm wrong. There is something left . . . rage.

I run to the closet to get the bat and smash the hell out of the TV. I march up to the glass coffee table and bring the weapon down with all my might. The flying glass and broken pieces are nothing more than confetti. It's only right; after all, it's a party! We are here to celebrate my friend rage—it's her coming-out party.

I get a running start and take the bat to the hallway mirror. It shatters in multiple glorious pieces! We can't stop now. The frenzy inside me demands more and more carnage. I latch onto the bat with both hands and aim for the shelf full of awards given to See Us over the years—yeah, they have to break too. I bring the bat up over my head once again and bring it down on the glass shelves. It rains glass confetti; so pretty!

The window calls out to me. It too wants to be part of the party. I close my eyes, lean on my back leg, and swing—but it doesn't land. I open my eyes. Uncle Ty is holding the other end of the bat. He's stopping me midparty.

I look in his eyes. They're flooded with tears. And now mine are too. The air is gone from my lungs. I crumple to my knees. A guttural cry escapes from my throat and tries to give voice to my pain. But it can't, because pain like this shouldn't exist. I weep openly on the floor as my uncle holds me. He can't save me from this, and I can't save him. So, we drown together . . .

Within the hour, groups of protesters from See Us and other organizations take to the streets, heading directly for the police station. The media follows the crowd and tries to get them to talk about what they feel. One Black lady turns to the cameraman and lets out a cry that is part rage and part sadness. The man is so taken aback that he almost drops the camera.

Leaders from the Black community march out in front of the pack and give interviews demanding justice. There are reporters outside our house, as well as crowds of protesters shouting their support. The news is filled with reaction footage throughout New York City. The crowd keeps growing, and police presence—per the mayor's request—has been heightened.

My uncle is trying to keep See Us from breaking down our doors to get me to speak to the media. Every few minutes, someone from the foundation is calling to plead with my uncle to let me speak. He refuses, saying I need time to let what's happening sink in. He needs time too. His hands are still shaking.

I'm standing in the middle of the house surrounded by the wreckage, and I wonder: What are the cops having for dinner? Will they have a regular meal, like, say, chicken and rice, or will they go all out with a celebratory feast? Will they invite their friends to join them as they cheer getting off? Oh my God, is there cake? Do people serve cake after getting off of shooting a woman in the head?

You're so stupid, Ayo! Don't you get it? They didn't shoot a woman; they shot an animal.

We're animals, but not like a small dog—white folks love, protect, and, for some strange reason, kiss them on the mouth.

We're creatures to be hunted and killed on a whim. And all this time, we've been playing a game here in the animal kingdom, called "How to not scare the white folks so they don't shoot us."

That's why we glob on chemicals to keep our hair from looking too Black; nappy hair scares them. We lower our voice, adjust our tone, and learn to code-switch because big, Black voices threaten them.

They creep into our homes and take what they like: our traditions, our culture, and our slang. But we don't protest; protest might startle them. Instead, we adjust. They feed us diced-up chunks of casual racism, and we make no mention of the bitter taste. We swallow quietly and don't make a fuss; a fuss would make them nervous. Nervous white folks are quick to shoot.

That's the object of the game: to live a life so small, so anemic, that white folks hardly know we're there. It's paramount to our survival. Is that why some of the icons of the civil rights movement were killed, because their lives were too big?

Medgar Evers.

Fred Hampton.

Malcolm X.

Is that the key to staying alive in this country—try as hard as you can not to exist? Would my mom be here now if she'd made herself smaller? What does that mean for all of us? How small do we have to make ourselves to not scare the white folks?

As night descends on Harlem, rallies become riots. People are throwing things through high-end store windows, then looting whatever is inside. The peaceful protesters and the rioters are mixing in, and it's hard to make out which group is which. All over Harlem, sirens can be heard as fires are being set in trash cans, stores, and cars. The cops rush on the scene in full riot gear.

The anger of the crowd is palpable. I know the rage that grips them; it has taken me too. And as the city begins to burn, I don't see wild, lawless thugs; I see spiritual, tribal men and women who are tired of begging the gods for a drop of justice. No more drops; they need it to rain. It's the only way to nurture the last seed of hope they have.

Sly News calls them criminals, and one commentator says the cops need to be even more aggressive so that the city can return to "order." The network actually has the nerve to suggest that cops have to be more forceful with us because Black people are somehow prone to acts of violence. They have people calling into the show talking about how Black people go to jail more often, due to our lack of self-control and discipline.

WTF? Sly News is full of idiots.

The protesters are dancers, retelling Alvin Ailey's *Revelations*. There's grace and beauty in their movement, even if it is fueled by fury and frustration.

See Us has given up on calling; the entire board is here at the house. I overhear them talking about the protesters who have been beaten over the head and tear-gassed while my mom's name falls out of their lips as they chant.

"They're risking their lives fighting for justice for Rosalie and her only child can't even make an appearance? They need to hear from her. Now more than before," Nate says.

He's right.

I never wanted anyone to get hurt, and if the only way to stop this is to speak to the crowd, then I will. I can hold back my fear and face whatever needs to be faced. But I don't know what I will say to them. How will I lead them with no real voice of my own?

I didn't want to say anything before because whatever I said would just add gasoline to the fire. I don't have it in me to take the high road. I want to burn down the police station and every damn thing near it. How do I find the strength to battle that rage and make something good out of it? How can I tell them to tame their anger when I can't tame mine?

I need you, Mom. I need your strength. And I'm going to get it.

I promised my uncle that I wouldn't leave the house tonight, but I have to. I have to go find the last key. It will tell me how to get my mom's strength and courage.

I text my friends and tell them to meet me at Devonte's restaurant. His family, sensing what was coming, boarded up the place, but he has the key, so we should be okay. He tries to tell me how sorry he is about the grand jury decision; I can't take any of that in right now. I stick the last set of clues in my back pocket, put the box in my backpack, and head for the door. I'm hoping my uncle will be too distracted to note that I am gone. I have a good shot at that, as they are all in the kitchen arguing.

Uncle Ty calls out to me just as my hand makes contact with the door. "Where you going?" he asks. Nate enters the hallway just behind him.

"I need to find out what my mother left me. It's important," I reply.

"Ayo, this isn't a game!" Uncle Ty shouts.

"I know! You think I don't see what's happening? Uncle Ty, people are getting hurt, and if this keeps going . . . I can't just stay here and watch everyone fight for our family but me. I want to speak out. I want to add my voice to this. But to do that, I need to find the last key my mom left me."

"Then I will come with you."

"No, I have to do this with my friends. We started the hunt together, and we need to finish together," I reply.

"You're not going out there. It's too dangerous," he says.

"Uncle Ty, has it ever been safe for us?"

He sighs, deflated. Hollow.

I turn to Nate. "Tell the media and the board to meet me in front of the police station. I'll be there soon. I'll address the crowd—I promise. But there's something I have to do first."

A light sparks in Nate's eyes. "Anything to get you out in front," he says as he takes my hand, ready to guide me through the crowd.

My uncle softly calls after me, "Ayo . . ."

I turn back to face him. The concern etched in his eyes makes my heart swell.

The past five weeks has aged him, and the grand jury decision all but broke him. I inhale deeply, preparing for him to argue with me. But instead . . .

He swallows hard and nods. "Be careful."

———

Black Harlem is pissed, and so white Harlem is nowhere to be found. All the rich and trendy spots we drive past are closed, even though it's barely seven in the evening. Nate drops me off in the alley near the back entrance of the restaurant. There are no lights on inside, but that is the way we arranged it. Only when I text him does Devonte turn the light on and come to the door. I get out of the car and run inside.

We enter the office in the back, where everyone else is waiting. It's a small space, with a large wooden desk that takes up most of the room. On the desk are stacks of invoices and mail.

There are only three chairs in the room, but that's okay— we're all way too hyped up to sit.

After we hug each other, they all tell me how sorry they are about the decision. Actually, they let out a litany of curses and angrily suggest that we let the whole place burn, since there is little to no hope of us ever getting justice.

"Hey, I was right with you guys—at first. But the fact is, Harlem is our home. And the people out there getting hurt are our people, so we have to stop it," I remind them.

"And you think you can find a way to do that?" Shawn asks.

"Yes—with help from my mom."

"Yo, hold up!" Dell says, seriously pissed off. "Do we have to stop the fighting going on? I mean, maybe kicking some white folks' ass is the way to go! Yeah, like giving them a little dose of what they have always given us."

Shawn sighs. "I'm not trying to hate on anyone, but yo, sometimes . . . they make it so hard."

"Let's remember there are white people marching with us too," I say. "I get the hate part, though. Trust. But we can't let it swallow us. And no matter what, I think we all agree we don't want anyone getting hurt, or worse, killed. Right?"

They nod, but it's easy to see that they are fighting the same rage I have been. The decision isn't just a blow to my family but to all of Harlem.

"I'm just say'n, maybe we need to let a few of the people in the grand jury get knocked out. See how they like it," Dell says.

"You don't have a violent bone in you," Nai says.

"Yo, don't get it twisted. I'm hard-core," Dell informs her.

"You can't even make it through the opening sequence of *Up*," Nai says, sounding totally sprung.

"Hey! That was pillow talk! You can't tell everyone!" Dell says, looking shocked and betrayed.

"Pillow talk? Did you two . . ." Shawn can't finish his thought.

"No! It's more like 'cuddle on the sofa' talk," Nai corrects him. "And you're right. My bad."

Shawn and I exchange looks of relief. These two are so not ready for that step yet.

"Yo—my dad just texted me. They're putting the whole city on lockdown in one hour! We gotta get going if we want to find this key," Devonte says. We quickly get down to business, the final set of clues:

Note:

This third and final key is long overdue.

You were ready to know.

I wasn't.

I am now.

Key #3

This ends where it started.

Take time to turn things over.

Follow Mr. Hathaway.

Seems simple, but "This ends where it started" could mean many things. It could mean start back at my house, which is where we first received the package. It could also mean that we have to go back to Dance Theatre of Harlem. There is also the possibility that the first clue is referring to the very first hunt my mom put together for me. Since there are so many possible outcomes, we decide to skip to the second part and see if we get lucky.

Take time to turn things over.

"Does she mean take time to think about things? Like turn things over in your head?" Shawn asks.

"No, I think it's more direct than that," I reply, looking over the note. I turn it over, and there's nothing written on the other side. I turn over the two other keys, and there's nothing engraved on them either.

"Yo, check it!" Devonte says. "Two clues that point to the same thing: the box. It's where this whole hunt started, and it's something you can turn over. If I'm right, there should be something on the bottom of it. Do you have it with you?"

I take the box out.

"Go ahead, Ayo. Turn it over," Nai says, placing her hand on my shoulder.

I turn the box over, and there's nothing carved on the bottom. There's no song lyric or poem to follow. There's just a little sticker with the label of the place my mom brought it from—

That's it!

"This is where I need to go," I tell the group. They lean in closer and read the small words printed on the tiny sticker: *Malcolm Shabazz Harlem Market.*

"Yes, but *where* in the market?" Shawn says.

"I don't know, but I'll find it somehow."

"What about the last clue, 'Follow Mr. Hathaway'?" Nai asks.

"I'm not sure about that. Maybe I have to go there and see first. I'll call you guys if I get there and can't find the last clue," I reply as I motion toward the door.

"What do you mean, call you? We're coming with you!" Devonte says, going for the door. Before he can reach it, I run out of the office and lock the door. They shout in protest and ask if I've lost my mind.

I reply through the locked door, "I'm sorry, but I can't take the chance that you guys might get hurt, given everything that's happening. I need you all to stay in there, where it's safe."

"Ayo, don't do this!" Devonte shouts. I wish I didn't have to leave them here, but I know its what's best. I get to the exit. I hear Nai banging on the office door and shouting behind me, "Ayo, you can't go out there by yourself. Something terrible could happen to you."

Nai, something terrible already did.

CHAPTER NINETEEN

Roots & Wings

The streets are even more chaotic than when I left my house earlier. It feels more like a war zone than it does a thriving city. The car alarms, sirens, and protest chants all mix to make one wall of harmful noise. The stores that could not close up in time are rushing to do so now. The homeless people on 116th Street, where the market is located, are scrambling to get to safety. The air is smoky and thick thanks to lingering tear gas.

I keep my head down until I make it to the market. The Harlem market is a row of shops that sell African crafts and textiles. You can find anything there, from printed shirts with African countries on them to high-end African sculptures.

I scour the row of shops, but most of the merchants have gone. The few who remain are trying to close up shop as fast as they can. I ask them if any of them know who Hathaway is or if they know what shop sells the box I have in my hand, but no luck so far.

Damn!

I check my cell for an update and learn that some of the protesters are now being tased, in addition to tear-gassed. There's also a report of shots fired, but no one knows who took the shots or why. The weight of the chaos brings my head down, and then the rest of my body. I'm sitting on the corner, hugging my knees, trying not to let the heaviness of everything crush me. And that's when I hear it: my mom's voice. She whispers softly in my ear.

"Ayomide, there is a job to do. Fall apart on time that is yours. This time belongs to our cause. Our people."

I drag myself back upright.

All right, Mom, I'm up. Now help me find the shop I need.

That's when I spot it through the window of a small hole-in-the-wall art shop—a painting of Donny Hathaway. He's not my mom's favorite male soul singer, so I'm not sure why she zeroed in on him, but it doesn't matter. I found it!

It's a shop called Roots & Wings, and they sell Black artwork in all mediums. There are also sweatshirts, handbooks on herbal remedies from Africa, a small collection of biographies, and a selection of essential oils. I run into the shop just as the young woman goes to lock the door. She's about my height, with full lips and a curly Afro mohawk.

"Wait! I need to get something in there," I plead.

"Girl, the streets are hot! You need to be home. Don't get caught up in all of this." She goes to lock up once again. I knock on the door and beg her to open, just so I can explain.

"I know you can't stay open. I just need a few minutes."

"Girl, it's not that serious. Come back tomorrow. On second thought, folks is mad. You might need to come back in a few days. This mess is about to get ugly. I can't believe they let them cops off. You know what—actually, I can believe it." She shakes her head angrily.

"I know I can't tell you how to run your shop, but please stay open just for a few minutes."

"It's not my shop, but . . ." She sighs and looks behind her. There's a man who just entered from the back room. He's tall, dark, and about the same age as my uncle.

"We are supposed to be closed, Randa," he says with a melodic African accent. But I can't make out which country.

"She says she needs something in the shop and it will only take a few minutes," Randa replies.

"Young lady, is it that important?" he asks.

"Life and death," I reply.

He smiles. It's brilliant. I've never seen a smile so . . . electric.

"Then in that case, you better come in. But please hurry. We need to close," he says as he disappears into the back room once again. I thank them both and enter. The space is small but has eye-catching pieces that I could spend days studying—if I had the time.

"I've been around here before. I haven't seen this place," I say as I take it all in.

"We just opened up less than a year ago," Randa replies.

"Well, your stuff is beautiful."

"Thank you. What is it you were looking for?" Randa asks.

"Um . . . I'm not sure."

Her face falls. I get it. She's ready to leave and go home, and all of a sudden some dizzy customer comes in with the intention of browsing for hours. I assure her that that is not the case.

"I know what I'm looking for, Randa. I just don't *know* what I'm looking for."

She rolls her eyes, obviously wishing she'd locked up before I got there. I try to think like my mom. She doesn't do anything random. It's all connected in one way or the other.

"Do you have the book *The People Could Fly*?" I ask.

"We ran out of that one. But we do have sweatshirts that have the cover on it," Randa says, pointing to the corner of the store.

There are about a dozen sweatshirts on the rack with the folklore book cover; it's the same cover as the box I have. All of them are about three times my size. I look inside the shirts, and there's nothing in the pockets. I look at the base of the rack; also nothing. There's no clue as to where the last key could be.

"Do you have any sweatshirts that are my size?" I ask, growing desperate.

She thinks for a moment and then says, "We had one, but we sold it to a sista wearing a pretty head wrap."

I bet it was Kizzy. She's helped my mom with past scavenger hunts. She always sports her signature Kente cloth head wraps.

"It was odd. She bought the sweatshirt, put something in the pocket, and then asked us to hold on to it and said that someone else would come to pick it up. We offered to ship it, but she said no and muttered something about tradition," Randa says.

I smile to myself. "Can I see it? I think it's for me."

"Really? Okay, I'll check. The person who bought it left the name of the girl who is supposed to come get it." She goes behind the counter, bends down, and comes back up with a white bag. She looks inside and sees a receipt. She holds the slip of paper close to her and says, "I need your name before I can give this to you."

"Ayomide."

"Yeah, that's you. Here you go."

She hands me the bag, and I take out the sweatshirt. I quickly put it on and reach inside the pockets. One is empty, but the other isn't.

While Randa continues her closing routine, I walk off into the corner. The envelope holds the final key and the last journal entry. I kiss the key and open the letter . . .

March 24, 2004

Dear J.J.,

Akin is back from Nigeria today, and I couldn't wait to show him what's inside the yellow envelope. I cleaned up the apartment, got dressed, and took deep breaths to steady my nerves. I was thrilled he was able to go back to the place of his parents' birth. He wanted to visit for some time, but life always had other plans.

When we first met at the Augusta Savage retrospective, his peaceful vibe and chill really impressed me. And during the Q&A, I loved how he weighed things before he spoke. We loved the same authors and frequented the same food joints. He knew where to get the best mac and cheese, and I introduced him to the spot with the best salmon croquettes.

And I loved that he needs soul music in the morning like most people need coffee — especially Donny Hathaway.

But what really drew me to him was his brilliant smile. He gave a whole new meaning to "tall, dark, and handsome." He delighted in the little things, like homemade ice cream and taking the long way home. And, like most artists, he's obsessed with art. His chosen medium was clay, but he was good with all sorts of materials, including woodwork. His day job as an accountant helped pay his bills, but every moment he could spare was spent sculpting.

Last year, he started accounting at a local firm. He was the only Black accountant. He liked to joke that he preferred his racism straight up, but in corporate America, they served it on the rocks. And as it turns out, watered-down, subtle racism is just as bitter. Sometimes those white folks are so subtle with it that Akin wonders if he's imagining it. He isn't. They're racist as hell at his firm.

On his first day of work, the security guard only asked him for ID, whereas the other newcomers just went right into the building. The company sent out a memo on "appropriate attire" after he wore a kente cloth tie. In staff meetings, his boss would tell him just how glad he was to have someone so "articulate" on his team. They'd ask him to explain the actions of the latest rapper or Black celebrity, as if Black folks held a meeting once a week to consult with each other.

It seems like little things, but it wasn't to Akin. I think each cut — however slight — began to fester. What made it worse is that after a few months on the job, the staff started to get really comfortable with him. It's never good when white folks get comfortable with us. It means they are about to open their mouths and start some mess.

He was at an office Christmas party and a coworker came up to him, drink in hand, and said, "Can I ask you something? I mean, I think I can because we're bros — so, what's up with the saggy pants and the gold-tooth thing?"

Racism is the hydrochloric acid rain that Black folks scramble to get out of any way we can. Some do the "good Negro" two-step: they never make waves, don't raise their voice, and pretend not to know which member of Wu-Tang is which.

Others try to get away from the liquid fire by buying a fast car and driving to their big mansions perched up on high. Only to learn that it rains up on the hill too. And some Black folks are just so traumatized by the rain and the fact that it's actually man-made, they just stand there and pretend it's not happening: What racism? Everything is all good, as the flesh slides off their bones.

Akin wasn't like any of the folks above. He understood racism in all its forms. He didn't pretend it wasn't there. He was just as well read as I was, if not more. He confronted things when they needed to be confronted and didn't back down. But a few months after he'd started his new job, I noticed his smile had dimmed.

The more injustice I saw, the more fired up I became; I joined civil rights groups, marched, and boycotted as much as I could. But Akin retreated inside himself. The stars I saw in his eyes were fading. He'd been reading biographies on James Baldwin, Marcus Garvey, and Josephine Baker. He read more but talked less. I guessed he was looking for answers.

Tonight started off well: Akin entered my apartment and we quickly embraced. It felt so good to be near him again. He'd been gone for a whole month. And yes, his smile was back; not only was it back, it was brighter than ever. He told me that as soon as he set foot on African soil, he felt a peace he'd never felt before.

"In Nigeria, when they address me, they address me as a man. Not a Black man, just a man," he said, absolutely beaming. "Lili, going to Africa was like finding a cure to an illness I didn't know had already been ravaging my body." He was practically dancing as he paced up and down my living room.

The only time he called me "Lili" was when he was excited about something. I was overjoyed to see him this way. I suggested maybe I could go with him the next time he visited. That was when he looked at me with a mix of joy and caution. That was when it started to click . . .

James Baldwin

Marcus Garvey

Josephine Baker

Akin wasn't looking for a way through; he was looking for a way out. My heart plummeted down to the soles of my feet. I felt chilly, although the apartment was warm. I put a hand in my pocket and rubbed the envelope like it was a person I was trying to comfort.

"You want to go back to Nigeria," I said.

"Lili, it's where I belong. I want a sweet life. A life where I know that if another man hates me, he does because of my actions, not because of my skin. I need to be in a country that knows how to pronounce my name."

I tried to let his words sink in. "Akin, I've wanted to go too. Many, many times. But what about everyone else?"

"This is about you and me, no one else. I would love for you to come with me —"

"Akin, I want to go with you, but . . ." I had to stop

and refocus. It was vital that he understood where I was coming from. The envelope was burning up in my pocket. I wanted to take it out and show it to him. I wanted that envelope to change everything, but something kept me from pulling it out. Before I gave it to him, I needed us to be on the same page.

I told him that while he was away, the *New York Times* had announced that Amadou Diallo's family would be settling for three million dollars with the city. They wrote up a succinct account of what happened like it was normal: a Black man was shot forty-one times by cops who wrongly suspected him of being a criminal. And so, the city pays a few bucks. The cops get off scot-free.

Then I told him about overhearing some of the students in the after-school program I volunteer with; they weren't struck by how utterly ridiculous it was to shoot an unarmed man forty-one times. They weren't upset that the cops were acquitted of his murder. Instead, they focused on the money. They asked each other what they would have done had their families come into that kind of jackpot.

"Lili, I'm sorry. I know that it's tragic that kids have to face that," he said.

"Akin, it's more than a tragedy. These kids have no idea how valuable they are. They don't know that the only thing that's changed in this country is the way slavery is packaged. We have to show them that the auction block has been traded in for the city blocks, and our bodies are still up for sale."

"You have done so much for those kids. You expect more from them than any of the other volunteers. You show up to their games, to their plays, and you stay until dark if they need to talk. You have done enough."

"It doesn't feel like it"

"Listen, Lili. I've shown my work to some of the professors at the University of Lagos. They have an artist-in-residence program, and they want me. I can sculpt and you can teach. We are always talking about what it would be like to live in a country that can pronounce your name. Live in a country where you don't have to march for the simple right to exist. This is it, this is our chance!"

"No, we can't give up on this place! We can't give up on those kids or this city," I reminded him.

"You are fighting so hard, Lili, fighting for a country that will never see you."

The room was too hot and too cold all at once. I felt like I was one step away from the edge and the ground kept shifting under me. Every muscle in my body tightened as I tried to force air into my lungs.

I walked over to him; I took his beautiful face in my hands. Maybe this failing was mine. My mama knows how to anchor my daddy so that he won't float out into the darkness. Had I failed to do that? Had I failed to hold Akin down so he didn't drift away?

"Akin, I love you. I know it's hard, I do. But we can't stop now."

"Us finding a way to live our lives, us walking away from the white gaze and choosing to be happy . . . That's a righteous, defiant act! That's its own protest!"

That was when I told him about an idea that had been brewing in my head for the past two years.

"Akin, I'm going to start a nonprofit, right here in Harlem. I know I can't change the entire world, but maybe I can do something right here. We can do it together," I pleaded.

He shook his head and looked at me in disbelief. He took my hand in his and spoke in a very gentle but resolute tone.

"Rosalie, every day here is a blow. If it's not a gut punch, it's a jab. If it's not a jab, it's an uppercut. Or a bullet in the back from the very people who swore to protect and serve. I love you, but I am done with America."

I was going to argue; it's what I do best. But his eyes told me he was serious. They also told me that he needed to do this so he could keep his smile.

"You're tired," I whisper, almost to myself.

"Yes, Lili, and I have to take what's left of my soul and go."

I kissed him, long and hard, because I knew I'd never get a chance to do it again. Akin was a wonderful man, but I'm not looking for wonder. I'm looking for strength. There was no way I could show him what was in the envelope, because to raise a child in America is to be in battle every day. Akin wasn't built for war; fortunately, I am . . .

I put down the letter; stunned. I guess Mom was finally ready to tell me . . .

"Young lady, did you find what you needed? We need to close up now," the store owner says.

His voice pulls me out of my daze. "Huh? Oh yeah. I did. Thank you."

Randa chimes in, "That's the girl the sweatshirt was being held for. Her name is Ayomide."

"I love that name. It is actually my great-aunt's name. She was a very special soul," the owner says.

"Thank you."

"That's such a lovely illustration," he says, looking at my sweatshirt. "I recently worked on a carving of the very same image, using a wooden box."

I take the box out of my backpack and show it to him. "Is this it?"

"Yes!" the owner says. "It was an online order. You must be involved in the organization that commissioned it. Are you happy with the results?"

I nod slowly as I study his face more closely.

"This is your first year in the market. Where was your shop before this?" I ask.

"All of my shops are in Africa. This is my first one in America. And to be honest, I'm not sure I will stay here. This country hasn't changed," the owner says sadly, then bids me good night. I put the box in my backpack, ready to head out and shake off what amounts to nothing more than a crazy vibe I feel.

The owner grabs the clipboard from the side of the cash register and makes his way to the back room, where he begins to hum a soulful tune. I smile to myself and head out the door. Randa comes to lock up behind me.

I hear her shout out to the owner, "That's a nice song, boss. What's it called?"

"'A Song for You.'"

By Donny Hathaway . . .

CHAPTER TWENTY

I Remember Now

I have about a million questions. But I do not go back inside the shop to ask them. That would be like holding a Q&A on the deck of the *Titanic*. Also, I'd like to open the box here and now, but the chaos is growing and I need to get off the street. I rush into the subway station and get off a few stops later. It only takes a couple of minutes, but every second feels like an hour. I've waited so long to find this info, and now that it is only moments away, the wait is killing me. What could the source of my mom's powers be?

I think it's a book. It has to be. And if I'm right, then I will have to skim it before I talk to the crowd. What if it's a massive book? What if it's like *War and Peace* and I have a half hour to read it?

Nah. It's probably a poem. She loves poetry. I bet a long time ago, she ran into a poem that changed her life and made her the woman she is today.

When I get out of the train station, cops are arresting people because the curfew is now in effect. I worm my way past the insanity and make it down the block, toward the restaurant. It's the only place I can think of to go. I can't go home; there's just too much going on there with the media and the board members of See Us. But here, I can open the box by myself but feel safe, knowing my friends are only a few feet away in the back office.

That's if they are still my friends after I locked them up.

I enter the restaurant, take the box out of my backpack, and place it on the counter. I unlock each lock one at a time. My fingers tremble slightly when I get to the last one. I put the key in the last lock but don't turn it. I need more time.

You don't have more time! Wait any longer and there won't be a Harlem to save! Ayo, open it!

I take out my cell and click on my news app. A small part of me is hoping that it will all go away. I picture myself turning on the news, hearing, "Cops indicted on attempted murder of . . ." and everything will be fine.

I watch a live news feed—the decision still stands. The city is still burning. And every second that passes, it's getting worse.

There are ambulances and police cars everywhere. The crowd in front of the police station is embroiled in a heated exchange with the cops, who have now formed a wall to prevent the crowd from going farther into the station.

"*Ayomide!*" my mom's voice screams inside my head.

"Okay, Mom. Okay," I say as I turn the key. I take a deep breath and open the box to reveal my mom's strength once and for all: it's a sonogram with a grainy outline of a baby. And at the bottom of the picture it says, *Ayo—twelve weeks.*

Me?

Me? I'm the reason my mom is so strong?

And suddenly a flood of memories washes over me. They are moments I took for granted and never bothered to take note:

My mom coming home at night exhausted from working and sneaking into my room, saying she just had to see my face . . .

All the times we'd be watching something awful on the news and she'd reach out and take my hand. She wasn't just reaching out to comfort me; she was recharging . . .

There were times she'd spend all day going head to head with politicians. She'd come home weary and empty. She'd come into my room and place her hand on the side of my face. And then I watched her light up. I didn't know it was her way of replenishing her soul . . .

And all the times she came into my room, I always thought she was avoiding work or that she was feeling bad because she'd been gone a lot, but that was it. She came into my room because she needed me. She needed my strength.

Can it be true? The firm, powerful voice I longed to have has always been in me?

For real, is that even possible?

Rosalie Bosia thinks I'm a force in this world. She's never wrong about these things.

Then that must mean . . .

"Oh my God, I'm dope!" I laugh.

I am strong.

Me! Ayomide Bosia.

Suddenly, I am no longer alone in the room. I'm surrounded by dark figures draped with stark white clothing and textured head wraps. They are all around me. They share my eyes; they have the same jaw line, the same full lips that my mom and I do. They stand before me, proud. They look at me with fire and determination in their eyes.

Yo, the ancestors are in formation!

"Y'all showed up for me?" I ask.

My mom's voice comes back to me from the night we went looking for monsters in the closet. *"Child, there are hundreds of people waiting in the wings to help you. Every one of your ancestors. All you have to do is use your voice and call to them . . ."*

That's when I see it in their eyes: they were waiting for me to find my voice and call on them. I see it so clearly in my head now. All the times I thought I was too weak to reach for what I wanted, what I needed, was time wasted. I won't waste any more time doubting myself. I am not a disappointment to Afros everywhere. I'm a freaking savage!

I run to the back room and unlock the door. My friends all look at me, startled. I don't have time to explain.

"Did you find the last key? Did you open the box?" they ask.

"Yeah. I found what I was looking for."

"What was in the box?" Devonte asks.

"Me."

—

My friends immediately put a call in to just about everyone they know to give my instructions on what to put on the posters we're going to take down to the protest. We hit up everyone in our school, and they are all willing to help.

The Knights are going to meet us with large speakers and mics and, of course, music. The Narcs—with their perfectly laid weaves and sculpted eyebrows—will be doing an Insta Live on the steps of the police station. They call for their followers to come and get their political activism on. The Vintage group —Mario Bros. forever!—will be there, as well as the basketball players, cheerleaders, and basically the whole school.

We also reach out to the Generals—they are bringing their entire domino group, which turns out to be larger than

I thought. The Water Ladies only do "civil" protests, but this time, they are showing up and showing out with their flare skirts and "God Don't Like Ugly" T-shirts.

But the ones that will stand out the most are a group of about two hundred Black women dressed like Spock. Tonight is their annual meetup, and they asked if they could go dressed the way they are, and we said, "Hell yes."

I call Nate and ask that there be megaphones for us to pass out to some of the members of See Us and the crowd. I ask Milton to gather info I need for my speech and to meet us in front of the police station.

Once we're there, the scene is unreal. All of Harlem has come out to fight, rage, and call out the system that seeks to end them. I find my uncle and assure him that I am okay about speaking to the crowd. The certainty in my voice throws him for a moment, and then he smiles to himself.

"What is it?" I ask.

"I see her. Right there, just now. I saw her in your eyes. You are ready."

Facts.

"I called the hospital and spoke to your mom's doctors. They promised me they would turn on the TV so she could hear you speaking to the crowd. I know we don't know if she can hear you, but—"

"Uncle Ty, she's listening. Trust me. And she's not the only one." I look out at the massive herd of ancestors who came here with me tonight. They spread out among the crowd. They've been guarding us. They've been rooting for us all along. This was never just our fight. It's theirs too.

Nate and the other members work on getting the crowd to settle. Everyone needs to find someplace to put that rage. It's taken a long time, but I know exactly what to do with it and the power it holds. I plan to share that with them and give them a place to aim their wrath.

I look out at the crowd and see Milton headed for me. He hands me the info I asked him to find. "There's a lot more, but these seven should start you off," he says above the chaos of the crowd.

"Thank you."

"These names are pretty big. I mean, they won't just go down like that. They will try to fight back. Are you sure this is the direction your mom would go? Do you think you're ready for it?"

"I'm not sure what she would do. I only know what I am about to do. And for the record, I was born ready."

He looks me over as if he sees something in my eyes that fascinates him. "Something is different . . ."

"Yes: everything. Everything is different now," I reply as I look over the notes he has for me.

"So, does that mean you're coming back to See Us?" he asks.

"Yes. I know you are the president now. That's fine. I don't care what my title is. I just want to be a part of it."

He shrugs. "It's okay. I never moved up in the ranks. I was just keeping your seat warm."

"You didn't announce that I left?"

"No."

I look at him closely. Wait, is Milton a nice guy? Huh.

"What else you need from me?"

"Hand this to our social media department," I say. "I need these three words hashtagged and trending. Also, let's lay claim to the three words by getting the domain name right now. And there's a handful of members here with extra signs—have them circulate and hand them out, please."

"On it."

"Milton . . . thank you."

The members of See Us who have been pleading and at times demanding that I speak begin to chant my name. The crowd shouts and swears about the grand jury decision and calls for revenge, just as much as they do for justice.

I look out at the sea of ancestors, giving me all their energy and support. I look to the side. I see my family, friends, and my community. I am not alone. And even if none of those people were here, I would still have someone, because my mom is here too. I know she is because I can feel her guiding hand on my shoulder.

Getti . . . all they need to hear from you is the truth, she whispers softly in my ear.

I exhale and walk to the podium. The crowd goes silent. I begin to speak.

"It's been almost six weeks since my mother stood on this very spot and asked the city of New York a question: How much? How much will we have to pay to finally be treated equally in this city, in this country? It is because of that question that she lies in the hospital, fighting for her life.

"My mom is my entire heart. Those two cops clawed right through my chest and ripped her away from me. They left a bloody, gaping wound where a heart once lived. It sent me into a hole so dark that I couldn't conceive of a time when there was light. But the people of Harlem would not let me stay in darkness. They reached out and reminded me of something I had forgotten:

"I am my mother's daughter.

"In this struggle for equality, my mother sometimes stumbled, faltered, and fell, but she never allowed herself to stay down. She never gave up. She never compromised. And she never allowed the system to break her will.

"I am my mother's daughter.

"There should not be any Black people left in this country, for all we've faced. We've been betrayed, beaten, and burned. We've been enslaved, entrapped, and entombed inside a system that was created with one purpose: keep us down, at all costs.

"They plucked olive branches and handed them to us,

branches from the very trees they use to lynch us. Our bodies cooked under the glare of their hatred; our minds softened and our souls shriveled into nothing. So how is it there are still Black people left in this country?

"Our ancestors.

"They didn't stop when the whip cut into their backs or when the dogs bit into their flesh. They didn't stop for water hoses, Klan rallies, and tear gas. What right do we have to consider giving up, even for a moment?

"My mother reminded me every day about where I came from. She did that because she knew there were people out there praying I'd forget. And I will admit it, I did. I forgot for a long time just what badasses the ones who came before us were. But I remember now. And I am here to remind you.

"If they think this grand jury will stop us from fighting for justice, then they don't know my mother. They don't know me. And they don't know you!"

The crowd roars to life. The sound fills the streets. I take a deep breath before I continue. It's a cleansing, freeing breath. There's no second-guessing my words or my thoughts. I'm standing at this podium, and for the first time in my life, I understand that this is exactly where I belong.

I continue once the crowd settles. "My mother is a force unlike any other. She's formidable, resilient, and tenacious. I am my mother's daughter."

I take a deep breath and share what I've learned. "My

mother's question to the city was: How much? I have the answer: Too much. We have overpaid and we are due for a refund."

The crowd cheers and begins to shout, "Pay us back!"

I gently hold my hand out to settle them. "And while my mother is my mentor, I am not her. I'm not here to ask another question. I'm here with a warning."

The crowd is hyped at a fever pitch. The energy and sheer excitement is practically moving the podium.

"For too long we have been pleading to be seen by America. We are done with pleading. We are here to tell you, while you may not see us, we damn sure see you!"

The crowd goes nuts and moves like they have caught the Holy Ghost.

"Do you hear us, America? The plainclothes cop who shoots before he identifies himself, the social media platforms that allow violence against our people to be turned into a joke, the police commissioner who turns a blind eye to the casual way Black men and women are killed without regard to their civil rights, and the corporations that back them . . . We. See. You."

The crowd roars again.

"ComX Inc., a company that advertises regularly on Sly News and stood by as the network made light of our pain. ComX Inc., we see you."

The crowd shouts the phrase back to me. I name the six other companies Milton got for me. Every time I call out a name, the crowd shouts back to that company, "We. See. You!"

"And we will be boycotting you from now on," I announce. The crowd cheers.

"Lastly, to the members of the grand jury, the cops who tried to kill my mother, and the entire NYPD—it is a mistake to think this is where it ends. We remember now who we are. And where we've come from. We will not be deterred. The monuments to systemic and institutional racism will not come crashing down right now. But mark this day: today is the day those monuments are no longer on solid ground. We. See. You."

CHAPTER TWENTY-ONE

Purpose

I didn't really want a birthday party, not while my mom is still in the hospital. It felt wrong to be here without her. I was there this morning and in the middle of reading a poem about the strength and resilience of Black voices called "This Is Not a Small Voice," by Sonia Sanchez, when it hit me: My mom has been in a coma for six weeks now. There is no sign of her getting better. Is she really never going to wake up? That's when I broke down sobbing.

I thought of skipping the party given for me by See Us, but I stayed and mingled, because I knew she'd want me to. Also, everyone had worked so hard to get folks to come to the rally, they deserved to blow off some steam.

The rally went better than any of us expected. I'm elated at the results of that night. Three out of the seven companies we called out have since pulled their ad money from the Sly network. And the others are now reviewing their partnership with them.

In the few days since the march, membership has rocketed up, and there are talks of expanding office space sometime next year, to accommodate the boom in membership.

I don't think of this party as being my party, because everything that happened that night was a result of everyone working together. I think of it less as my birthday party and more like a celebration of unity. I tried to explain that to the adults in the room, but they insisted that the party focus on me.

So, here we are at See Us headquarters, in the middle of a large birthday bash, complete with a four-layer cake, fabulous gold and pink decor, and a table full of gifts. The music is banging and everyone seems to be having a good time.

I started my birthday at my mom's bedside. There's no real change in her condition, but I promised myself that I would try to enjoy tonight because everyone worked so hard to put it together.

I've been trying to talk to Nai, but every time I head toward her, someone wants a picture with me or wants to discuss See Us. I take as many pics as they need in order to write us a check. I play twenty questions and smile even if I don't feel like it. I don't mind, because I know it's a good cause.

Finally, I get a free moment, so I take Nai and usher her out to one of the small offices so we can talk. "Hey, are you okay?" she asks as I close the door behind us.

"Yeah, I'm good." I signal for her to take a seat. "I saw you and Dell. You guys look so cute, it's ridiculous."

She laughs. "Yeah, we do got it go'n on."

"I actually brought you in here to say I'm sorry," I begin.

"For what?"

"You never miss a chance to take care of me. I can't think of a better best friend. And I haven't given you half as much attention as you've given me. I should have checked in with you more often. We were in the same house and yet I let you go through everything with your mom alone."

"Ayo, your mom is my mom too. She's hurt, and that's where your attention should have been. And don't worry; I wasn't alone. I actually talked to Dell almost every night."

"Really?"

"Yeah. I'd call him, we'd talk about my mom, and he'd listen. Then we'd talk about . . . everything, I guess. I even got him into *The Great British Baking Show*. And now, that's our jam! Girl, don't trip. We good."

I choke back tears and clear my throat. "I have something for you."

"It's *your* birthday. That's not how it works."

"Excuse you, I do what I want—I'm fifteen now."

"Oh, excuse me!" she says playfully.

I hand her an envelope with fancy lettering. She opens it. Her mouth drops. "Ayo . . ."

"I thought now that you and your mom are cool again, maybe you two could use a mother-and-daughter day."

"An all-day pass to a spa for two? It's too expensive. I can't take this."

"It didn't cost me anything. My mom helped the owner out with an issue she had, and she gave it to us."

"Don't you want it for you and your mom? She's gonna wake up, Ayo, I know she will," Nai says, suddenly panicking.

I place my hand on top of hers. "Yes, Nai, she will. And when she does, we will pig out and argue over what show to binge. The spa isn't really our thing. And besides, I think she'd want you to have it. So take it already."

"Okay, fine! But only because you're so pushy."

I laugh and embrace her. We pull apart just as Dell bursts into the office. "Yo! I've been looking for y'all everywhere— guess who's in the stairwell kissing?"

We all run out to the staircase, just in time to watch Milton and Shawn midkiss! We should be mature, composed, and chill about the whole thing. We aren't. We start clapping and cheering like we've lost our minds. They try to play it cool, but we can see they are just as giddy as we are.

After a few hours, I manage to duck out of the party so I can meet Devonte. He offered to skip track practice to join the party. But I didn't want to share him with a crowd. I wanted us to be alone. So, we go to his house, sit on the sofa, and watch Berry Gordy's *The Last Dragon,* and he makes me hot chocolate. It's a really chill and relaxed vibe, and exactly what I wanted after the party. Oh, and we make out—a lot. And when the movie is over, I hand him a small black ring box.

"This is kind of sudden, but yeah, I'll marry you!"

I playfully roll my eyes. "Ha ha. Whatever. It's not a ring."

"What is it?"

"Open it, genius."

He opens the box and finds a simple silver chain with a pendant of winged feet.

"It's more than just a track-and-field symbol. Hermes, the Greek god it's modeled after, could travel between worlds. There was no limit to where he could go. I feel the same way about you. No limits for you, at all. I want you to always remember that."

He doesn't say anything. I'm wondering if this was a terrible idea and he hates it.

"It's okay if you don't like it. I can take it back to the—"

He takes my face in his hand and gives me a long, lingering kiss.

I guess he does like his gift.

Later, I find my way back to my mom's hospital room. The nurse looking after her is letting me spend the night because it's my birthday. I enter my mom's room and wedge myself between her and the bed rail. I recount my whole day to her.

"You should have been there! The guy was only going to

donate two thousand bucks, but by the time I was done with him, he donated twice as much, and he said there might be room in his budget to hire three paid interns for the summer! Don't worry, we already contacted all the kids in the summer program and told them about it. Oh, and also, there's a tech company I think we should check out. We might be able to talk them into supporting our entire Black Girls Code program . . ."

I drone on about everything from Dell and Nai to the box of cupcakes I gave the nurse. I keep talking even as my eyelids get heavy. I whisper to her, "We had a deal: I won the hunt. I get my wish, Mom. And that's my wish—for you to wake up."

Sleep takes me. The next thing I know, the sun is up. I open my eyes and find my mother awake and softly smiling down at me.

I lose my mind and hug her so tight that I'm sure I'm hurting her. I call the doctors, the nurse, just about everyone. And as they tend to her, I look out and see them all around the room: dark figures, dressed in stark white clothing and textured head wraps. They nod toward me, glide out the window, and take flight.

Thank you, ancestors.

Thank you for returning my heart . . .

EPILOGUE

Six Months Later

"You are shameless!" I shout as I wag my finger in front of my mom. She vowed that we would finish the newest season of *Insecure* next week. The rules were very clear. And now, I come home and find her in front of the TV on episode five! Five! That's half the season. I place my hands on my hips and demand, "What do you have to say for yourself?"

"I didn't even know what I was doing, Getti," she says. And now she's going to play her new favorite card. "You know my head ain't too good."

She has a ways to go before she's fully recovered, but the doctors are really happy with her progress. They told us it's nothing short of a miracle. There's even more good news: I've been talking to my dad!

When I first went back to the shop and told him who I was, I thought he'd die of shock! It took a little while for the news to sink in. He never imagined he'd be a dad. But once he found out, he delayed his trip back to Nigeria so we could get to know each other. He's showing me how to make jollof rice! He's also started introducing me to relatives on his side of the family. It turns out I have about like a hundred uncles and aunties.

He was really upset with my mom for not telling him about me. But in the past three weeks or so, he's let that go—mostly. He wants to try and fix things between the two of them so that they can be friends and parent together. He talked about moving here permanently, but I can tell that's not where his heart is and I talked him out of it.

He loves Nigeria, and there's no reason he should have to give that up, but he's promised to come back to the United States every two months to check on me. Also, next year, I get to go to Nigeria and meet my new relatives in person!

I take my cell out from my back pocket and view a series of pictures my dad and I took the last time we hung out. I have his eyes and his smile. I look in my contact list and see the word "Dad." It feels good to see that.

Something pulls me out of my thoughts—a figure trying to get up the stairs without being noticed.

"Rosalie Bosia, what are you hiding?!" I ask.

She shrugs and bats her lashes like she's just a sweet innocent little girl. But it's clear she's hiding something behind her back.

"All right, lets see it, missy!" I order.

She shows me what she's been hiding—a half-empty container of Häagen-Dazs rum raisin ice cream. There was a sale, two for the price of one. My mother had hers yesterday and now she's moved on to mine.

"That's it! You cannot be trusted. From now on—all desserts will be regulated by me! I'm sorry, but you have shown yourself untrustworthy." I take the ice cream, and she comes after me.

"Just one more scoop!" she begs.

"No! You have to learn."

"Aw, c'mon, Getti, you have to let me have the rest."

"Why is that?"

"It's a rule. People that get shot in the head get as much ice cream as they want," she says with a straight face. I crack up and hand her back the container. She feeds me a spoonful and then eats the rest.

"Are you packed already?" she asks. It's spring break and all of us, including Milton and Devonte, are going to Miami Beach. Uncle Ty and his wife have a rental place and invited all of us to come hang out for a week. It's all we've been talking about for weeks. I was supposed to be packed already, and I'm not.

"I'm gonna pack now," I tell her.

"The guys will be here in half an hour, girl, get going!" my mom shouts from downstairs.

I quickly throw whatever is clean or clean-adjacent into my suitcase. I jump into the shower and rush to get dressed. I come downstairs and into the living room. "Are they here yet?" I ask my mom.

My mom doesn't respond. She's transfixed with what's happening on the news. I look on as the reporter repeats, "An unarmed African American woman, Lashay Horton, is dead after officers mistook her apartment for that of a murder suspect . . ."

My mom gets on her phone and starts making calls immediately. I'm right behind her; my first one is to Milton. He tells the rest of the group. They're in a cab headed this way. I continue to make calls. We need to put a meeting together quickly and see how we want the youth division to respond to this. I'm already on my sixth call when my mom taps me on the shoulder.

"Hang on, Mom, I gotta see how many people we can get to meet tonight, and I have to call—"

"Spring break, remember?" she says.

The trip.

"Oh." I put my cell down.

"It's okay, Getti. You can help out when you get back. Go, have fun and be safe," she says, then kisses me on the forehead.

I smile sadly and walk out the door. Everyone is piled into

the cab across the street, waiting on me. I look at Devonte. He grins, making his already handsome face that much sexier.

He motions for me to hurry and get in the car. I look down at the ground but remain in the doorway. He gets out of the car. He's read my troubled expression.

"I heard. Milton told us. We can help when we get back," he says.

I don't reply.

"Ayo . . . we've been planning this forever."

"I know."

He sighs and shakes his head in dismay. "Milton is in See Us. He's going on the trip."

"I don't know Milton's heart. I only know mine." I walk down the steps and stand close to him. "Go. Have a good time."

He strokes my cheek. "If you ask me to stay, I will."

"I know."

He looks deep in my eyes. "Ayo, ask me to stay . . ."

I can't meet his gaze. I don't know how to tell him that there's no room for the two of us. But when I finally risk looking into his eyes, I can tell he already knows that. And although he's not saying anything, his silence is screaming at me. It's asking me a hundred questions:

Why can't we make it work?

Why can't I be both an activist and his girl?

Why must I choose?

"Devonte, the girl who struggled to choose between her social life and social issues is gone. Some people can stay in the fight part time. And some of us are full-time warriors, who don't get to pause or take a day off. You know which one I am."

He pleads, "I get it, but you don't have to be. Ayo, you shouldn't have to give up your whole life."

"No, I shouldn't. But then again, we shouldn't have to change our names on job applications because the 'Black names' go to the bottom of the pile. We shouldn't have fear be the first emotion we feel when a cop is near."

"You fought to have a life and now you do. Ayo, I *know* you. I know that you can do both."

"I'm sorry."

He clenches his fist, "Argh! C'mon! What happened to the girl before? The one who told me off?! The girl who was fire and did her own thing? What happened to her?"

"Her mom got shot in the head."

His eyes are glossy; he blinks back tears he'll never admit were there in the first place. He brings me close and whispers, "Ayo . . . I love you."

"I love you too," I manage to say before the tears come. He brushes them away from my face. "You can't fix the whole world, baby girl."

I smile. "No but maybe Harlem. Harlem's a good start."

He kisses my cheek and walks back to the cab. I run inside

because I don't want to see them drive off. My mom quickly ends her call when she sees me enter crying.

"Are you sure about this?" she asks as she lovingly strokes my back. I put my head on her shoulder and sob.

Then, I take a deep breath and remember who I am and the enormous sacrifices that were made to get me to this point. "I'll cry on my own time. Right now belongs to Lashay Horton. She deserves justice." We get back on our phones and brace for one of many battles ahead.

The wind picks up outside, a tree branch taps on the window, like an old friend trying to get my attention. I look out and watch in amazement as color seeps back into Harlem. The rich reds, browns, and golds that I had drained from my beloved city have returned. This is Harlem saying, "Welcome back, daughter . . ."

ACKNOWLEDGMENTS

I would like to thank:

My patient and phenomenal editor, Margaret Raymo. (You are officially invited to the cookout!)

My superagent, Adrienne Rosado. (Thanks for talking me off the ledge ~~almost~~ daily.)

My cover artist, Sopuruchi Ndubuisi. (Thank you for the stunning artwork.) And also Celeste Knudsen, who designed this beautiful jacket.

Last, to my friend and assistant, Shannon Ariss. Hey, Shan, we survived the writing process. We survived!